ANA DIPINTO

Scorned In Blood

*To my mom*

Neck wrapped in velvet
Wrists bound in chains
Love and hatred
Are one in the same
Abandoned in darkness
Disappear in the flood
Through a river of red
Scorned in Blood.

# Contents

# Acknowledgement

Special thanks to Joseph Ellis, who created the awesome vampire teeth on the cover of this book. Maryellen Maglione, who supplied me with the picture that I used to create the background for the cover, and Umi Haft-Funke, who provided her professional graphic design skills to help me put the cover together.

# Chapter 1

S he stepped forward, each movement in slow motion as she inched closer towards him until their bodies were almost touching. Her once familiar face, which used to be so full of life, now took on the look of death and the color of an ashen grey. The intensity of her eyes made them almost glow, like that of a nocturnal animal, in the total darkness of the room. His gaze stayed transfixed upon her. His heart pounded hard against his chest. Both fear and curiosity consumed him. He tried to step back, but his legs felt too heavy, and his feet stayed frozen in place. He stood motionless as she inched closer to his face and softly touched his lips with hers, gently parting her mouth as he followed her lead. Her tongue wrapped around his, pleasure and pain enveloped him as she bit down. Then suddenly, she disappeared.

Zaine awakened, his forehead sweating from the nightmare. The taste of salt lingered on his tongue. He put his hand to his mouth wiping the blood away. *Must've bitten my tongue in my sleep,* he thought to himself as he reached out, dipping his finger in the white powder that lay on the nearby table. He brought his finger to his right nostril snorting the substance. The clock across the room read 12:00 am. When had he even fallen asleep? His mind felt like it was in a state of confusion. He rose from the worn-out black leather couch he had been sleeping on and walked into the kitchen. He grabbed a cold beer from the fridge and his cell phone off the counter.

"Babe, what are you doing? Come on over."

"No. Zaine. Caleb is asleep, and I am not going to wake him."

"But Babe, I really need you. Ask your mom to watch him."

"I can't. I got to go. It's late."

The call disconnected. Zaine stood there, staring at the screen, cursing his girlfriend. "Bitch." He mumbled to himself. He had met Nita about six months ago when he had just gotten out of jail. She was working at the bar he frequented, and they hit it off right away. He remembered the first time he saw her. She was coming off her shift, and he was going in to have a few beers with his best friend, Chris. They were there celebrating his homecoming. Nita was wearing tight skinny jeans and a black deep V-neck t-shirt. She had tattoos on her arms and piercings in her face. She was the exact opposite of his ex, Harper. She was taller too but just as thin. That was about the only thing the two women had in common, their slim but curvy frame. Nita was exotic looking. Her eyes slightly slanted, her small nose perfectly positioned on her face, and her full lips always shiny with lip gloss. Everything perfectly proportioned, he thought. She was beautiful. Then she spoke. Her voice was soft and sensual, and he was instantly captivated.

Zaine and Nita started dating shortly after that first meeting. Suddenly they were going everywhere together. She would drive him to his odd jobs until he had finally saved enough money for a car of his own. Accompany him to all his hangouts.

She brought her son Caleb over to meet him and introduced him to her mother. She would spend every night at his apartment when Caleb was spending time with his father. He realized quickly she was falling for him, just as Harper had done. Zaine was charismatic and charming, and she was willing and ready to dote on his every need. Nita would do anything he asked, come when he called, putting him first and foremost above everyone and everything. But lately, she'd been changing. She began making excuses, saying she had to work or take Caleb somewhere. But he knew in his gut there was something else going on. She was avoiding him. Was she seeing someone else? Cheating on him? Who was this other guy? What did this guy do for her that he couldn't? Sure, Zaine was unemployed, but he made his money in other ways.

"Fine then, Fuck her. I can have any other girl I want to come over here." He said to himself. But after a few unsuccessful attempts, he put his phone back down on the counter and went back to his tiny dark living room. The truth was things had changed after what happened to Harper, and he went to jail. Now, most of the people he'd known before, except for Chris, just tended to avoid him.

Zaine took a swig from the beer bottle he still held in his hand. The crisp carbonated beverage was almost refreshing as it glided down his throat. He sat back down on the old worn leather couch, took another hit of the cocaine on the coffee table, set the beer bottle down, and turned on the tv.

\* \* \*

She was dressed in dark clothing, her long straight black hair falling down her back. She walked through a door into the grand entry foyer of an old-fashioned house. Brass candle sconces lined the walls, dimly lighting the entryway. She strode up the elegant grand staircase gliding her hand along the dark wood railing until she reached the second floor. Gracefully, she walked down the long hallway until she came upon a set of double doors. She opened the doors and stepped into an elegant dining room. Inside sat a long mahogany dining table. Along the table were matching chairs made with ornate wood and red velvet seat cushions. There were silver candlesticks placed along the table, each lit with a single candle. Two large crystal chandeliers hung from the high ceiling. Heavy dark red drapes covered the windows. No food was on the table, but clear crystal wine glasses sat at each place setting. Each glass had been filled with deep red wine. A wine so red and dark it resembled the color of blood.

Zaine continued watching this scene unfold in the dining room as if he saw it on a tv screen. The room was silent, but he noticed two men and a young woman seated at the table. Both men appeared to be tall, even in their seated positions. Both dressed in all black. With dark hair and intense eyes, their faces held a firm appearance and expression. The young woman, however, had more delicate features. Long, bold red hair fell into curls around her face. She wore a red lace dress, the same color as her hair. A multi-strand pearl necklace hung from around her neck. Beaded bracelets and gold rings adorned her wrist and fingers. She looked young and beautiful, but there was something else about her. It was something different about her complexion; her skin appeared almost translucent. Actually, there was something off about

4

all of them. With their almost mystifying appearance, they all seemed slightly inhuman.

Zaine continued watching as the familiar figure of a girl he'd once known walked over to the man seated at the head of the table. He took her hand, bringing it to his lips. He kissed the inside of her wrist, though Zaine felt he held it there a bit too long. When she finally took a seat at the table in the chair to the left of him, Zaine noticed a third man in the other seat beside her. A man that he hadn't seen before. This man had a square jawline, a scar was present across his right cheekbone, his facial features much stronger than the other two men at the table, but his skin had that same translucent look though it may have been slightly darker. He also seemed to be somewhat shorter than the other two, but he appeared to have a more robust, stockier build.

Each person sipped the dark red wine from the glasses set in front of them at the table. The one seated at the head of the table was now looking straight ahead towards the large double doors at the room's front. A sinister smile crossed the man's face, and Zaine felt as if he was staring straight at him. His nerves stood on edge. He began to sweat, and his heart was now racing. As the man's smile grew wider, two long fanged teeth appeared dripping with blood.

Zaine woke up again with a start. He hadn't even realized he had fallen asleep. Small beads of sweat were dripping from his brow; his heart was pounding in his chest. The darkness of night had faded, and the early morning sun was shining through the window of his apartment, even with the blinds closed. The tv was still playing some infomercial in the background. He searched around for the remote, finally finding it in the couch cushions. He turned off the tv, took a sip of the warm beer that was still on the coffee table in front of him, then got up and walked into the bathroom. He splashed some water on his face and looked at his reflection in the mirror. His eyes were bloodshot; his wavy hair looked greasy.

What was going on with him? Why was he having these dreams, these nightmares? He thought to himself, *why am I dreaming of her, of Harper?* He had to do something to distract himself, get rid of these dreams, and get Harper off his mind. He paced around his apartment for a while, scrolling through his social media accounts. Not much was going on there. He checked his email and text messages for any new work coming in. After a few hours of this and still not getting Harper out of his thoughts, he called Chris, pulled on a pair of jeans and a grey t-shirt, and ten minutes later, he was on his way to the bar to meet him.

"What's up, man? What's going on with you?" Chris had greeted his friend while seated at the bar, wearing his usual jeans and flannel shirt with the sleeves rolled up.

"Not much, man. Just needed to get out of the house." Zaine greeted him back with a handshake and pat on the back.

The two men sat there talking, occasionally glancing up at whatever sports game was on the tv set above the bar. The bartender came by and placed two beers in front of them. Just then, Nita walked in wearing her usual uniform of tight jeans and a t-shirt, ready to start her shift. She noticed Zaine at the bar, walked over to him, wrapped her arms around his neck, and kissed his cheek. He smiled lightly at her and kissed her other cheek before she walked into the backroom of the bar.

"Man, what's up with you two?" Chris asked, sensing a little distance between the two lovers.

"I don't know, man. She's been acting weird lately. I called her to come over last night, and she refused. She never used to do that before, but lately, there always seems to be some excuse. Every time I need her, she says she's busy, has to work, or take Caleb somewhere."

"Well, you know she works a lot and is trying to take care of her son. I'm sure it's nothing."

"Maybe." Zaine shrugged.

They sat at the bar for two more hours until Chris had to leave for work. Zaine hung around even after Chis had left. He shot a few rounds of pool and played on the electronic poker machine at the end of the bar. He ordered some food and another beer and waited for Nita to finish her shift. Afterward, they drove back to Zaine's apartment. There, he told her about his nightmares from the night before, although he decided it was best to leave out the fact the girl in his dreams was his ex-girlfriend instead pretending he dreamt of a face unknown.

"It was probably something you saw on tv. Maybe you should ease up on the late-night scary movies." Nita laughed, making lite of Zaine's fears as she cleaned the kitchen, putting the dishes away, and then wiping down the countertops.

"Yeah, right," Zaine responded grimly.

Once the kitchen had been cleaned, they cooked dinner together and sat in front of the tv while eating. Caleb was staying the night with his father, so Nita was free to keep up the night with Zaine. After they finished eating, Nita got up and put their plates in the kitchen. Zaine followed behind her. He wrapped his arms around her and turned her around, so she was facing him. He moved his hands up her shoulders and across her neck until he had her face in his fingertips. He leaned in and kissed her intently. He then moved his hands back down her body to her waist and lifted her onto the countertop. She wrapped her legs around him, and then he carried her off to the bedroom.

Zaine got up from the bed. He looked down at Nita lying there. She looked peaceful and innocent. He brushed the hair from her face, leaned down, kissed the side of her cheek, and left the room, allowing her to sleep. He went to the kitchen, grabbed a beer from the fridge, and began searching the kitchen for his stashed cocaine. He knew it was there somewhere. He checked the metal tin in the upper right kitchen cabinet. Nothing left in there. *Ugh.* He looked in the steel jar on the countertop. Still, he found nothing. He was beginning to get frustrated. He checked the pocket of his denim jacket, pulling out a pill bottle. Not what he was looking for, but it would have to do for now. He opened the bottle, pouring two pills into his hand, then swallowing them with a swig of his beer. He sat down, laying his head against the back of the couch, and closed his eyes.

Once again, she was there. Harper was standing in front of him in his living room so close they were almost touching. Her hair was long and dark with blunt bangs cut across her forehead. Her skin was pale, her lips bright red, and her eyes were a vivid, sparkling green. The full moon outside cast an unusual light that surrounded Harper in his otherwise darkened living room. He stood staring at her once again, unable to move, and for a moment, she didn't move either. Then slowly, she reached up and touched his face. Her touch was cold against his cheek; it sent a shiver down his spine. She just stood there with her cold hand against the side of his face, never saying a word. He couldn't turn his eyes away. He stared transfixed into Harper's eyes until she broke their gaze. Once his eyes were free to roam again, he looked her up and down from head to toe. She wore a black knit top and a black velvet choker with a silver heart pendant hung tightly around her neck. She wore black jeans that showed all her curves. A long navy-colored jacket which she kept open in the front, hung over her shoulders. Black lace-up boots with a stiletto heel were on her feet. He'd always liked it when she wore high heels, and tonight, she looked as sexy as ever before. He could remember all the times they had been together. Every moment they spent together in his old apartment or hers. But he had to stop thinking of her like that. Nita, his girlfriend, was sleeping in the next room. And Harper was long gone. So why was she here? Better yet, how was she here, standing right in front of him, so real, so alive? But he was sleeping, and she was dead. He knew that because he'd killed her.

# Two

Three years earlier

Harper sat at a small corner table in the Aura Springs cafe where she worked. She had just finished her shift and was waiting on her best friend Cloe to meet her there. Harper had just moved to the town of Aura Springs a few months earlier. Her family had moved nearby into a neighboring town years ago, first her parents, then her sister and brother-in-law with their kids. Now she was ready to be close to them again, and Cloe was the first person she had met when she arrived. Cloe lived in the same apartment building a few doors down. About a month after Harper moved in, the apartment complex had its annual summer resident picnic. She almost didn't go, but then at the last minute, she decided maybe it would be a good idea to meet some of her new neighbors. Cloe had come up to her and sparked a conversation. She was such a friendly person, and they became instant best friends. Ever since that day, they had become almost inseparable. It was nice having a close friend like that again. She hadn't had many close friends since high school. She had gone on a separate path from all her friends. While they had all gone off to college and to pursue careers, she stayed behind. She began hanging with a different crowd, had spent her time in bars, and going to concerts and parties. But then her family slowly started moving away. They had always been so close, and she was beginning to feel like it was time to get her life together, figure out who she was and what she wanted to do. So, she gathered all her savings, quit her job, said goodbye to her roommate, and left her old life behind. She had settled in this new town only a few miles away from her parents and sister. She was living alone for the first time and working at the café. She started taking art classes at the community college, and then she met Cloe.

Harper noticed Cloe walking into the café, waving to get her attention. Cloe was short in height, probably only about five feet. Her shoulder-length curly hair fell around her face, and she wore her usual outfit of tee shirt, skinny jeans, and black ballet flats. Harper stood up from her chair and hugged her best friend, then they both took their seats at the little round table. They sat there a few minutes sipping their coffees, then got up to head off on their shopping trip. Tonight was the end of semester showcase at the community college, showing the art students' work and featuring one of Harper's paintings.

"So, where do you want to start? It's your big night." Cloe asked

"I figured we'd just go to Jolie's. And I don't want to make too big a deal about this, ok. Please stop calling it my big night." Jolie's dress shop was located along the main street of this small town, just a few blocks from the café where Harper worked and not far from their apartment building.

"Well, it is a big deal. You're a great artist, and it's about time you are showing your work, but ok. Let's go." They walked side by side the four blocks to the dress shop. Once inside, Harper tried on a few dresses before deciding on a simple one-shoulder black cocktail dress with black pearl detailing on the shoulder and a chiffon overlay on the skirt. Harper paid for the dress, and the two walked back to the apartment so Harper could get ready for the event.

The college was holding the showcase in the gallery on campus. The students' paintings and photographs, and computer illustrations hung on the bright white walls while the sculptures and pottery pieces were placed strategically around the gallery. Harper walked around the gallery taking in all the fantastic work the other students had completed. The click of her shoes against the black and white tiled floor echoed in her ears. Cloe and Jace, who was Cloe's boyfriend, were going to meet her there after Jace got home from work. Harper stopped in front of her painting. She had worked on it for weeks for her final project. They could use any medium and capture any subject they wanted so long as they showed the techniques they learned in class. She chose to use gouache on a stretched canvas. It was a little tricky, but she loved the effect of the gouache paint and just had to be sure to use minimal water and keep the paint creamy. In the end, it came out better than she'd imagined. She had always been a fan of vampire literature and folklore and used that as her inspiration. Her painting depicted a white coffin with blood dripping from the corner, spilling into a puddle on the floor. The figure of a woman with long black hair in a white dress was walking away from the coffin. In the upper left corner were the white teeth of a vampire with blood dripping from the fangs. All of this was painted on a grey background that got gradually darker toward the bottom. The whole painting was created in black, grey, and white, with the red of the blood being the only bright color used. She remembered being nervous about showing it to the class, but it got great reviews from her classmates and professor.

As she stood there looking at her painting on the wall, a cool breeze swept against her neck. She thought she saw something or someone nearby but saw nothing when she turned her head. She was in this corner of the gallery alone. Must have just been another student or patron walking by, she thought to herself. The goosebumps suddenly rose on her skin, and she wrapped her arms against her stomach. She rubbed her hands up and down her arms to help warm herself. She shook off whatever eerie feeling she was having and began to move around the gallery to see if Cloe and Jace were there yet. She pulled her cell phone out of her tiny purse to text Cloe since she hadn't found her yet.

Harper was looking down, typing into her phone, when she bumped into something. When she looked up, she realized she hadn't walked into something but someone. It was Zaine Brantley. She had seen him around town a few times, and he came into the café once in a while, but what was he doing here at the showcase? Did he know someone in the school? She had heard he didn't have much family and mostly kept to himself save for a few friends, mostly Chris. But everyone always said what a nice guy he was. She opened her mouth to apologize, but the words wouldn't escape her lips.

"Sorry." He said to her first. "You're Harper, right? You work at the Café?"

"Yea, that's me. I'm sorry. I walked into you. Was texting

and walking. Should've been watching where I was going." She said with a slight laugh feeling mildly embarrassed.

"No, it's ok. I wasn't paying attention either. I was looking for my sister; she's a graphic art student at the school. She's supposed to be here."

"Oh, that's really sweet of you to support your sister. Well, I'm going to look for my friends. Have a good night." Harper turned to walk away when Zaine grabbed her by the wrist. She turned to him with a quizzical look on her face.

"Sorry, I shouldn't have grabbed you like that. But before you go, do you think we could go out sometime? I mean, I've seen you around a few times. I wanted to ask you the other day at the café, but you were busy." He smiled down at her. His eyes sparkled in the overhead lights from the gallery.

"Sure. Just give me a call, I guess. I really got to go. My friends just got here." She said, turning away to meet Cloe and Jace at the door.

"Was that Zaine Brantley you were just talking to?" Cloe asked her immediately on sight.

"Yea. You know him?"

"Not personally, but everyone knows who Zaine Brantley is. His uncle owns Brantley Developers, and everyone says Zaine is poised to take over the company one day since Mr. Brantley's sons don't want it."

Harper turned to Jace, "Hi Jace. Thanks for coming." Then turning back to her friend to continue their conversation, she told them how she bumped into him while texting to see where they were and that he asked her to go out sometime. She told them how she had accepted and told him to call her. As the women gushed over Zaine's gorgeous smile and how lucky Harper was that he had asked her out, Jace rolled his eyes.

"He's the lucky one, Harper. You're a great girl. Any man would be lucky to get to know you better. Just be careful. I know everyone acts like he's some kind of stand-up guy, but I hear he could be a real asshole."

"Thanks, Jace. It's sweet of you to look out for me like that. But we've only had one small conversation and may go out on one date. It's not like we're getting married or something." Harper laughed and looked at her friends, knowing she was already lucky to have these two-great people in her life.

The next morning Harper awoke to a text message on her phone from a number she didn't recognize. She tossed her phone to the side, not bothering to open the text. She went out to her kitchen, grabbed a cookie out of the tin on the counter, and started the coffee. She had to work in a couple of hours, so she went to take a shower and get ready for her shift at the café.

Once she was finally done getting dressed and applying her makeup, she poured herself a cup of coffee and made a decent breakfast of egg whites, toast, and a small bowl of fruit. She grabbed her phone off the bed and finally read the text message that came through earlier that morning.

*Hi Harper. It's Zaine. I was wondering if you'd like to get a coffee or something with me this morning. Let me know.*

She looked down, smiling at her phone for a minute before replying.

*I have to work this morning, but maybe after my shift. Meet me at the café around 4. I should be finished up by then.*

A few minutes later, her phone pinged with a new message.

*Sounds good. See you at 4.*

Harper grabbed her jacket and purse on her way out the door and headed to work with a smile on her face. As she walked to the café, she thought about how her life was coming together. She had great new friends in Cloe and Jace. Her family was nearby again, and she would be seeing them the next weekend. Her classes were going great though she was looking forward to the break between semesters. And now, Zaine. They hadn't exactly talked yet or gone out on a date since they had only officially met last night, but she was still hopeful and excited.

As her shift ended at the café, Harper watched as Zaine walked in precisely at four o'clock. He looked so put together in his dark wash jeans and a button-down shirt. He had his shirt sleeves rolled up, revealing the tattoos on his forearms. Harper waved to him, finished wiping down the counter, and motioned she'd be with him in a minute. She walked into the back room, removed her apron, grabbed her purse, and headed into the employee bathroom. She checked her reflection in the mirror, brushed out her long black hair, and reapplied her makeup. She changed into a mauve-colored t-shirt dress, slipped on her denim jacket, spritzed on some perfume, and walked out to meet Zaine.

Zaine was standing by the counter, holding two to-go cups of coffee. He held one out to her, and she took the cup from him. She thanked him, took a sip of the coffee, and they both headed out of the café. As they walked out, Harper thought she noticed a dark figure by the front window, the same as the other night at the showcase. It sent a chill down her spine. But as they came closer to the front entryway, she didn't see anyone. Once outside, she looked again, but there was no one in sight. The parking lot was empty. The early evening sky still showed a bright blue as summer was finally approaching.

"I was thinking we could take a walk on the boardwalk. What do you think?" Zaine asked while leading her to his car.

"Sounds great," Harper replied, smiling.

Zaine opened the passenger door to allow Harper to get into the car. Once in the driver's seat, he turned on the car and pulled out of the café's parking lot. They drove east towards the shore, and Harper peered out the window taking in the sights of this tiny shore town. Though it was only a short drive, Harper loved looking at the small beach cottages with their little white fences and the old-fashioned red brick train station. They pulled into a nearby parking lot, and Zaine paid the parking attendant. They got out of the car and walked up the sidewalk to the boardwalk. The night was bustling with people, couples, families with children, groups of friends just hanging out for the night. They walked along talking, and Zaine put an arm around Harper. He led her down a small sandy path onto the beach. They sat in the sand for a while, watching the waves crash onto the shore and the sun set as it disappeared into the horizon. A cool breeze was coming off the ocean. Harper felt a chill across the back of her neck, and a tingling sensation ran through her whole body. Her heart began to beat a little bit faster. She suddenly had this uneasy feeling of someone watching them. She looked around but again saw no one. She took a few short breaths and shrugged off the chill and uneasiness, determined to enjoy this moment.

Just then, Zaine turned to face her. He looked into her eyes, ran his fingers through her silky hair, then leaned in and kissed her.

After a while, they walked back to Zaine's car, and he drove Harper home, dropping her off in front of her apartment building. She thanked him for the lovely night, and they agreed to see each other again. She walked up the stairs to the front door of the apartment lobby. As she was fishing through her bag for her keys, a small breeze brushed against her neck, sending chills down her spine for the third time that night. Her heart dropped down into her stomach. Her bag fell to the ground. That same uneasy feeling from earlier of being watched had returned. She looked behind her to the parking lot. Zaine was still parked in front of her door. She waved goodnight to him, picked up her bag, and opened the door to her building. As soon as she was inside, the nervousness subsided, and she texted Cloe to meet her at her apartment. She walked through the lobby to the elevator. Once upstairs, she noticed Cloe was already standing at her door and holding a bottle of wine.

"How did it go? I brought some wine over. Figured if it went well, we celebrate, and if it was bad, we could drown your sorrows. Either way, we drink." Cloe said with a laugh.

"It was amazing. Zaine text me this morning asking me to get coffee. I had to work, so I asked him to meet me at the café."

"Tell me all about it."

The two ladies walked into Harper's apartment. Harper pulled a couple of wine glasses down from the cabinet as Cloe searched for a corkscrew and opened the bottle of wine. Harper grabbed some cheese cubes and fruit from the refrigerator and a box of salted crackers from the counter. They took the food and wine into the living room, setting everything on the coffee table, and they settled onto the couch. They sat there eating their snacks and drinking the wine while Harper told Cloe all about the events of the night. She told her about Zaine coming into the cafe and ordering them coffee while he waited for her. She told her how he opened the car door for her and drove down to the beach. She recounted how they walked on the boardwalk and down into the sand and how Zaine had kissed her.

"Oh my god! Girl! It was so amazing.'" Harper was gleaming with joy recounting the events from the night.

"That's so great. I'm so happy for you. And don't worry about what Jace said last night. Those are just rumors, and he's just looking out for you, but you never know this could be it. He could be the one."

"Well, let's not get ahead of ourselves. It was just one evening."

"One very amazing evening by the smile on your face."

Both girls laughed and continued talking. They had one more glass of wine each, then Cloe had to leave to meet up with Jace. Harper said goodbye to her friend. She poured herself another glass of wine. She sat back on the couch, turned on the tv, and settled in for the night.

# Three

The next few months had gone great. Harper and Zaine were spending more and more time together, and lately, he had been spending more time at her apartment than anywhere else. He had told her he loved her, and she had said it back to him. Every day was as impressive as the first. But then, Harper had started a new job at an art gallery in town. She worked the gallery job while still taking her art classes and working at the café twice a week. Zaine wasn't too happy about it. They had begun to have arguments over all the time she was spending away from him. He would tell her she didn't have to work so much that school and one job were enough. He couldn't understand her passion for her art nor her loyalty to the café. She was noticing other changes in Zaine as well. He wasn't spending as much time at the office with his uncle or at the job sites. He seemed to be sleeping less and drinking more. It seemed every time she saw him, he had a beer in his hand. He was also becoming short-tempered and withdrawn.

So, the day she had asked him to go with her to her family's house for her niece's birthday party, she was actually glad he had refused. Only he got mad when she still went. Then when she returned home later that night, she found him waiting for her at her apartment.

"Hey." She had said to him, somewhat surprised to see him there.

"What took you so long. I needed you here." His tone was bitter and sharp.

"I told you it was my niece's birthday, and I was spending the day with my family. You could have come. I invited you. You were the one who said you didn't want to." She snapped back at him.

"Well, I needed you here. You are never here lately." He yelled back as he stormed out of the apartment, slamming the door behind him.

Harper stood there, stunned, staring at the door. She threw her purse and jacket on the edge of the couch and walked into the kitchen to pour a glass of wine. After a minute, she had begun to calm down. She took out her cell phone and checked the time. The screen displayed 9:00. She dialed Cloe's number into her phone and waited for her to answer.

"Hey, how was the party?" Cloe asked soon as she answered.

"It was great. I had a wonderful time with the family, as always. They all said to tell you hello, and sorry you had to miss it."

"Yea, it sucked I had to work today, but I heard some interesting gossip while there." Cloe worked as an event planner at the local hotel, and she always heard all the town gossip when she worked a party being held for any of the locals.

"Ooh, juicy gossip. Do tell."

"Have you talked to Zaine today? I heard his uncle fired him."

"What? What do you mean Zaine was fired? He hasn't told me anything. I guess that would explain his foul mood when I got home tonight," Harper said as she went back over the details of the night since she arrived home in her head.

"Yea. Apparently, a rather large amount of money had gone missing from one of the company's accounts a few weeks ago. They're saying Zaine stole it, and when his uncle figured out it was him, he fired him immediately."

"What? That doesn't make sense. Cloe, I have to go. I'll call you back later." Harper hung up the phone, grabbed her jacket and keys, and hurried out the door.

Harper got in her car and drove toward Zaine's apartment. He lived in a luxury apartment building just a few miles away from Harper in the center of Aura city. His mother had bought it for him when he graduated from college. She knew she was sick and only had a few months left to live. She wanted to make sure he would always have a place to live. After she had died, his uncle hired him on at his company. Grooming him to one day take over. It didn't make sense that Zaine would steal money from the company. He didn't need to. Not only had Zaine's mother left him an apartment, but she also left him a decent-sized inheritance. Harper had to find out what was going on. She had to see Zaine.

She pulled into the parking lot of his apartment building. She parked her car and walked towards the front of the building. The night sky was dark and cloudy. The street lamps in the parking lot seemed to be out, leaving only the moon's faint light, which was hiding half behind a cloud to light the way. Harper heard a sound above her. It sounded like the flapping wings of a large bird. She flinched and looked up into the dark sky, where she saw a rather large bat flying around the building. She began to pick up her pace as she moved closer to the front door. A strong breeze came through. Fearing an oncoming storm, she ran until she finally reached the front steps. She struggled with her keys, looking for the one to Zaine's apartment. It was hard to see in the dark. The light above the awning was out as well. She took her phone out of her purse so she could use it as a flashlight. As she searched through the few keys on her keyring, she realized the keys to Zaine's building and apartment were gone. She flashed the light of her phone on the keypad on the sidewall pressing Zaine's apartment number. She rang the bell a few times. The buzzer echoed loudly in the otherwise silence that surrounded her. He didn't answer. She tried to call his phone. No answer. Feeling defeated, she stepped off the front steps and ran back to her car. It had started raining, and still feeling startled by the bat, she just wanted to get back home.

The next morning Harper awoke, looking to her cell phone for any kind of message from Zaine. There were none, no missed calls or voicemail, nor any text. She placed the phone back on her bedside table and rolled back over in bed, covering her head with the blanket. She would have stayed there in bed all day if she hadn't had to work later that afternoon at the café. Thirty minutes went by, and she checked the screen on her phone again. Still, nothing from Zaine, just a text sent from Cloe asking if she had talked to Zaine and if she was ok since she'd never called her back the night before. She put the phone back down, not responding to Cloe. She made her way to the kitchen, made some coffee, and took a granola bar from the pantry. There was a knock on the door, and she could hear Cloe calling her name. She wasn't ready to talk yet, so she crept to the bathroom and turned on the shower.

Later that day, Harper arrived at the café for her shift. She went straight to the back room and took her apron from the hook she kept it on. She checked the dry erase board on the wall; she was working the counter that night. She pulled her hair into a ponytail and went back to the front to start work. She spent the next few hours making coffees and serving customers various pastries and sandwiches. All night she kept an eye on the front door hoping Zaine would walk through ready to talk to her. It was rounding nine o'clock, and the café was getting ready to close. Still, there was no word from Zaine. She was feeling worried. Zaine had never taken this long to call her. He was usually the one calling her first or coming by her house. If she had called or text, he would call back or respond within a few minutes. Harper continued to clean up and close out her register. She handed in her till from the day and walked out of the café into the cool brisk night.

She heard someone call her name. Startled, she turned, and there was Zaine. Her face lit up with a smile. She walked over to where he was standing at the corner of the building. He wrapped his arms around her, pulling her close to his chest. She could smell the beer and cigarettes on him. They stood there in a silent embrace for a moment. Rain began to fall from the sky, and Zaine took Harper's hand and led her towards his car. They drove to her apartment, still not speaking a word. Harper was just glad to see he was ok. She wanted to give him the chance to talk first, but her mind was reeling from the rumors she heard from Cloe. It was only a short drive from the café to Harper's apartment. So short, in fact, that Harper always walked to work. Once upstairs, Zaine sat in Harper's living room. She came in and handed him a cup of coffee from the kitchen. He placed it down on the table and glared at Harper. When he still wouldn't say anything, she finally broke the silence.

"What happened with your uncle? Why didn't you tell me something was wrong? I heard some things. I just want to know what is going on." She spoke calmly, but he continued to just glare at her for a moment. When he finally spoke, his tone was stern. She expected he would apologize, but instead, he lashed out.

"So, you believe everything you hear? You're just as bad as everyone else." He kicked the table in front of him like a kid having a tantrum. The coffee mug spilled over, dripping coffee onto the floor. Harper jumped up and ran to the kitchen to get a towel to clean up the spill.

"What the hell?" She screamed at him while she bent down to clean the coffee spill. Zaine got up from the couch and began pacing around the apartment. They continued to argue as he yelled at her that she hadn't been there for him and she didn't know anything. She argued that he was the one being distant and keeping secrets. He kept saying that he needed her support, and he needed her to be more present for him. She rose from the floor and put the coffee-soaked towel in the sink. When she turned around, he was standing directly behind her. He was so close she almost knocked right into him. He pulled her close as he had in front of the café. He stroked her hair and whispered to her.

"I'm sorry." He said as he hugged her tighter.

The next few weeks were more of the same. Harper would go to work at the café or the gallery. Twice a week, she went to her classes at the community college. Zaine would argue with her that she didn't know anything about the things he was going through. He would say how he needed her and lash out when she had to work or go to class. She began visiting her family less and spending less time with Cloe to please Zaine. It was easier than arguing all the time. But he still managed to find things to argue about. He was drinking more and more, and his temper flared whenever she disagreed with him. He would say he was sorry for screaming at her. He'd say it was the stress of not working and the situation with his uncle. She felt bad for him. His uncle believed he stole the money, but he denied it. He claimed he was somehow being set up, but he wasn't allowed anywhere near the office or any of the job sites to find out by who. Harper believed him. She thought, *why would he steal that money?* It wasn't as if he needed it. He owned the apartment, and he still had his trust fund that his mother had left him. He began taking day labor and freelance jobs. He said he didn't want to live off his trust fund, that he wanted to earn his money. But something didn't quite feel right to Harper. She felt there was something more going on than what he was telling her.

Then one night that she was staying at his apartment, he left her there alone. He said he would be back soon but wouldn't tell her where he was going. She waited up for him, but as the hours went by and he didn't return, she began to worry. She pulled out her cell phone and called him. A phone rang in the other room. She walked out of his bedroom where she'd been waiting for him, following the sound of the ringing. She found his phone sitting on the kitchen counter. He had forgotten it. She picked up his phone from the counter, turning it over in her hand a few times. She noticed he hadn't put a passcode on his phone. She placed the phone back on the countertop but then picked it up again. She opened it to the home screen and pressed on the icon for his text messages. She scrolled through the names on the screen. Most of the texts came from her or Chris. There were a few from his uncle and his sister. But a new message came through from a name she didn't recognize. The name on the screen read Lizbeth.

Harper heard a noise from the other room. Her heart dropped down to her stomach. It sounded like a knock on the window, but Zaine's apartment was on the top floor so it couldn't be that. She walked into the living room, still holding tightly onto his phone. She peered out the window to see the same large bat from the other night. It must have hit the window. That must have been the sound she had heard. She looked back down at the incoming text on Zaine's phone. She clicked open the message to read the conversation. The bat knocked against the window again, and she jumped. She decided to turn down the blinds to block the view. Somehow that made her feel a bit safer. Looking back down at the screen on the phone, she read the incoming text from Lizbeth.

*Mr. Vladescu is looking for his money. He says to be here with it tomorrow night.*

That was all the message said. But who was Lizbeth, and who was Mr. Vladescu, and why did Zaine owe him money? There were no other messages from whoever this Lizbeth person was. Harper decided to scroll farther down his list of texts to see if she could find any messages from this Mr. Vladescu guy. She didn't see anyone named Mr. Vladescu in his messages or in his contacts. She put the phone down on the coffee table. She paced back and forth, feeling confused and worried about this text, then she walked back into Zaine's bedroom. She walked over to the small wooden desk he kept in the corner of the room. She opened the drawer and started pulling out papers. What she found baffled her. Her hands were shaking as she read through the documents. They were bank statements showing large withdraws until the ending balance was left to only a few hundred dollars. She kept searching. This couldn't be his only bank account. He had to have another one. He couldn't have run through all of his trust fund. She continued searching through the desk, but she didn't see any other bank statements. Then she spotted a black notebook in the drawer. She pulled it out and flipped through the pages. The pages were filled with meaningless words and numbers that she didn't understand what they meant. She saw no coherent sentences. It looked like the writings of a mad man. She closed the notebook and put it back in the drawer. Her mind was reeling. What had Zaine gotten himself into? Had he actually stolen that money from his uncle? Was this Mr. Vladescu person the reason why he needed the money? She continued looking through his things, searching for anything that would give her any sort of clue as to what was happening. She began checking the pockets of his clothes and his bathroom cabinets when she heard the front door open. Zaine walked into the apartment. Harper walked out of the bathroom to greet him.

"What are you doing awake? I figured you'd be asleep by now." He'd asked when he saw her.

"I couldn't sleep. I was worried about you. I tried to call, but you left your phone." She pointed to his cell on the coffee table.

"Oh. Sorry about that." He picked up the phone without saying anything else and walked into the bedroom. Harper began to follow him when he suddenly turned around. Rage showed on his face.

"Have you been going through my phone? And my desk too?

What is this?" He yelled as he picked up the bank statements from the desk. She must have forgotten to put them back in the drawer.

Harper went to open her mouth to respond, but no words came out. She had never seen him this angry and full of rage. They argued plenty, but there was something different in his face this time. He continued yelling at her.

"You don't trust me that much you have to go through my things? Why can't you just take what I tell you; no questions asked. You always have to ask so many questions, and now you're going through my personal things."

"I...I just..." She tried to say something to explain, but still, she struggled for words. He came closer to her. She backed up against the wall. He raised his fist, and she flinched, closing her eyes tight. A loud bang like that of a hammer hitting the wall echoed in her ears. She turned her gaze to see his fist against the wall, inches from her face. She shifted her body to move away from him, but he grabbed her by the throat and slammed her back up against the wall. Still, he continued yelling in her face. His breath reeked of booze and cigarettes.

"What? You just what?" He was yelling.

Tears began to stream down Harper's face. Zaine's hand still wrapped around her throat. She tried to choke out a word or two, but before she could make out an answer, he threw her down. Her head hit the table. A sharp pain traveled down the whole of her spine from the nape of her neck to her lower back, and then everything went dark.

# Four

Harper sat on the chaise lounge, looking out the window at the bright blue moon. It was a clear night, and she felt she had made it productive. Now she just wanted to use the remaining hours of darkness to relax and read her book. She didn't read very much in her old life except for a few novels here and there, but now in her life of the undead, it had become something she enjoyed. It was something that allowed her an escape from the new reality she never really wanted to face. For her, it was a way to stay connected to life. She missed her old life except for maybe those last few months. She had grown up in a moderate lifestyle to two middle-class parents. She had a sister, aunts, uncles, grandparents, and great friends, all who she loved and who loved her back. Sure, she had ups and downs just as anyone else, but overall, life wasn't all that bad. That was, of course, until she met Zaine. Zaine was charming at first. He was handsome and tall, respected in the community. He was unlike anyone Harper had ever met before. He didn't have much family. His mom had passed away when he was just twenty-three, and his dad left long before that when Zaine was only a child. He had no memory of his father and didn't seem to care to find him. He had a sister and an uncle, but they'd had a falling out after Zaine's uncle had fired him from the company for stealing money. So, when Zaine would get mad when she couldn't be with him because she had some family thing or when he wouldn't attend any family functions with her, she would just make excuses for him. She would tell herself he just didn't understand because he didn't have a close family as she had. She believed he would change eventually if she would give him some time. Time, she tried to give him. So much time and so many chances, but things had only progressively gotten worse as time went on. Instead of trying to embrace her family, he tried to alienate her from it. His alcohol and drug problems began to surface. Harper began to realize how Zaine was manipulating her and trying to make his life hers, and the more she tried to pull away, the harder he grasped onto her. They began to argue every day, and each argument grew worse and more aggressive until finally that fateful night, the night of the accident, when everything changed. Except it was no accident, and Harper was no longer alive. Not in the way she used to be. And Zaine was the cause, and Zaine would pay, and Harper would get her revenge.

"Shake it off, Harper." She thought out loud to herself. Thinking about Zaine made her angry inside, but for now, she needed to calm down. She had done all she was going to do for the night. Zaine had seen her. He had felt her touch. He was beginning to question her presence in his dreams and what he believed to be dreams. Harper knew her revenge would take time, and she needed to be patient. She wasn't like Dac or Nikolai, who were each at least a couple of centuries old. She wasn't even as old as Quentin or Emmaline, who is still considered young for vampires have been around for decades.

No, she was a brand-new vampire, only a few years old. She still needed to grow into her powers and strength. Nikolai was the one who made her, and because he was ancient and powerful, she was much stronger than other new vampires but still not strong enough. And she needed to be stronger, much stronger, because once her plan was complete, Dac would never forgive her, and she'd be on her own, and she needed to be prepared for that.

\* \* \*

Harper remembered the moment Nikolai had made her. She could see it in her mind as if it had only happened moments ago. She felt herself rising out of the water, feeling herself entwined with another being. She could feel his firm grasp around her waist and the soft leather of his jacket. The cold water was dripping from her hair, and her soaked clothing clung heavily to her body. Her head was dizzying. His sharp fangs pierced the skin of her neck. She shivered. He drained the blood from her veins, and she was consumed with a mixed sense between pain and ecstasy. Then he pierced the flesh above his collarbone with the sharp pointy nail on his fingertip, dragging his nail across the skin, creating a gaping wound.

Harper wasn't sure if this were real or she was dreaming. Her head was still spinning, and her vision was blurry. She felt his hand around the back of her head, drawing her lips close to the gash. She thought she heard him whisper something in her ear, but she couldn't make out the words. It was almost as if he were speaking to her mind, but her brain couldn't register the distant voice. The blood was now pouring out from the gash in his neck. Almost instinctively, she placed her lips over the bright red blood and began to drink. With each drop of his blood that she swallowed, it was as if she were now connected to him, to his life, to his past. She saw his bright blue eyes in the shadows. She saw a young woman with long black hair, much like her own. She saw the dark dungeon-like room with chains hanging from its walls. One set of those chains was locked around the woman's wrist, constraining her. She could see her struggling, the tears in her eyes, and she could hear her begging for her life. Then she saw another man. He was tall with the palest skin and the shiniest black hair, but it was the redness of his lips, which she noticed most of all. The man reached out and grabbed the woman's neck. He pulled her close. Then she saw the man open his mouth and sink his sharp fanged teeth into the woman's neck. He drank until the woman was drained of all blood and all life. Then he tossed her aside as if she were nothing and disappeared into the darkness. Harper could feel the pain in Nikolai's heart, and at that moment, she realized why he had chosen her. She looked just like the woman in the vision.

She awoke the next night with a thirst, unlike anything she had ever experienced before. She was inside a room unfamiliar to her. The strange room was large, and she was lying on a massive four-poster bed, covered in the smoothest silk sheets and softest comforter. The bed was made of rich mahogany wood, like something out of another period in time. There was also a large mahogany armoire and a vanity table across the room. A crystal chandelier hung from the ceiling, and a small lamp stood on the bedside table. The walls were made of stone, and the floor was wood with a beautifully patterned area rug that covered the space between the end of the bed and the vanity set. While the room was elegant and beautiful, she sensed something wasn't right. Something else besides the unfamiliarity of this place puzzled and alarmed her. This room had no windows.

Harper rose from the bed and walked over to the vanity. She glanced into the mirror, startled by her own appearance. Her skin was paler, and her hair was shinier, and the color more vibrant, like the man in her dream. But that wasn't a dream, was it? Where was she? She looked down at her hands; her nails were longer, forming into sharp tips. Remembering the man from her dream, she looked back up into the mirror, opening her mouth to examine her teeth. What she saw shocked her so much that she almost shrieked. Her two fang teeth were now longer and sharper. She touched the upper left fang tooth with the tongue. The sharpened tooth pierced her tongue, drawing a small amount of blood. Just then, she heard a light knock on the door. As she turned, she noticed the door slowly opening. Her heart was now pounding hard in her chest. Something had altered her appearance. What was happening to her, and who was coming into the room? Was it her capture?

A man then walked through the door. His dark hair was straight combed to one side, resting at his chin. She noticed it was shaved underneath. He wore black jeans, a black button-down shirt, and black calf-length boots. Who was this guy?

"Ah, you are awake. I brought you something for nourishment. Figured you'd be thirsty." He held in his hand a large steel goblet. He tried to hand it to her but placed it down on the nightstand next to the bed when she did not take it. "You should drink this. It will quench your thirst."

"Who are you? Where is this place? Why did you bring me

here, and what the hell did you do to me?" She yelled back to him.

"Drink first. Then I will tell you everything. You'll need your strength first'"

"I am not drinking anything!" She yelled back in defiance.

"Suit yourself. I will come back once you've calmed down a little. I understand this is all very confusing, but if you don't drink soon, you will start to feel the pains of your thirst, and you will become weaker. You need nourishment." At that, he calmly turned around and walked out of the room.

Harper looked down at the goblet. The thick liquid swirled inside the cup. It smelled almost sweet like wine and was red like the color of blood. Was it blood? Whose blood was it? What was going on here, and why was she craving whatever was in this cup? Unable to resist any longer, she picked up the heavy steel goblet and drank its contents. She drank until it was empty. The liquid was thick and sweet. But didn't blood taste salty? So, it couldn't be blood, right?

She placed the goblet back on the nightstand and cautiously opened the bedroom door. Slowly she stepped out into a long hallway. She walked carefully along the corridor, searching for the man who had brought her here or an exit. Finally, she came to two double doors at the end of the hall. She stepped into the room, first noticing the bookshelf filled with books covering the opposite wall. There was a fireplace to the right of the room with a fire burning in it. Harper also noticed it was another room without any windows. Across the room was a desk, and there sat the man from her room earlier. The same man from her dream with the bright blue eyes. The one who carried her out of the water. What a terrible nightmare, but what the hell was actually going on? All that could not have happened, could it?

"I knew you'd come. Unfortunately, the events of last night were no nightmare. I will explain as best I can. Please have a seat."

Was he reading her mind? She shook her head slightly to shake the thought. That was impossible. People didn't read minds. She sat in a red cushioned chair next to the fireplace. The room was drafty, and the warmth of the fire felt comforting. They both sat in silence for a moment, and then the man began to speak again.

"My name is Nikolai. I know you must be very confused right now. Yes, I can read your thoughts, but only the ones you leave open to reading. One day you will become conscious of which thoughts you are leaving open for others to read and which ones you are not. I don't know what you remember from last night, as most of your thoughts are closed off. You are very guarded. But that is good. Anyway, as I was saying, I don't know what you remember from last night, but there was a terrible accident. I pulled you from the water. Then I bit you and allowed you to drink from me."

"What do you mean, you bit me? What the fuck kind of crazy person are you? What the fuck is going on here?" She interrupted him. But he stayed calm, answered her questions, and continued with his storied explanation.

"I realize how this sounds, but you will come to see the truth of it soon enough. I am a vampire, and now you are too. When I pulled you from the water, I had to turn you. It was the only way to save you."

With those words, he flashed visions into her mind, evidence he was telling the truth. She saw him in a foreign country and clearly in an earlier time. Which year it was, she was not sure, but she could tell it was centuries ago. A man was coming up to him inside a small cottage. She saw the moment he was transformed. His hair was still the same length as it was now but styled differently, parted down the middle. He wore a narrow-sleeved black coat, a grey waistcoat, and breeches. On his feet were black riding boots. The other man similarly dressed came up close behind him, drawing his sharp fanged teeth into Nikolai's neck. And then she saw the image of the night before. Nikolai's arms wrapped around her waist. Her hair and clothes were soaked with water, him sucking her neck and then her drinking from the wound in his.

"You did this to me! You stole my life to turn me into whatever this is you are!" Harper furiously screamed at him, rising from her chair.

"I did what I had to do to save you! He stole your life! I gave you your life back! It might not be the same as before, but it is what it is now?" Nikolai yelled back, losing his patience with her. They both stood silent for a moment.

Harper sank back down in the chair, remembering the earlier events of the night before. Her argument with Zaine and him pushing her down. She remembered the feeling of hitting her head against the coffee table and the rapid pain shooting down her back. Her voice shaky, she asked, "You said it was a horrible accident, but it wasn't an accident, was it? He killed me, didn't he?"

"Yes, well, almost. When I pulled you out from the water, you were dying, and you would have if I hadn't done what I did." Nikolai replied. The sadness and pity showed in his bright blue eyes. "I had noticed you a few weeks ago. I sensed you were troubled, but I wasn't sure why at first. I began to watch and keep a close eye on you as much as possible. I would enter your thoughts whenever I could, and then one day, I saw you with him. I sensed something about him was dangerous, and it was only a matter of time before he hurt you. I had to protect you. You reminded me so much of someone I used to know a very long time ago."

*The woman I saw in the vision,* Harper, thought to herself.

"Yes, the woman you saw when you drank from me. She was my wife."

"You've really got to stop reading my mind like that." She said with a sarcastic smile.

"Sorry occupational hazard." He gave a little smile back.

"She was very beautiful, your wife. You must miss her a lot. I felt your pain and heartache last night. I'm so sorry for your loss."

"Yes, I loved her with all my heart, and I've missed her every day since. I wasn't strong enough to save her then from the one who murdered her. But I am strong now, and I couldn't let you die. I just wish I could have saved you sooner."

"The vampire who made you, he killed your wife?"

"No, his brother killed her before I became a vampire. The one who made me, he came to me later. He offered me a new life with a strength I'd never imagined and the chance to avenge my wife and unborn child."

"And did you avenge them?"

"Yes, but in truth, it didn't heal the pain and loss that I felt. And times are different now. Now we only fight and feed for survival. And even that is rare. That is the most important thing you must remember. Dac has made it so that we no longer need feed directly from humans. I will teach you all you need to know about the new powers and strength you will soon experience. And as you age in your new life, you will grow stronger, and your powers will grow stronger, but you must remember only to use them when necessary and never murder for revenge or pleasure. I realize you may one day want to go after the ones who you hurt in your old life, but you mustn't do that. It is the one rule Dac has for all of us. He is the one who made me, and he is the head of this house. If you break that one rule, the others will come to destroy you, but most of all, Dac. He will view it as a sign of betrayal against all he..." Nikolai paused; "we have built. As I said, it was long ago when I became a vampire, and times were different then. Dac brought me into the middle of a feud between him and his brother. His brother was a ruthless predator, and he killed for sport. The ones he fed on, he preyed upon and tortured them first. He'd bring them to the catacombs within his castle, chained them up like animals, tortured, and beat them. Then he would suck them dry of all their blood and toss them aside for their corpses to rot. He had no respect for human life even though he was once human himself."

"That sounds so horrible. How did this vampire get your wife?"

"Everyone in the village knew of the rumors and vampire folklore. The older generations told stories of a vampire named Luca. Luca was a man who had gone missing from our village about a hundred years earlier. He had never been found despite his family's search for him. Everyone said he just vanished without a trace. After a while, people began saying vampires had abducted him, and some years later, rumors had surfaced that he had been sighted lurking around the village in search of victims. He, along with other vampires, was said to live up in this castle in the mountains. But you see, that was all it was, so we all thought anyway. Sure, some of the older generations still believed, but it was just silly superstition for most of us. The castle appeared to have long been abandoned. No one in our little village had ever actually seen or known anyone to come or go from there, nor had anyone actually seen a vampire. We heard rumors for years of people disappearing if they got too close to the castle, but most people didn't dare venture out that far into the mountains as it was heavily infested by wolves. We mostly believed the ones who disappeared had been attacked and eaten by those wolves.

"But that night, the night Luca took my wife, I was gone, I was helping another friend in the village with his horses. A visitor was coming into town who wanted to buy the horses from him. I was helping my friend prepare for the sale. I wasn't expecting to be gone that long, and when I returned home, my wife was gone. A neighbor told me she heard screaming and saw my wife being dragged away in the direction of the castle by a dark, powerfully dressed man." Nikolai paused for a moment. Harper could sense the pain he was feeling from recollecting that night.

"It's ok. You don't have to say anymore. I saw what happened."

"I tried to save her. I went to that castle, but when I got to that room, it was as if I were frozen in place and all I could do was watch in torment as he killed them. I don't even know how I got back to my cottage, but that was when Dac came to me. I agreed to let him turn me into a vampire like him and help him in his fight against Luca. He taught me how to use my strength and powers, and together we fought against his brother. It was a tough fight, but in the end, we overcame Luca and destroyed him. The others that lived with him fled, and we never heard from them again. At first, we searched for them, so we could destroy them like we had Luca. But after a while, we decided they weren't any risk to us without Luca. So, we kept a low profile to avoid the townspeople and eventually left our home country. It was after that we agreed to build a better coven, a safe place for other vampires like ourselves. There are four of us who live here now, but there have been others in the past. And we all live by the same code in order to ensure our existence."

\* \* \*

"Hey. Reading again?" Emmaline asked as she entered the library, breaking Harper from her memories. She was wearing her usual lace dress and Victorian-style boots. Tonight's color was a deep purple. She wore a necklace of multiple strands of beads around her neck and fingerless gloves on her hands.

"Hi, Emmaline. No. I've been holding on to this book for hours, but I haven't been able to concentrate on it. I guess I just got a lot on my mind. I was thinking of my first night here, actually."

"I remember when you first got here. You were so shy and reserved. You've really grown into your new life here over the last couple of years."

"Thanks. I really appreciate it. You guys really are like family to me."

"I think I should tell you, though; we all know what you've been up to. We know where you've been going these past few nights. Just be careful, ok. Please don't get too caught up in getting revenge. That can only lead to trouble. If you take this thing with Zaine too far, you know what will happen.

41

You are very special to Dac and to Nikolai. Dac will tolerate a lot because he cares very much for you, and Nikolai feels protective of you for his own reasons, but Nikolai's protection will only reach so far if Dac feels betrayed."

"Don't worry; I won't do anything foolish. I just wanted to scare Zaine a little bit. Make him think he's going crazy or something. That's all. OK?"

"Just be careful, please." With that, Emmaline turned to leave the room, and Harper gave her a little wink.

# Five

"You need to talk to Harper, Nikolai. You need to get her under control before she takes this revenge thing too far. She shouldn't be going to see Zaine like that. She's putting us all at risk."

"I know, Dac. I thought she was moving past her anger, but it's becoming clear she is not. You know it's the anniversary of the accident of her death and rebirth as a vampire. I guess it's just hitting her a little harder this year, but I will talk to her."

"Be sure you get through to her. She needs to stop this." Dac demanded as he walked out of the room.

Nikolai sat back in his chair, remembering the first night he saw Harper. It was a warm summer night, but there was a cool breeze coming through. The sky was clear; the moon and stars were exceptionally bright, sparkling against the midnight sky. She was standing alone on the boardwalk, staring out at the waves crashing against the shore. Her long dark hair was blowing slightly in the light breeze. She reminded him so much of his late wife, and when she turned around just enough for him to see her face, the resemblance was uncanny. He could see in her eyes that she was upset. He heard her repeating, "I just want my life back," over and over again in her thoughts. He felt so connected to her but also scared for her. He began to have this overwhelming feeling to protect her. He sensed she was in some sort of danger but wasn't sure what it was.

For the next few weeks, he watched her. Every night he would look in on her to make sure she was ok. He watched as Zaine argued and yelled at her. He saw the way Zaine manipulated her into doing things she clearly was uncertain about doing. He realized this was what she had meant that night by wanting her life back. He recognized now that the danger she was in was coming from Zaine. Then one night, he saw as Zaine pushed her to the floor. He saw her head hit the table. He watched Zaine lift her up and drag her out of the apartment, shoving her into the passenger side of his car and then drive off. The car was moving fast and swerving along the road, then suddenly it veered off into the grass and down the hill into the deep end of the lake. He saw as Zaine emerged from the water, but where was Harper? It was at this moment that it became clear this was no accident. Zaine had planned to drive Harper into the lake and leave her body there. Nikolai dove into the water, pulled Harper from the car, and up and out of the lake. He had her wrapped in his arms. His mind and heart were reeling with emotion and memories of the night Luca had taken his wife from him. He had to save this girl, but he could feel she was close to dying. There was only one thing he could do. He sunk his teeth into the side of her neck. "Please forgive me." He whispered as he continued to suck the blood from her veins. Feeling such a deep emotional connection to her, he took his fingernail, cutting into his own flesh. The blood began to pour out from the freshly created wound. "Drink," he whispered to her. As she drank the blood spilling from the gash in his throat, he could feel her coming back, and he carried her away to the home he shared with Dac and the others, knowing she was finally safe.

Bringing his thoughts back to the present, he placed his head in his hands. He knew he had to talk to Harper. He had to talk her out of continuing to see Zaine. What was she doing showing herself to him like that? Why was she provoking him? Nothing good could come of her being so hell-bent on getting revenge. Harper had been so distressed after her murder. Payback was always on her mind, and when she found out that Zaine had convinced everyone that it had been a car accident and only received a few months in jail for reckless driving and a DUI, she was furious. Nikolai had stayed close by Harper's side in those first days, teaching her how to be a vampire. He also tried teaching her ways to channel her anger. He thought she was moving past it and finally becoming comfortable and accepting her new life. Lately, though, Harper had been becoming distant. She was sneaking far off alone at night, and everyone knew she wasn't going to feed. They didn't need to.

Dac provided more than enough food supply with the blood bank that he ran a few blocks down. Every night they would all meet in the dining hall. Dac would sit at the head of the table, Nikolai to his right and Harper to his left. Emmaline would sit next to Nikolai, and then there was Quentin, who would sit next to Harper. They would drink from wine glasses and discuss the books they read, things they'd watched on TV, or the places they visited the night before. Except for Quentin, they rarely wandered out alone and always after they had fed in order to resist temptation. Quentin was different in that he didn't feed off the blood, but instead, he fed off the energy of other living beings. All of them, however, were the same in that they tried to live the simplest of lives to blend in with the living. But lately, Harper had been going out alone early in the evening and arriving at dinner late, long after everyone else. Dac was becoming suspicious, so Nikolai asked Quentin to follow her one day.

"Don't let her see you. You're great at concealing yourself. We need to see what she's been up to; I'm worried about her."

"Us too. Emmaline and I have been talking. We've noticed changes in Harper. She's withdrawn worse than when she first got here. I'll be careful she doesn't see me and let you know what I find out."

"Thank you."

Quentin left Nikolai's office that night and returned later with the news. He had successfully followed Harper to an apartment near the beach in Aura Springs. He watched through the window as she stood in front of a man. Without speaking, she embraced him in a kiss. As she pulled away, Quentin saw the blood dripping from the man's mouth. He watched as the man wiped his mouth in horror, and Harper vanished. He hurried after her. She was headed back in the direction of the house, so he stayed behind a while so she wouldn't notice he had followed her. When he returned, describing the man and all he'd seen, Nikolai realized it was Zaine. Harper was going to see Zaine. He told Quentin to continue watching Harper. He needed to know what she was doing, and he needed to protect her.

"I had a feeling you'd want to speak with me. I figured I'd save you the trouble of coming to look for me." Harper said to Nikolai as she walked into his office.

Nikolai looked up at her. Her hair was as long and shiny as ever, her lips bright red and full but not red from lipstick. It was what happened after they drank the blood of humans. Was it Zaine's blood? What had she done?

"Don't worry. He's not dead." She said to him, reading the worry on his face and the thoughts in his mind.

"What is going on, Harper? What have you been doing going to Zaine like this? You could be putting us all in danger."

"Please don't be so dramatic. He doesn't realize what is happening. He's an addict. He thinks he is hallucinating, and that is what I want him to think. I want him to think he is losing his mind. Terrify him a little bit, that's all."

"Harper, you need to let go of this revenge and anger you harbor inside of you. This is not good for you. It will eat you alive."

"Alive! I am not alive! I haven't been alive for three years, and it is his fault! I miss my family, and I miss my old life. And that is his fault and your fault too. You should have let me drown in that lake that night. You should have left me to die."

He saw the tears form and fall from her eyes. He wrapped her in his arms and stroked her hair.

"I love you, Harper. I will always protect you, just as I did that night. Just as I am trying to do now."

"Love me? Protect me? Is that what you call it? You took my life from me that night just the same as he did. Only what you did was worse. You took me here and made me a part of this life of immortality that I never asked for all because I look like your dead wife. I hate Zaine for what he did to me, and I hate you too!" She screamed as she pulled away from him, turned on her heels, and stormed out of the room.

Nikolai stood there, stunned for a moment. Harper's hateful

words were sinking in and filling his mind. His heart was now aching. He had never thought of it like that, but was she right? Had he been just as bad as Zaine?

\* \* \*

Harper marched down the hall. She hadn't meant for the words to come out like that, but how could he say he loved her and protected her? She was fuming with anger. She had to get away. She needed to clear her head and get back to her plan. She couldn't let him or the others get in the way, and now she knew they had been following her. It was probably Quentin. She'd have to talk to him. Get him on her side. Convince him to help her. But first, she needed to be alone. She grabbed her jacket off the bed, her phone and earbuds off her dresser and left the house, and headed out of Aura City towards Aura Springs to her favorite spot, the beach.

She walked up to the end of the boardwalk and sat on her favorite bench next to the old soda shop. This was her favorite spot when she was alive and still was. It was peaceful and quiet. The soda shop had closed up years ago, long before Harper had moved to the area. There was nothing else on this end of the boardwalk, so it was long forgotten and deserted, just as she liked it. She could look out at the ocean waves crashing onto the shore or look out past the horizon and imagine being anywhere else. Then suddenly, she realized she wasn't alone. She looked over and saw Nikolai standing against the side of the old soda shop, one foot up against the wall. He was dressed in his usual all-black from head to toe, staring down at her. His bright blue eyes were showing through the dark hair falling in front of his face.

"What the hell are you doing here? I came here to be alone. How did you even know I'd be here?"

"This is where I first saw you that first night three years ago, so I figured I'd find you here tonight. You were standing right there leaning against the railing staring out the ocean that night. I used to come here too when I wanted to be alone, away from the house. Everyone seems to forget this spot exists. It's so quiet and secluded here, away from everything and everyone. But anyway, I came to apologize. I wanted to say I'm sorry. You were right. I'm no better than Zaine."

"No. I should apologize to you. I shouldn't have said those terrible things. The thing is, I don't hate you. All of you have become my family now. It's just sometimes I really miss my human family, you know?"

"Yea, I get it. I miss my wife every day, and that was centuries ago."

"But you got your revenge. You destroyed the one that killed her, right? So at least you got that."

"That doesn't heal the pain, though, Harper. It doesn't make it hurt any less. Only time can do that. You've got to get revenge out of your head. You know what will happen if you don't. You need to let this go. Please, will you promise me you'll let it go? Channel your anger some other way. Read your books, go back to painting like you used to."

"I quit painting the night I died."

"Please just find some other way to deal with the anger other than revenge. Please." He begged her.

"But then he never has to pay for what he did to me. He just gets to go on living his life as normal. I'm sorry, Nikolai, I can't promise you that, but I can promise I won't kill him. I won't let him realize what's really going on. He'll only think it's a bad dream. He'll go a little crazy, and then I'll leave him alone. OK? I just want him to feel the guilt of his crimes."

Nikolai sat next to her on the bench, put his hand over hers, "I know you want him to pay, so do I, but I wish you could just be happy with us. We all love you so much. Especially Dac, but if he feels you betrayed him, I won't be able to protect you; none of us will."

"I know. I love all you guys too." She rested her head on Nikolai's shoulder, and together they sat there silently staring into the night sky.

# Six

It had been a few nights since Zaine's last nightmare. He was relieved about that. He still had a scratch on his neck from the last one. In his previous dream of Harper, she had stood again in front of him in his living room. Unable to move, it was like she had put him in some type of trance each time she appeared. This time she had placed both her hands on each side of his neck, holding him in a tight grip. He felt a sharp sting as if being cut by a knife; he realized it was one of her fingernails. She pulled her one hand away and placed her lips against his neck, where she had cut him. She had licked his neck softly at first, and then she began sucking harder and harder. His knees began to buckle, the mix of pleasure and pain so intense he could barely stand. She let him go, and he fell to the floor. She was gone, and he awoke weak and feverish in the very place he had fallen in the dream. His dreams were getting so intense he was beginning to sleepwalk and apparently cutting himself. These nightmares were also making him ill, so when the last few nights his dreams had been quiet, he'd been happy about it. When Nita had asked what had happened to his neck, he made some excuse about cutting himself shaving, but he could tell she knew it was a lie. How could he tell her he was dreaming of his dead ex-girlfriend, the one he'd murdered?

He had a job lined up for today, which was good because it had been a few weeks since his last one. He'd be building a shed for a family down the street. It was for a single mom of three named Janice, and they had just recently moved into the area. She had bought a small house, but it didn't have a garage or much storage space, so he'd agreed to build her a shed in the backyard for her kids' bikes and stuff. He'd told her he'd start this afternoon around two o'clock. He looked at the time. He had about ten minutes to get over there. He pulled on a pair of jeans and a t-shirt. The sun was shining so it wouldn't feel too cold, especially once he'd started working. He grabbed his toolbox and started out the door.

He arrived at Janice's house right at about two o'clock. She opened the front door just as he was about to ring the bell. She was wearing dark blue jeans and a lavender-colored scoop neck sweater with the sleeves pushed up. She had black flat boots on her feet and a dishtowel in her hand. Her hair was pulled back into a low ponytail. She looked good for a mom of three, probably in her early thirties.

"Hi, Zaine. How are you? The little one is taking a nap didn't want to wake her. All the supplies are in the backyard. You can go straight back and get started."

"OK. You sure the noise won't wake your daughter?"

"Her room is on the other side of the house, so it should be alright. Would you like something to drink?"

"Water will be fine. Thank you."

Zaine walked to the back of the house to survey the supplies to build the shed as Janice went to grab him a bottle of water. He started sifting through the pile of wood stacked on the ground. He was starting with the floor today, and maybe he'd get to the frame. Finish up the walls and roof the rest of the week and paint it when it's done. Janice came out briefly, handed him the bottled water, and told him if he needed anything, she'd be in the kitchen and to just go right in. He began putting the pieces together for the shed flooring, working well into the evening hours. Once he laid the floor down, he began to put up the wood framing. Janice reappeared a short while later, offering him a break.

"Would you like some dinner? The girls are all playing in their room. You can come inside and take a break if you'd like."

He was getting hungry, so he agreed and followed her into the house. "Thank you. May I use your bathroom to clean up a bit?"

"Of course. It's right down the hall, first door on the right."

The house was small, so the bathroom was easy to find. It was not surprisingly a tiny space. Kids' toys were in the bathtub, a lime green towel was hanging on the towel rack, and cosmetics covered the sink's counter space. He stared into the mirror for a second, examining the cut on his neck almost all the way healed. He reached into the pocket of his jeans and pulled out a small plastic bag. He snorted a little bit of the white powder over the small bathroom sink, washed his hands, and walked back out to the kitchen. Janice had a plate of chicken, rice, green beans, and a small dinner roll set out on the kitchen table for him. He ate quickly, barely tasting the food, thanked her for the meal, and went back to the yard to continue working. By this time, it was well past dark, it being the fall season and all. He turned on the backlights and returned to his work on the shed.

It began to mist, and Zaine could see the dense fog rolling in. A dog was howling somewhere in the distance. He hurriedly covered the part of the shed he had built and the remaining wood with a tarp. He packed up his tools and headed to his car to return home. As he began driving, the fog was becoming thicker, making it hard to see. He didn't have too far to go, so he continued driving even though his vision was limited. His cell phone pinged with a message. He quickly glanced over at the screen, picking the phone up from the passenger seat, trying not to take his eyes off the road. The name on the screen read Lizbeth. His heart rate picked up a few beats with the sight of her name on his phone. He hadn't heard from her in three years and hoped to never hear from her again. He tapped on the screen to open the message.

*Mr. Vladescu wants to see you. Meet at midnight tomorrow night—the old spot. You remember.*

Just then, his car rolled over a bump in the road. He didn't remember there being anything there before. He slowed down his car but then decided it was best just to keep driving, figuring it was probably just some animal, or maybe something fell off the back of some truck or something. He decided he'd check his car in the morning.

He arrived at his apartment building, parked his car in his usual parking spot under the tree, and walked up the stairs to his apartment. As he unlocked the door and stepped inside, he threw his keys down on the side table. He sat on the now worn black leather couch, rested his elbows on his knees, and ran his hands through his hair. He hated this place whenever he actually gave it any thought. He used to own a luxury apartment in Aura City with all the modern amenities. It had brand new hardwood floors, large windows throughout, and central air and heat. The kitchen had all the modern stainless-steel appliances. The building had a clubhouse, a pool, and a resident gym. It had a full parking lot and also a covered parking garage for residents. Too bad he had to sell it soon after his release from jail after Harper's death. It was a good thing Harper's body was never found in the lake. He told everyone he hadn't seen harper in two days since the night he surprised her at the cafe, and he was able to convince everyone his car ended up in the lake because he was driving drunk.

His new place was a garden-style brick apartment building in Aura Springs, not far from the beach. It had only a tiny parking lot and street parking access. The grounds were always unkempt and filled with litter. The lighting surrounding the place rarely worked. There were no building amenities, not even an onsite maintenance crew. The inside was dated with old carpet and old cabinetry, and old appliances. But it was affordable, and he needed the money from the sale of his old apartment after he exhausted most of his trust fund when he got involved in high-stakes poker games with Mr. Vladescu and Lizbeth. Now Mr. Vladescu was attempting to contact him again through Lizbeth the way he always had.

Zaine knew he had no choice but to meet with him tomorrow night, but he couldn't help feeling it was a bad idea. After his short time in jail, he told himself he wouldn't get involved in such things anymore, not that he could afford to. He had lost so much money that he had owed Mr. Vladescu tens of thousands of dollars in the end. He ended up stealing money from his uncle's company and getting fired, losing any opportunity to run the company one day as he had planned. He had become so stressed and short-tempered that he'd accidentally killed Harper when he caught her snooping through his personal things. He never meant for her to get hurt. Yes, he was angry with her, and he was rough with her, but he didn't mean to kill her. But she had fallen and hit her head. When he couldn't wake her up and saw the blood coming from the fresh wound on her head, he had no choice but to carry her out of the apartment and drive her into that lake. Things in his life were getting bad enough, and he couldn't risk getting caught with anything else, especially if it would somehow expose Mr. Vladescu and Lizbeth. Vladescu was dangerous, and Zaine was already in way too deep.

After he had gone to jail, he hadn't heard from Vladescu or Lizbeth, and when he returned home and still hadn't heard anything from them, he figured Mr. Vladescu had just cut his losses and moved on. He knew that it was naive to think that, but it had been years since he'd heard anything about either of them. He still owed Vladescu a few thousand dollars, so he must be calling to collect, but Zaine didn't have that kind of money anymore. He was barely getting by on his odd jobs and day labor work. The thought of this meeting tomorrow night was getting to him. He went to the kitchen to grab a beer but decided he needed something stronger tonight. He poured himself a glass of whiskey instead.

The next night Zaine drove to the spot where he was to meet with Mr. Vladescu. It was an old two-story colonial brick building on the outskirts of town. Tall weeds stood overgrown in front of the building. A narrow concrete walkway led up to the dark green front door. He texted Lizbeth to say he was there so she could meet him at the door as she always had in the past. She opened the door and led him down the hall. The inside was as dark and damp as he remembered. They came to the door at the back of the house that led to the basement. Lizbeth ushered him into the darkened room ahead of her and closed the door behind them. Zaine walked silently down the creaky wooden steps, with Lizbeth following closely behind him. He took each step with careful precision as he tried to adjust his eyesight to the darkness surrounding him. The warmth of Lizbeth's breath brushed against the back of his neck, and sweat began forming on the palms of his hands.

"Welcome, Zaine. Please have a seat." Vladescu said as he gestured to the seat across from him. He was seated at a round poker table. The candles set on either side of him flickered in the darkness giving off little light. His dark hair and pale skin reflected against the candlelight. His dark eyes were piercing right through Zaine. For a moment, Zaine thought he saw a flicker of red appear in his pupils.

Fear enveloped Zaine as he walked across the concrete flooring of the unfinished basement. Zaine clenched his fist and swallowed hard. He took the seat offered him across from Vladescu. Lizbeth handed him a glass of whiskey and then took a seat at the only other chair next to Mr. Vladescu.

"Do you know why I asked you here?" Mr. Vladescu asked

"The money I still owe you. I...I don't have it all, but I can get it if you can give me just a few weeks." Zaine answered back, his voice shaking with blatant fear.

"I have a game coming up. I'm going to give you a chance to win your money back. It's a very high-stakes game—more than you've ever played. You won't have to put any money in. I'll cover that. When you win, I'll take my cut and the back pay you owe me, and you will be left with more money than when you first came to me three years ago."

Zaine remembered that first night. He was out looking for

something to do. Harper had been working and studying so much, leaving little time for Zaine, and he was growing restless. He met Lizbeth in a bar that night. She told him about this secret poker game happening nearby and invited him to attend. There was a luminescent appearance to her skin and an intense sparkle in her wide eyes. She stared deeply into his eyes, holding his gaze for what seemed like an eternity. His mind became hazy, and almost as if he had no control of his own body, he followed her out of the bar. The first few nights, he had won generously, but after a while, he began to lose with each game and each bet he made. He lost more and more money until he was so in debt to Mr. Vladescu that he lost everything, including his freedom.

The thought of getting into another high-stakes game made Zaine anxious, but as he looked at Mr. Vladescu with his hand on the silver 9 mm handgun set on the table pointed in his direction, Zaine knew he didn't have a choice. "When is the game?" He asked.

"You will receive a text with the location. At that time, you will go to the designated spot immediately. The text will contain instructions, including how long you have to arrive at the game. Do not be late." Mr. Vladescu told him and then motioned to Lizbeth.

Lizbeth rose from her seat next to Vladescu and motioned for Zaine to follow her. Zaine rose to his feet. His legs were weak underneath him, and he prayed they wouldn't betray him and leave him lying on the cold floor. However, he somehow managed to keep his composure even with his heart pounding fast in his chest. The last thing he wanted was to get caught up back with these two, but what choice did he have? He followed Lizbeth back up the stairs wanting nothing more than to get out of this house and away from her and Mr. Vladescu.

"It's been a long time Zaine. You look good." She said to him as they entered the central part of the house.

"Yea. Thanks," Was all he could muster back in response.

She took his hand in hers. The soft skin of her hand was cold against his. She led him up another flight of stairs to a second-floor bedroom. The room was furnished with a small bed in the middle of the room, a small side table in the corner containing a single dull lamp, and heavy drapes drawn closed over the windows. The sweet scent of her heavy perfume assaulted the inside of his nostrils. She turned to face him, her lips crimson red, her rich dark auburn hair fell in loose waves grazing her slightly exposed breasts. She stepped closer to him until their bodies were touching. Suddenly he felt warm all over as the heat rose inside him. He kept thinking he shouldn't be there, yet he couldn't turn away from her. She looked straight into his eyes then gently kissed his lips. He embraced her as she slid her cold hands down the sides of his face and then around the back of his neck, sending a shiver down his warm body. She pulled her lips away from his placing them on his neck. Her sharp teeth then broke through his flesh; a prickling sensation ran through his nerves. His knees grew weak as she sucked the blood from his veins. He held onto her waist to steady himself, pulling her in closer.

The next morning, he awoke in a feverish state, unsure of where he was. The room looked vaguely familiar from last night, but what had happened, and why was he here? He rose from the bed in a state of confusion and walked over to the window peering through the thick drapes out the window into the morning sunlight. He remembered then the conversation with Mr. Vladescu in the basement and then coming up to the room with Lizbeth, but that was all he could remember. The rest of the night was all just a blank.

He left the room and found a bathroom across the hall. He stood for a moment staring at his reflection. His skin was pale and ashen, and sweat was dripping from his forehead. He splashed his face with water and went to look for Lizbeth or Vladescu. The house was empty. They were gone.

# Seven

Dac sat, staring at his computer. The screen cast a blue light across his face in the otherwise darkened room as the breaking news story stared back at him. He clenched his jaw and fists as he read the news article on the screen.

A young woman found dead in the middle of the road early this morning, it read. While it first appeared to be a hit-and-run accident, upon further inspection, she was found to have two puncture wounds on her neck just above her collar bone. She had been mutilated and suffered a significant loss of blood. The authorities are assuming a wild animal attacked her. Although there was evidence that she had been run over by a car, it appears she had been dead for some time before that. Comments from the family expressed their deep sadness and grief of this tragic incident as they were left wondering how someone could just run her over and not stop, even if she had already been dead. Police are warning the public to beware of wildlife and stray dogs in the area.

Dac slammed his fists down on the desk. He knew this was not the work of a wild animal. A vampire killed this woman. He ran his fingers across his face and through his hair. This was not good. He had spent so many years keeping a low profile, never risking exposure, and now this. The only good thing was that humans no longer believed in vampires. By the time he and Nikolai left their home country, vampires were becoming mostly a thing of legend and folklore. But still, the risk of exposure was too significant to their existence.

Thinking of this young woman made his mind race back to a time long ago before he and Nikolai killed his brother Luca. He remembered how he first discovered the horrific things Luca had been doing. He remembered how Luca turned him into a vampire like himself, expecting Dac to join him in his evil reign.

Dac had been only fourteen when Luca had first disappeared, and rumors suggested he was dead. He had spent the next ten years searching for Luca, never believing that his brother had died. Then one night, just as he was ready to give up hope, Luca appeared to him. Their father had just died, and their mother had died just a year before that. Dac was facing a new life on his own. He was alone in the darkness of his room, ready to succumb to the very misery of his mind when suddenly Luca was standing in front of him. Elated at the sight of him, Dac jumped up to hug his long-lost brother, but Luca instantly backed away. He studied his older brother for a moment sensing something was wrong. Luca's appearance hadn't changed in 10 years. Luca was 12 years older than Dac but staring at him now, they looked to be around the same age.

"I want you to come back with me to my home. It is up in the mountains. There I can keep you safe." Luca had said to him.

Though he could sense something off with Luca, he was

so happy to see him, finally reunited with the brother he had mourned for so many years that he packed his things and went with him without question. Outside, a horse-drawn carriage was waiting to take them to Luca's home. They traveled all night through the woods and up the mountain. The thick fog of the night left little light. Wolves howled in the distance, and bats swarmed the sky around them. Dac sat nervously in the carriage, hoping they would arrive at their destination soon. As they rode farther up the mountain, a large stone wall with iron gates came into view. They rode through the gates down a long path to a large castle. They entered through the large doors, and Luca called to a man in the next room who was clearly a servant. The man entered the foyer. He was an older man with grey hair, and he stood slightly hunched over.

"Please take my brother to his room. Then you may go." The man bowed slightly to Luca then picked up Dac's case, which contained the few clothes he had brought along with him. Dac followed the older man up a flight of stone steps to a door at the end of the long hall. Inside, the room was furnished with lavish drapes to cover the windows. A large bed sat in the middle of the room, and an armoire stood in the corner. A small table and washing station were against the wall. The old man sat the case down on the floor, then closed the door behind him. Moments later, he returned with a tray of food and water then retook his leave. Only this time, when he left, he locked the door behind him and didn't return. Dac jumped to his feet and ran to the door. He pulled on the door lever, but sure enough, the door was locked. What was this? Was he now a prisoner in his own brother's home?

The next few nights went exactly the same. The old hunched-over man would come and leave food for him a few times a day. Whenever Dac would question him, he would just say it was in his best interest to stay in that room until his brother had called for him. Each time Dac would slink down onto the bed and pick at his food, and he would sit and wait. Until finally, one night, he heard the lock in the door, but instead of the old man, two women appeared in the doorway. The first had long auburn hair and was dressed in a light blue gown with a lace trim surrounding the low square neckline. Her eyes were dark and intense, and her skin glowed. The other, dressed in a similar fashion, had bright golden hair that fell in loose curls past her shoulders. Her eyes were a softer shade of blue. The woman with the auburn hair spoke, "Your brother would like to see you now. Come with us." Both women turned to leave the room. Dac stood up, brushing out the wrinkles from his clothes, and followed behind them. They walked down the same long hall and down the same stairs he had walked up that first night. The two women brought him to a large room where Luca was waiting for him. Without saying a word, they both retreated, leaving Dac and his brother to be alone.

"Hello, brother. I trust your accommodations have been to your liking." Luca said to him

"My liking? I do not like being held prisoner! What is going on here? Why are you keeping me locked up in that room?" Dac demanded.

"It was for your own protection. Come now. Please allow me to show you around, and I'll explain everything." Luca explained calmly.

Dac followed his brother as he showed him around the sparsely lit castle. He explained all of the portraits that hung on the walls as they passed each one. "This is your family and your legacy," Luca said to him. "This is the secret our parents never wanted us to know. I found out ten years ago, and I joined my rightful place here amongst all this, and now it is time for you to join me. But there is something else you need to know." Luca led him down another flight of stairs that took them under the castle into the damp catacombs. As they walked, Luca told him stories of the vampire and explained that he had become one. Dac listened fearfully as his brother spoke. Luca's voice barely registered in Dac's mind as if it were far off in the distance, although they stood side by side. Dac could hardly wrap his head around the words he was hearing. Finally, they reached the end of the tunnels and stepped into another large room. The room was cold and dark. A few large candlesticks stood in the corners of the room, giving off the only light. Shackles lined the walls, and blood stained the floor. Dac looked around, horrified.

"I knew you wouldn't come into this willingly. I've been watching you for the past ten years. Watching you grow from a boy into a man, waiting until you were ready, but you are soft and sensitive. But this is your birthright even more so than it was mine, and I am about to give you more wealth and power than you could ever imagine." With those words, Luca lunged at him. Dac saw the red glow in the dark pupils of Luca's eyes. He put his hand out in an attempt to defend himself, but Luca grabbed him by the throat. He was too strong for Dac to fend off. Before he knew what was happening, Luca had his teeth in his neck and was draining the blood from his body even as he struggled. But what Dac hadn't realized was that Luca was filling the wound with his own blood as he drank, making the exchange that would turn Dac into the vampire he was now.

The next night Dac awoke on the cold stone floor. The

memories of the night before came rushing back to him. Distraught at what had become of his brother and now to himself, he searched for a way out. He roamed through the many halls and corridors until he finally found an exit and escaped the compounds of this dreaded castle. It was only then that he realized he had nowhere to go. He wandered through the woods and back down the mountain from which he came a few nights earlier. The wolves were again howling in the background. Their sounds rang in his ears. The bats were flying above in the cloud-covered sky. An eager thirst came over him as he walked through the wooded mountainous terrain towards the village he called home. He reached the clearing faster than he could have imagined. The thirst in him was growing stronger. The scent of nearby humans filled his nostrils. He continued walking along the edge of the woods, unsure of where he was going but knowing he needed to get far away from here.

He walked along the edge of the woods. The leaves rustled in the wind. The crunching sound of movement across the earthy ground caught his attention. Out of the shadows, a young boy appeared. Instinctively he reached out and snatched the boy up by his throat. Before he could make a sound, Dac snapped the boy's neck. With his new vampire teeth, he tore into the boy's flesh. The blood spilled violently out of the boy's now open throat into Dac's mouth and down his shirt. A warmth infused within his body. His chest and arms tingled as he not only drank the boy's blood but took the very essence of his life. When the blood ceased to flow, he dropped the boy's body to the ground. As the euphoric state he had been in began to fade, he looked down at his blood-stained hands and shirt and realized what had just happened. Horrified and hating his brother for what he himself had just done, he pushed the body into the woods and ran into the darkness. When he finally stopped running, he found himself at the cemetery where he had not long ago buried his parents. Sitting at their grave, he cried out and vowed his vengeance.

\* \* \*

Dac rose from his seat at his desk and began to pace the room. Sometimes he envied Quentin's needlessness for blood, although he would occasionally drink it to give himself a more human flesh-toned appearance. Still, Quentin had never been human, so he didn't share that same connection to human life. Who would be careless enough and so brutal to leave a person lying in the road to be run over and discovered? Back before he established the blood bank to provide them nourishment, they had to feed on humans or even animals at times, but they had always been careful to dispose of the bodies in a discrete and respectable way. They were selective in those they chose to feed upon; they chose those already near death or with no families to miss them or wonder about their disappearance. Dac had to know who was responsible for this before there were other bodies to be found.

He called the others to meet him in the study. He needed to talk with them. One by one, they each came into the room. First was Nikolai, concern clearly showing on his face. He must have heard or seen the news already. Next, Quentin arrived stone-faced as always. Emmaline was not far behind him, but where was Harper? They waited another thirty minutes for her before she finally came into the room to join everyone. They all stood around and listened to Dac tell them the story about the young woman who had been found dead.

"This can't continue to happen. If they found one body already, there are surely others. We have to find the vampire or vampires responsible and put a stop to this." Dac said to the group.

Emmaline and Quentin shared a glance between them, then turned their eyes towards Harper. "Do you think...?" Emmaline began to ask a question, but Harper caught their stares and interrupted before she could finish.

"You can't possibly think this is my fault?"

"It's just that you've been out there stalking Zaine lately. Maybe some other young one got the idea from you." Emmaline replied.

"It's possible someone did see you, but we can't speculate. We just need to find out who is doing this." Dac interrupts.

"This is ridiculous!" Harper yelled as she stormed out of the room, slamming the door behind her.

The few books on the wall shelf toppled over from the door slamming. Nikolai started for the door to chase after Harper, but Dac stopped him; placing a hand on Nikolai's shoulder, he said, "Let her go for now."

The rest of the group continued their conversation, discussing different ideas on finding the vampire who left that woman's body where it could be discovered. They ultimately decided to have Quentin go out and investigate the situation. He would check out the area and keep an ear out for other vampires. They hoped that they would find whoever it was, Quentin would bring them to Dac, and hopefully, they could teach them a better way to go about things, figuring it was probably a young vampire who possibly didn't know any better. Maybe whoever made them left them on their own without teaching them to fend for themselves and cover their tracks. It was what happened to Emmaline. Emmaline became a vampire in the year 1969 at the age of twenty-one. She was young and carefree, totally immersed in the hippie culture of the time. The vampire who made her picked her out of the crowd at a music festival. Shortly after, he disappeared, leaving Emmaline all on her own. Dac found her scared and alone, hiding out in a mausoleum. He brought her back to the house with him, and she has remained there faithfully ever since.

Emmaline and Nikolai left the room, leaving Quentin and Dac behind to discuss the investigation's first steps. Quentin decided to look around the area the young woman had been found and search for any clues proving a vampire had been there. He promised to report immediately back to Dac anything he found at the scene. Quentin agreed to start tonight. In the meantime, Dac had to see Harper.

Harper had stomped down the hall towards her room in total disbelief of how the others, primarily Dac, could blame her for the actions of some other vampire. She could expect such accusations from Emmaline. She pretends to be nice to her and be her friend, but she's heard Emmaline say things to Quentin. But Dac, how could he agree to such an unfounded accusation, and why hadn't Nikolai stepped in and defended her? Could he possibly think she was responsible for this too? And maybe that woman was just attacked by some wild animal? How could Dac know for sure it was a vampire who had done this.

Harper slammed the door to her room and plopped down on

her bed. She needed to clear her head, and more importantly, she needed to get back to her revenge on Zaine. She had left him alone for a few days since she realized Quentin had been following her. Now it was time to put the next phase of her plan into motion. Everyone would be occupied with the investigation into the dead woman. Harper decided she could use that to her advantage. She just needed to map out her next steps.

Moments later, Dac knocked on Harper's door, quietly entering her room. She was sitting stretched out on the bed, pretending to read a book. She sat up straight, placing her feet on the floor when she heard Dac enter. He sat next to her, silently stroking her hair with his jeweled ringed fingers much like he had the first night he had come to her. They had an unspoken bond between them since the first moment they had met. It was a strong, undeniable attraction. Dac knew that Nikolai had brought her here because she had reminded him of his late wife. He knew the connection Nikolai felt towards Harper was deep and protective, but he also knew that Nikolai would never betray Una's memory. Nikolai felt the loss of his wife and unborn child so profoundly and had never gotten over it. In all these years, he'd never seen Nikolai get close to another.

Harper turned to face Dac sitting next to her. His intense eyes were staring back at her, his face showing remorse. She reached her hand up to touch his face. He leaned into her. His lips grazed her neck. He sunk his teeth into her artery, allowing the blood to fill his mouth. They lay on the bed entwined as one in the intimate exchange of vampire blood as he took in her life and love, and she received his return.

# Eight

It was early Saturday morning Zaine was on his way over to Janice's house to put the finishing touches on her shed. Chris had come by the day before to help attach the roof. Today the two men were going to attach the doors and paint the shed. Afterward, he had plans to meet up with Nita since he hadn't seen her all week.

When he arrived at Janice's house, Chris was already there waiting in the backyard. Zaine pulled out the cans of paint from the car and brought them to the back. He and Chris then walked back towards the car to retrieve the remaining paint cans, tools, and paintbrushes. An older man walked by, looking frail and sick. He stopped for a moment looking in the direction of the two friends. Chris waved to him, but he just turned and continued walking.

"Yo, man. I've been seeing that guy everywhere lately." Zaine said to his friend.

"Maybe he lives around here or something."

"Maybe, but I've never seen him until recently. He's kind of creepy man."

"Yea, well, he seems harmless to me. Let's just get to work."

The two men made their way back to the yard to finish up

the shed. The morning sky was beginning to darken with grey clouds. Zaine and Chris quickly hung the doors to the shed. According to the weather forecast, it wasn't supposed to rain despite the cloudy skies, so they decided it was safe to start painting. Zaine was ready to get this job done to be over with it. They worked well into the afternoon and finished up the painting. Chris cleaned up the yard and put all the tools into the cars while Zaine met with Janice to get paid. Afterward, Zaine gave Chris his share of the payment for helping out, and the two went their separate ways.

On the drive back home, Zaine saw the old man again. He was standing near the edge of the road watching the passing cars. As Zaine drove past, the man appeared to be staring right into his car. He couldn't help feeling as if this man were somehow watching him. He would see him near his apartment, at the store, and now he'd seen twice today. *Stop being paranoid*, he told himself. He needed to get home and get ready to meet Nita.

When he arrived at his apartment a few minutes later, Nita was already there waiting for him. He was surprised to see her dressed in her usual work uniform of jeans and a black t-shirt with her hair pulled back into a ponytail. He got out of his car, walked up to her, put his arm around her, and together they walked up to his apartment.

"I thought you were off today." He'd said to her.

"Johnny called me in. I could really use the extra money, so I said I'd go." She replied.

Zaine gritted his teeth when he heard this news. They had made plans, and now she was going to blow him off to go work. They began arguing as Zaine expressed his frustrations. As the yelling between them grew louder and more intense,

Zaine reached out and grabbed Nita by the neck. She grabbed onto his arm, struggling to release his grasp. He finally let her go knocking her against the wall. She stared at him in wide-eyed disbelief. He had never become physical with her before. She had heard rumors about him but had never experienced this side of him for herself. Her eyes began to fill with tears, and she turned and ran out of the apartment. Zaine slammed the front door that Nita had left open and then slammed his fist into the wall. He stomped over to the kitchen grabbed a beer out of the refrigerator and the pill bottle off the counter. He poured the last pill in the bottle down his throat and chased it down with a large gulp of the beer.

He could hear the waves crashing in the background, but the fog was too thick; he couldn't see the water. As a matter of fact, he could just barely see his hand in front of his face. He heard what sounded like a melodic voice whispering his name and pushed against the heavy wind in the direction of the harmonious sound. Something brushed across his leg, and he flinched. A bright white light flashed before his face, but it was gone in an instant, leaving him in the pitch of darkness once more. The voice grew louder and louder as he continued walking, and as he got closer, it became a deafening screech. Zaine covered his ears with his hands, but it didn't drown out the sound. Something grabbed him by the neck, holding him in his place. He waved his arms around though he never made contact with whatever had him in its clutches. He winced from the pain of the creature's sharp claws digging into the skin of his neck as he continued in vain to break free.

Zaine awoke on his couch a few hours later to a buzzing coming from his phone. He did his best to shake away the memories of his latest nightmare and reached in his jeans pocket, pulling out his phone to check the screen. He rubbed his neck as he read the text that had come through from Lizbeth. The exact text he knew was coming. The very text he had been fearing.

*11:30 warehouse one on the marina.*

He stared at the words on the screen. His hands shook as he held a tight grip on his phone. He knew he had no choice but to show at the warehouse. He checked the time. It was 9:30. He had two hours. He decided he should go by the bar and apologize to Nita. He had lost his temper with her earlier, and he needed to make things right.

He arrived at the bar about thirty minutes later. He walked directly over to the bar and ordered a drink from a bartender he didn't know. He must be new. Zaine knew just about everyone who worked at the bar except for maybe the people working in the kitchen. He noticed Nita taking the order of some customers at a nearby table. As she turned away from the table, she saw Zaine sitting at the bar. He waved to her, but she turned her head and walked away into the kitchen. He stared intently at the back of her head as he watched her walk away. He had come there after all to apologize, and he wasn't just going to let her ignore him. He finished his drink and ordered another while waiting for her to come back out of the kitchen. She couldn't hide back there all night.

When she finally came over to the bar to grab a drink for her table, he reached over and grabbed her wrist before she could walk away from him. The new bartender looked at her then glared over at Zaine. He had a muscular build with a sleeve of tattoos down his arms and a scar across his upper right arm just below his shirt sleeve.

"Nita, you need anything?" The new guy asked.

"She's fine," Zaine replied before Nita could answer. Then he turned to Nita. "I just want to talk to you."

"I'm busy right now, Zaine. I'll have to talk to you later." Nita replied. The bartender was still standing by serving his customers but keeping a watchful eye on Zaine.

"Please just give me one minute. I have to be somewhere soon, and I just want to apologize for earlier." He begged.

"Fine. Just let me drop this off at my table." She snatched her arm from his grasp and carried the drinks to her customers, waiting patiently at their table. She returned to the bar shortly after, turned to Zaine, and said. "You have five minutes." Then she led him out the side door as the bartender kept watch.

They stood at the side of the building. The night air was cold, and he could see Nita shivering. Zaine reached out to wrap his arms around her, but she pushed him away. He looked down at her with what he hoped was sorrow in his eyes. As she looked back up at him, all he saw was contempt on her face. Again, he reached out to her. This time brushing the loose strands of hair away from her face, and again, she pushed his hands away.

"What did you want to say. I don't have all night, and you said you don't either." Nita said rather impatiently.

"I don't know what got into me earlier. I know you're upset with me. I'm really, really sorry. Please forgive me." He continued to beg. He tried once again to wrap his arms around her. This time she allowed him to hug her. He pulled her in close to his chest. She could hear his heart beating fast, and she let out a soft sigh. She pulled away from him and looked into his eyes though this time with a little less contempt.

"I don't know, Zaine. You really scared me earlier." She said back though her tone had softened from just moments ago. He began to protest and again beg her forgiveness. But she just turned to him and said. "Please, just give me some time."

Frustrated, he stormed off to his car and pulled recklessly out of the parking lot. Realizing he probably never paid his tab at the bar, Nita went straight inside to the bartender to take care of it.

"Don't worry about it. Just be careful around that guy. He's bad news." He said to her. Nita thanked him and went back to waiting on her tables.

Zaine sped out of the bar's parking lot, not sure where he was heading. He still had some time before he had to be at the marina, and he just needed to find someplace to calm down. He found himself coming up on Janice's house. He noticed the lights on in her living room, so he pulled up in front of her house. They had become rather friendly since he'd been working on building her shed. He went up the front walkway and lightly knocked on her door in case her kids were sleeping. She answered the door wearing a pair of black yoga pants and a tank top. Her hair was pulled into a messy high bun on top of her head, and just socks were on her feet. In her hand was a glass of wine, and her eyes were red and puffy as if she'd been crying. It was clear she hadn't been expecting anyone, and Zaine felt a bit embarrassed for her.

"Oh. Hi Zaine. Sorry please excuse my appearance. I wasn't expecting anyone." She looked at him puzzlingly, a bit surprised he was standing on her doorstep.

"It's ok. I was just in the neighborhood and noticed your lights on. I could go if it's a bad time. I know it's pretty late."

"No. Please come in. The girls are with their dad. I was just watching a movie enjoying a rare quiet evening alone."

"Oh, ok. It's just... well you looked..." he began to say as he entered Janice's house, realizing he didn't know quite the right words to say.

"Oh. I've been watching this love story. It was so sweet it had me in tears." She laughed at herself as she explained the apparent redness of her eyes. "Would you like a drink? I don't have very much pretty much just water, apple juice, or wine."

"Sure, A glass of wine. Thank you," He said as he began to feel less awkward now that he realized she hadn't actually been crying.

She walked into the kitchen and came back with a wine glass and filled it from the bottle of red wine she had on the little side table next to the sofa. Zaine took the glass from her and sat down on the couch a few inches away from Janice. They sat there for a while, talking, laughing, and drinking the wine, refilling their glasses as fast as they emptied them. Zaine could feel the buzz from the wine beginning to take effect, and he could tell by the redness appearing on Janice's cheeks, so could she. He sat for a moment studying the soft features of Janice's face as she kept on talking. Unable to deny his obvious attraction to her, he leaned his face in closer to hers until finally, their lips were touching, and he was kissing her. For a moment, she kissed him back as his hands felt around her body and under her shirt until she suddenly pulled away from him.

"I'm so sorry," He said as he jumped up from his seat on the sofa and headed towards the door. "I should get going." And then he was gone out the front door.

Back in his car, he stared out into the darkness in front of him. In the distance, he could see someone looking towards him. As he focused on the figure standing out there in the dark, he realized it was the strange old man he's been seeing all over town. The man with the grey and ailing face. Who was this man, and why has he been seeing him everywhere? It was almost as if this man was following him. Just then, he glanced down at the clock on his dashboard. The time read 11:20. It was time to go to the marina.

He pulled into the warehouse parking lot, parked his car, and stepped out into the cold night air. There was a fog hovering over the water of the marina. The sky was dark, covered in clouds. A swarm of bats was flying over the warehouse. He looked around the parking lot and saw the old man again standing near the water at the opposite end of the pavement. A mist of rain began to fall from the sky. Zaine walked briskly to the warehouse door. As nervous as he felt about going inside, he was more worried about staying out here.

# Nine

Zaine opened the door to the warehouse and stepped inside to a large open room. The air was thick despite the cold outside. The room was dark, lit only by a few dim overhead lamps hanging from the ceiling. In the far corner was a bamboo cherry red bar. A few glasses and liquor bottles sat atop the wooden bar top. A man stood behind the bar, ready to serve the patrons. On the opposite side sat a large wooden desk where Mr. Vladescu was seated in a plush black leather chair. Beside him stood Lizbeth in a long red evening dress that complimented her dark auburn hair and luminescent skin. She wore a multi-layered diamond and emerald necklace around her neck, and on her right ring finger, she wore the matching ring.

In the middle of the floor sat a single large round poker table made of the same bamboo cherry wood as the bar in the corner. Six black leather chairs were placed around the table. A woman with golden hair met Zaine at the door. She was dressed in a black floor-length evening gown with a deep v neck and jeweled encrusted tuxedo collar. She wore little jewelry, just a pair of diamond-studded earrings and a solitaire diamond ring embedded in white gold on her left middle finger. Her nails, long and sharp, were painted in a deep red. She gently grabbed his hand. Her touch was cold like Lizbeth's. She led him over to the table and to his seat. He remembered her as the dealer from the games three years ago.

Seated at the table were four other men, three of whom Zaine did not recognize. However, the fourth man looked awfully familiar, and when he turned to face Zaine, he realized why. It was Jace, Harper's best friend's boyfriend, or was he her husband now. Either way, he didn't really care. There was definitely no love lost between the two of them. Zaine figured this was going to be an interesting night to say the least.

"What are you doing here? I didn't think this was your sort of thing?" Zaine said to Jace as he sat down at the table.

"It isn't, but I got an invite and figured that I'd find you here, so I came," Jace answered back, the animosity radiating from his voice.

"You have something you want to say to me?" Zaine asked him.

"The woman you were building the shed for, Janice. That's my cousin. You stay away from her. You hear me. I don't need her ending up like Harper."

"Listen, I didn't do anything to Harper. I don't know what happened to her." Zaine demanded. The tension between the two men grew with each passing word.

"We all know you killed her. She wouldn't have just disappeared like that, and no matter what you say, we know you were the last person to see her." Jace took a sip of whiskey from the glass in front of him.

Just then, Mr. Vladescu walked up to the table, placed a hand on Zaine's shoulder, and looked down at Jace with a wicked smile. "Gentlemen, shall we begin?" He said as he motioned to the woman with the golden hair to deal out the cards.

As the next few hours passed, Zaine couldn't quite believe the luck he was having. He was winning almost every hand played. When he looked down at the chips in front of him, he knew he'd have enough to pay back his debt to Mr. Vladescu and still have some left over for himself. He shouldn't have been surprised, though, since Vladescu had told him this would happen. It was then he realized that this game was fixed. Had it been the same three years ago? Is that why he could never win a hand back then? It must have been. But if that was indeed the case, then what was Vladescu's end game? What happened to the guy who won back then, and what would happen to Zaine when this was over? Suddenly Zaine felt the fear and apprehension rise against his nerves. Sweat began to form on his palms and drip down from his brow. He looked down at his cards and across the table at the golden-haired dealer. His vision had started to blur, and everything suddenly felt millions of miles away. Then the loud crashing sound of glass shattering shook his attention bringing his surroundings back into focus. He looked around at the guy behind the bar, who was now cleaning up glass from a broken bottle. Jace rose up from his seat, threw his cards down on the table, collected his money, and left. Two of the other men got up and left as well, one of them with Lizbeth and the other with the card dealer. The fourth man walked out shortly after, and the bartender followed not far behind him. At that moment, Zaine realized he was left alone with Mr. Vladescu.

"Nice game tonight. You played well." Vladescu said to him as he handed him an envelope full of cash.

"Right," Zaine said, trying to sound confident, hoping his voice wouldn't betray him.

Mr. Vladescu extended his hand to Zaine, who shook his hand in return. Vladescu covered Zaine's hand with the ice-cold touch of both his hands, and Zaine shivered.

"I will see you again soon. Be safe until then." Vladescu said to him with a wink and a crooked smile, and Zaine saw the flicker of red in the man's pupils again. He nodded to him, withdrew his hand from Vladescu's cold grasp, and turned to leave the warehouse.

Outside the warehouse, Harper stood in the shadows. The dense fog made it easy for her to conceal herself. She knew Zaine would be inside, and she was just waiting for him to come out. She watched as people began to leave, but one person caught her eye that she hadn't expected to see. What was Jace doing there? This wasn't his usual crowd. One thing she did know was that these people were dangerous, and she needed to make sure Jace stayed far away from them. Zaine would have to wait as she decided to follow her old friend.

The car's headlights had shown brightly through the front window as Jace pulled into the driveway of his small bungalow home. Footsteps echoed against the pavement as he walked up the small front porch. Inside, the two small bedrooms at the back of the house were empty. The front living room and kitchen were dark and quiet. He must have moved in recently. Harper didn't recognize this place from when they were friends. The front door opened, and Jace walked in, heading straight to the kitchen. The open refrigerator briefly cast a faint light on the floor as Jace grabbed a beer and then continued through the darkened house into the living room. He settled into the oversized chair that sat in the corner of the room. Next to it was a small sofa. A tv hung on the opposite wall. He placed his beer on the side table and switched on the lamp next to him, only dimly lighting the room. That's when he noticed her.

A small gasp escaped his lips. He jumped up from his chair and reached out to her, but Harper quickly retreated backward. The look of shock on Jace's face somewhat amused her, but she kept her composure. She knew he'd have questions about where she'd been and probably about her appearance, and she needed to keep this visit short.

"Oh, my God! Where have you been all this time? We all thought you were dead. Does Cloe know you're here? She'll be so excited. She's missed you so much. And your family. Have you seen them yet?" He rambled on, surprising them both. Jace wasn't typically one to express so much excitement.

"Slow down, Jace. No, I haven't seen any of them, and you can't tell anybody you saw me."

"But why? I don't understand. What is going on, Harper?"

"Listen to me, Jace. I know this is going to sound unbelievable, but I can explain. I am dead. At least my human form is dead. Zaine killed me that same night he drove his car into the lake. It was no accident."

"I don't understand." Jace began to say, but before he could ask her how all this was possible, she lunged at him, grabbing ahold of his neck and shoulder. She held him tightly in her grasp and sunk her teeth into his throat.

With her mouth on his throat, she bit down on her own tongue to make it bleed, mixing a tiny amount of her blood with his. Through this small exchange of blood, she could show him what she wanted him to see without changing him. Through her, Jace could see the argument that had taken place between her and Zaine on the night she died. He could also see the aftermath of that fight. She showed him the moment Nikolai pulled her out of the water and made her into the vampire she was now. Once she decided Jace had seen enough, she dropped him down into the chair. She sat down on the edge of the coffee table in front of him and placed her hand on his knee to calm him. As she felt his nerves begin to relax, she looked up at Jace into his eyes and said gently, "I need you to stay away from the people you were with tonight. They are dangerous people. From this point forward, you will stay far away from them."

She left Jace sitting in the chair, stunned and staring off into the emptiness of the dimly lit room. It would only take a few minutes before he would awaken from the trance she had put him in. And once he did, he'd probably have more questions. She took one last look at him as she exited through the front door. He blinked his eyes as if trying to regain his focus. He reached his hand up to his throat and then stared questionably at the blood on his fingertips. He looked around the room for Harper, but the house was now empty. She was gone.

# Ten

Quentin searched around the wooded area where the young woman's body had been found the day before. He found no sign of any wild animal that could facilitate that type of attack. He concluded that Dac's suspicions had to be right. They were looking for another vampire.

He began to walk down the road leading in the opposite direction of the center of town. If it were a new vampire, they might be hiding someplace secluded away from anywhere too populated. As he walked, he kept his eyes open to any clues he might find along the way. He also kept his ears and mind open to listening for any thoughts or conversation from any other that may be vampire nearby. If it were a young one, they might not know how to keep their thoughts private, but so far, all was quiet. Then suddenly, he noticed someone not far ahead of him walking in the street. It seemed quite odd that someone would be walking on this stretch of the road any time of day, let alone at night in the dark. He quietly crept closer, concealing himself as not to be seen. As he came closer upon the person ahead of him, the scent of human blood informed him this man was definitely not a vampire, but something was noticeably off about him. He wore only grey sweatpants and a sweatshirt, no coat or jacket despite the cold air. When Quentin looked down at the man's feet, he saw that he wore only socks and slippers. His complexion was pale, almost greyish, the sides of his face appeared sunken in as though he suffered some severe ailment. Then Quentin noticed something alarming about the man. He had two round scars on his neck. This man had been bitten. He had the mark of the vampire. But why had he been kept alive? This was definitely not the doing of a young vampire. They were looking for someone older, more experienced.

Quentin decided to continue following the man hoping he would lead him to the vampire who had bitten him. He had to be especially careful in keeping his presence concealed, however, since whoever had bitten this man may now be able to see through his eyes, and he would be able to see things even the man himself could not see. Quentin had to be careful not to be spotted. He slowed his pace slightly as he continued to follow the man down the road and off a path leading to a small house sitting on a few acres of land. With no other neighbors nearby, this would be a perfect hiding spot for a vampire. Quentin stood back and watched the man enter the house. A light from the tv shown through the front window. He crept up to the house and peered through each of the small windows around the house. There was no sign of anyone except the man sitting back in a reclining chair watching the tv. There was a door on the ground that led to the basement. He unhooked the latched and opened the heavy wooden door. He quietly descended down the concrete steps into the cold, bitter basement. He brushed away the cobwebs that hung from the ceiling. An old rusty bicycle leaned against the far wall, and some old tools and a wooden workbench sat in the corner. Other than that, the place was empty. No sign of any vampire having been here at all. Figuring the man must have been coming home from the vampire not going to see him, Quentin decided to leave and report back to Dac. He wasn't going to learn anything new tonight.

As he traveled on his way back home, something, or more likely, someone else, caught his eye. Was that Harper? What would she be doing out this way? He decided he would follow her. It looked like she was headed in the direction of the beach, and he knew she would go there sometimes. She had this spot where she would go and sit when she'd want to be alone. He also knew that Zaine lived over that way now. He really hoped she wasn't going to see him again. It seemed that she decided to leave him alone, but what if she hadn't. What if she were still keeping to her revenge? Most of all, the questions bothering him were where she was coming from and where had she just been? She wasn't coming from the direction of the house, so what had she been doing? Only then did his foot hit something hard. He caught his footing before tripping to the ground, and when he looked down, there was another body. He bent down and turned the body over, examining the neck.

Just as he'd suspected, there above the collarbone were two puncture wounds. He looked up, realizing he had lost sight of Harper. Suddenly a chilling thought ran through his mind. Had Harper done this? Was she behind the other one too? He didn't want to believe it, and he had no proof. Maybe it was just a coincidence that a moment ago, he'd seen Harper coming from this exact direction. Either way, he had to get rid of this body and get back to the house. He picked up the corpse and carried it away. He decided he'd drop it in the marina leading into the ocean. Hopefully, the water would take it away. In the meantime, he knew now he'd have to keep a close eye on Harper.

Back at the house, Quentin met with Dac in his study. Nikolai was there as well. He described to them the man he saw walking and how he followed him to his secluded house but found no evidence of any vampire having been there. "Whoever it is, is not hiding out at this man's house." He told them. He decided to leave out the fact that he saw Harper on his way back to the house, and she was coming from some unknown place. He also didn't tell them about the second body he fell upon on his way back home. He wasn't ready to accuse Harper just yet. He had to find out more and be absolutely certain if he were going to tell these two. They both cared for Harper too much; he couldn't tell them anything until he knew for sure.

After telling Dac and Nikolai everything he knew, for now, Quentin left the room and decided he'd go back and look for Harper. He passed Emmaline in the hall and asked her, "Have you seen Harper tonight?"

"No. Why?" She replied with a tiny bit of hostility.

"No reason. Just looking for her." He decided to keep it vague. He wasn't ready to confide in anyone yet, not even Emmaline. Lately, she'd seemed a little annoyed with Harper. Quentin thought it best to just keep his suspicions to himself for now.

Emmaline shrugged him off, and he continued down the hall and out the front door. He headed back in the direction of Aura Springs, where he had last seen Harper. As he passed the marina where he'd just dumped the dead body, he felt a chill down his spine. The docks were empty as most people had already brought their boats in for the coming winter months. The water seemed calm, but he knew underneath the dark blue waters lay a disturbing secret.

He walked on toward the beach. Maybe Harper was there at her quiet spot. As he came upon the boardwalk, he looked around for her. No sign of her so far. He walked all the way to the end of the boardwalk, where he knew she sometimes went. She wasn't there. He leaned against the railing, looking out into the ocean, watching the waves as they crashed against the shore, trying to get a feel for what Harper was up to and where she could have gone. He could see why she liked it here so much. It was calming with the cold breeze coming off the ocean and the sounds of the crashing waves. It was also the place closest to Harper's old life.

As he stood staring out at the ocean, trying to think where else he may be able to find her, he saw someone walking across the sand far out in the distance. Though he couldn't see the person's features clearly, he could tell it was a woman, a preternatural woman. She was wearing a dark-colored jacket, much like the dark navy jacket Harper sometimes wore. She had the hood pulled up over her head, making it even harder to see her face. He could see strands of what appeared to be her black hair peeping out from under her hood. Although he couldn't see her face from the far distance, it had to be Harper.

He decided he should try again to follow her. He noticed she was walking up towards the boardwalk in his direction. He couldn't let her see him, so he hid behind the side of the building next to him and concealed himself. As he turned back to where he had seen her, she was gone. That was the second time that night he had lost sight of her. Feeling defeated and knowing the sun would be up soon anyway, he turned back and went home. When he arrived back at the house, he opened the door to his room, and that's when he saw her. "What are you doing here...."

# Eleven

Zaine walked into his apartment, closing the door tightly behind him, making sure to lock the bolt. He threw the envelope containing his winnings from the night down onto the coffee table. He sat down onto the couch and just stared down at the envelope for a moment. He couldn't believe his luck. Though it wasn't really luck at all, was it? Those games were fixed, but why had Mr. Vladescu chosen him this time? He may never know the reason why, and he didn't exactly care if he was honest with himself. He liked the money, and Mr. Vladescu promised he'd be bringing home a lot of it. He was sure the man would eventually want something in return, or maybe this was just his way of making his money back. Either way, Zaine was enjoying the win for now.

He leaned back on the couch. The rain was picking up outside. It had been misting all night, but now the rain was falling heavier. The raindrops pounded hard against the windows, and the sounds of the incoming storm were rolling in. Suddenly a loud crash of thunder sounded followed by a bright flash of lightning, and the power went out. Zaine was left sitting in total darkness. Another flash of lightning came lighting up his living room for a brief second. At that moment, Zaine almost swore he saw a figure standing across the room but with another flash of lightning, the image was gone. Zaine shook his head. Using the flashlight from his cell phone, he got up from the couch and went to his room. It had been a long night, and his mind was beginning to play tricks on him.

The next morning Zaine awoke dry-mouthed and groggy. He rose from his bed and went straight to the kitchen in search of water. He pulled a glass from one of the kitchen cabinets and filled it with ice and water from the refrigerator. The cold water was refreshing. Good thing the power hadn't been out too long overnight. He walked out onto the back balcony of his apartment through the sliding glass door off the kitchen. He lit a cigarette and surveyed the area outside. He could see the ground was moist and covered with wet brown and yellow leaves from the storm the night before. A few small tree branches littered the small parking lot, but there was no apparent damage. When he finished smoking, he put out the cigarette, flicked it over the railing, and then went back inside.

Back inside the apartment, he noticed the envelope from the night before sitting out on the coffee table in his living room. He went over and scooped it up, deciding to put the money in the small lockbox he kept on a shelf in his bedroom closet. He removed the metal box from its place on the shelf and set it on the bed. He took the key from its hiding place behind his desk drawer and unlocked the box. He hadn't opened the package in such a long time he couldn't even remember what was in it. When he looked inside, he saw some old papers and an old photograph. It was a picture of his mother before she had gotten sick. She was at the beach standing on the boardwalk, leaning on the railing with her back to the water and the waves crashing against the shore behind her. She was wearing a light blue sundress with a white shawl draped over her shoulders, and a rose in her hair. She was smiling and looked so happy. He wondered who had taken the picture. He couldn't ever remember seeing it before. He sat there, staring at it for a minute. He asked himself what she would think of him now. Good thing she was dead and couldn't see what a terrible wreck he had made of his life. Feeling his eyes begin to fill with water, he pushed those thoughts out of his head. He put the photograph and the envelope in the box, locked it, and put it back in the closet. He then looked around the room for his phone, finding it on the floor next to his bed. As he bent down to pick it up, he found a small plastic bag sticking out from under the bed. He picked up the plastic bag examining the white powdery substance inside, then slipped it into the front pocket of his jeans. He was going to need that if he was going to get through the day, he thought.

Zaine had another job this afternoon, a fence repair at a house just a few streets down from Janice. Maybe he'd stop by to see her after his appointment. Jace's little threat last night only made him want to see her more, and with the way Nita was acting last night, he figured he'd give her some time to cool off and maybe explore his options.

He changed into a new pair of jeans and a semi-clean t-shirt, grabbed his toolbox, and went outside towards his car. The sun had finally come out from behind the clouds, and the ground was beginning to dry. It was unseasonably warm today, considering the time of year and the fact it had rained the night before, but Zaine wasn't going to complain about that. With most of his jobs being outside and the winter vastly approaching, he knew money was going to slow down very soon as it would be too cold to work outside. It was a good thing he was making money with Mr. Vladescu. He decided he would be smart with the money he was winning and save it up to help him get through the winter months since he wasn't sure how long Vladescu was going to have him win. He only hoped Vladescu would let him out before he chose someone else to start winning. The last thing he needed was to be in debt to Mr. Vladescu again, but he wasn't going to think about that now.

Zaine had never met this client before today. He had called him saying someone had recommended his services. He pulled his car to a stop outside the address the man had given him. Butterflies formed in the pit of his stomach, and his palms were clammy. He looked around the area before deciding to get out of the car. The house was set on a large piece of land with no sign of any neighbors nearby. Lots of tall trees surrounded the open land on each side of the house. The house itself was small and rundown, with a wooden fence encasing the backyard. Zaine strolled up the muddy walkway towards the front door, all the while thinking there was plenty he could do to fix up this house. Maybe after he finished up the fence, the man would offer him more work. If only he could shake his trepidation.

Zaine knocked on the front door of the house. No one answered the first knock, so he banged on the door a few more times. When there was still no answer, Zaine turned away, starting back down the walkway when he heard the creak of the door opening. He turned around to face the person opening the door. His heart dropped to his stomach. His heart rate sped up a beat. He hoped the expression on his face didn't betray the apprehension he felt as he faced the grey-faced frail man who was now standing in front of him.

"Good afternoon Mr. Brantley." The man said as he held out his hand to Zaine.

"Hello," Zaine replied, and he shook the man's hand.

"Come, follow me to the backyard. I'll show you where the fence needs repair." The man turned and slowly walked down the path leading to the backyard. Zaine had it in his mind to make an excuse and leave, but instead, he followed behind him.

The man reached over the wood panels and unhooked the latch to open the fence. As Zaine passed through the gate into the yard, he took in his surroundings. The overgrown grass had turned brown and fell dying. Brown, yellow, and red leaves lay scattered across the ground. The rusty rake leaning against the side of the house seemed ironic since it plainly hadn't been used in quite some time. There was a wooden door positioned on the ground that Zaine figured led down to a basement. He couldn't help wondering what the man might have kept down there.

Zaine watched and listened as the grey-faced man showed him the broken panels in the fence, which needed replacing. There were new wooden panels laid out on the ground nearby. Zaine set down his toolbox and began removing the first broken panel. The man walked away back towards the house but then sat down in a lawn chair on the back patio, watching as Zaine worked. A cool breeze came through, causing the leaves on the ground to stir. A bit of dirt blew into Zaine's face. He wiped it away with the sleeve of the flannel jacket he wore over his T-shirt. He wanted to get this job done and never come back to this house again. He continued working until every new board was in place, and he repaired the fence entirely. Just as he was finishing up, he felt a cold hand on his shoulder. He flinched and turned around to see the old man standing behind him. He hadn't even heard him walk over. As he glared at the old grey-faced man, something familiar struck him though he couldn't place it. And not just because he had been seeing him around town lately, but it was something more as if it were something from a long time ago.

"Come into the house so I may get your payment, and I have something for you inside." The old man said as he turned away and led Zaine towards the back door of the house.

Zaine was overwhelmed with the smells of frankincense and garlic as they walked through the door into the small house's kitchen. He looked around. There were cloves of garlic hanging in the windows and crucifixes strategically placed over the doors and walkways. The old man handed Zaine a white envelope with money in it. Zaine took the envelope, feeling the weight of it in his hand. He could tell it was much more than they had agreed on. Before he could open his mouth to refuse the extra cash, the old man took Zaine's hand in both of his insisting he kept what was in the envelope.

"Please," he said. "I have one more thing for you. Wait here."

The old man walked through the doorway into the small living room, pulling a cedar box down from a bookshelf. He reached inside, pulled something out, and returned to the kitchen where Zaine was waiting. The old man was holding a vial containing some type of clear liquid. It had a black cord attached to it, and Zaine realized the old man was wearing something similar around his neck.

"Please keep this with you for protection. There are those

out there that would do you harm. This will keep you safe from them. Please take it and keep it with you at all times, my son." The old man placed the vial in Zaine's hand and, without saying another word walked back into the living room, settling himself in his reclining chair. Zaine was left standing awkwardly alone in the old man's kitchen. He put the envelope and vial in his pocket and left out the back door.

Back in his car Zaine sat for a minute staring at the old man's house. The last two words, the man said, still echoing in his brain, "my son." It couldn't be, could it? This man couldn't be Zaine's father. Zaine ran his hands through his hair, turned on his car, and drove towards home. The whole drive home, he kept trying to figure out why this man suddenly seemed so familiar to him today. Why had it hit him so hard when this man called him "my son?" It was probably just an expression Zaine kept telling himself. But something just wasn't sitting well with him right now. He hadn't seen his father since he was young. He barely remembered him. More importantly, though, what did he mean about people wanting to do him harm, why did he care so much, and how could the liquid in the vial he had just given him keep him protected. The old man had to be crazy.

All this was making Zaine feel like he was crazy. He turned his car around the next corner, and instead of going home, he went to the bar instead. He needed a drink and a clear head. He pulled into the bar parking lot. He was glad to see Nita's car wasn't there as he realized he didn't want to deal with her tonight. As he walked inside, he noticed the new guy behind the bar. He rolled his eyes but sat at one of the bar stools anyway and ordered a beer. Looking around the bar, he saw Jace and Cloe sitting at one of the tables. Great, he thought to himself, just what I need, another run-in with Jace. But the couple were looking pretty intense at their table, so they hopefully wouldn't even notice him. He turned on his stool, looked towards the tv above the bar, and drank his beer.

Zaine jumped when he felt a sudden pat on his shoulder. He turned to see Chris standing there behind him, laughing.

"Man, you nearly scared me to death."

"I see. What's up, man? What's got you so distracted." Chris replied, still laughing at his friend.

"Nothing. I just came off a job. Turned out to be that creepy old man I keep seeing around town. I almost turned right around and left, but I need the money. What are you doing here?"

"Just got off work, saw your car in the parking lot. Figured I'd stop in." Chris answered as he waved over to the bartender.

Chris ordered two more beers for himself, and his friend and the two men moved over to one of the high-top tables. As they sat there drinking their beers and watching the game on tv, Zaine was relieved for the distraction. The last few weeks, especially today, were beginning to get to him.

Later as Zaine pulled up in front of his apartment complex, he noticed Nita's car in the parking lot. What was she doing here? He let out a deep breath and braced himself for the confrontation. The evening air was much cooler now that the sun was setting. As he walked up towards his apartment, he saw Nita sitting on the steps leading up to his front door.

"What are you doing here?" He asked her not at all, trying to hide the tension in his voice.

"I was hoping we could talk." She said.

"Talk? For what? So, you could tell me some more what a horrible person I am? I don't want to hear it. Go home." He yelled as he pushed past her, almost knocking her down the stairs.

Nita grabbed hold of the railing to catch her balance so she wouldn't fall. She stood there, stunned at his reaction to her. She watched him enter his apartment and slam the door behind him. The tears began to fall from her eyes as she stormed off to her car.

Meanwhile, Harper was standing at the corner of the building, watching this scene unfold between the two. She felt the anger start to boil inside her. She almost couldn't believe how he treated this girl, but then the memories came flooding back of the way he had treated her. She felt as though she was reliving that fateful night when he screamed at her, pushed her down, and he ultimately killed her. The anger inside was now more than she could control. She stood there in the shadows staring hard at the numbers on his front door. The world around her grew dark. The wind picked up to a howling speed. The front door to Zaine's apartment flew open, and the glass window shattered into a million pieces. Inside, Zaine blocked his face with his arm as the pieces of glass from the window came crashing into the living room. He ran into the hallway away from the shattering glass as the rain continued pouring into through the now broken window.

\* \* \*

Harper stood at her private spot on the beach. The wind was blowing fierce as she watched the waves crashing angrily onto the shore. She was realizing now that her powers were growing stronger. Strong enough, she thought, to avenge her death and protect herself from the fallout.

Suddenly a dark shadow formed over her, and an even darker presence could be felt all around. Dac was standing behind her. She turned to face him. He looked down at her with his intense dark eyes. His expression radiated a seriousness that made her nerves stand on edge. Her muscles tensed as she stared back at him.

"You were out early today." He said, and Harper nodded in response. "I see your powers are growing stronger, but they are fueled by your anger." He spoke to her softly, but there was a force behind his words.

She opened her mouth to speak, but he raised a finger to silence her. His long black talon-like nail grazed her lip. The stone-like complexion of his skin radiated force. His aura was dark and powerful. For the first time since she knew him, she felt how dangerous he could be. The moonlight reflected off the rings he wore on his pale fingers. He slid his cold hand down her face and rested it against her neck.

"You are taking this thing with Zaine too far now. Your foolishness risks exposing us. I will not let you endanger the rest of us and destroy all I have built. It is time for you to stop this." He clutched her neck a little tighter. His nails were rigid against her skin as his firm hand exuded his strength. He stared deep into her eyes as if he could see down into the very depths of her soul. Then leaned in so close, his lips brushed against her ear, and he whispered, "I love you, Harper, but I will destroy you." Then before she could even take a breath, he was gone.

Harper stood, staring angrily into the night. The dark clouds came rolling in with the heavy winds that started up again. Hard rain began to fall, and far out in the distance over the horizon, lightning struck the water.

# Twelve

Zaine rushed back to the broken window carrying some cardboard he'd grabbed from the back closet and a roll of duct tape. With the rain starting to pour into his apartment, he quickly covered the window with the thick piece of cardboard and taped it in place. The front door was still wide open from the force of the wind. He pushed the door closed with his shoulder and bolted it shut. He looked around in disbelief at the glass and leaves scattered across his living room floor. Rainwater soaked the carpet. What the fuck had just happened? The sky had been clear all day, and there had been no mention of an upcoming storm. Then, out of nowhere, a fierce, heavy wind came through, blowing the door wide open and the glass out straight out the window. Now he had broken glass and leaves everywhere. He grabbed a broom from the kitchen and swept up the mess. In all the chaos, he hadn't noticed the blood running down his arm, but now as things began to calm down, his skin was stinging where the glass had cut him. He moved over to the sink to clean his wounds.

The night sky had grown darker with the setting of the sun. Unfortunately, the sudden storm had knocked the power out again. The apartment was pure darkness. He tried to search for a flashlight, feeling around the drawer in the kitchen where he thought one might be, but it was so dark it was no use searching any longer. Zaine walked back to the living room, feeling his way through the dark room so as not to bump into anything. He sat down, running his hands across his face. He leaned back onto the couch, staring into the emptiness of the room until finally, the darkness overcame him, and he closed his eyes to fall asleep.

A grey fog filled the room, and Zaine could feel a dark presence around him. Was it Harper, he wondered? But this felt different than the times that Harper had appeared to him. This presence was stronger, darker, but he couldn't see anyone through the dense fog. The hair on his arms stood up, and fear began to take over though he stood there defiantly. He called out, "Who's there?" No one answered. The earlier storm seemed to have passed, but the air around him was moist and almost suffocating. He thought he saw a shadow in the corner, but it was hard to tell in the dark. He moved to turn on a light, but the power remained out, so he stayed put in total darkness. He called out again, but still, no one answered. He could hear the howling wind outside. The loose pieces of glass from the broken window chimed in the harsh breeze. The presence around him grew more assertive. When he tried to move, he couldn't, and a cold firmness wrapped itself around his throat. When he tried to speak, his voice only came out as a weak grunt. He swallowed hard as he felt a sharp scraping down the side of the neck. A gravelly voice whispered his name. A frigid air tickled the back of his neck. Then suddenly, the room grew still, and the fog around him began to disappear. The presence was gone, and he was alone again.

Zaine awoke to a loud buzzing and a bright light flashing around him. It was a message coming into his phone. The room was still dark, but he could see the morning light approaching. He picked up his phone to silence the buzzing and checked the incoming message. A text from Lizbeth displayed on the screen with the date and time for the next game. He put the phone back down on the table. At least that would be a distraction, he thought to himself as he realized his nightmares were coming back again.

Not wanting to go back to sleep for fear of another nightmare, he rose up from the couch and went to the kitchen to make some coffee. He reached up into the cabinet above him and took down the bottle of whiskey inside. He poured the whiskey into his coffee cup along with the coffee. He stood in the kitchen for a moment sipping his whiskey spiked coffee. It was too early still to do anything. Everyone he knew would probably still be sleeping. He couldn't call Nita after the way he had treated her when she had stopped by his place the night before. He was starting to feel a little crummy about that, but he just wasn't ready to deal with her yet. Maybe he'd call her in a day or two and apologize. Perhaps he could try Janice. He thought of stopping by her place yesterday, but then he had been so distracted by the old man's words after he finished the fence that he'd forgotten. He went to the bar instead and then went home. Guess it was good he had come home when he did. Otherwise, his living room would have gotten more soaked from the rain than it had, and God only knows what else would have happened since he wouldn't have been there to shut the door and board up the window. He'd have to get that fixed asap. He decided to log on to this laptop and put in a maintenance request, and hoped someone would come today to fix it. Thankfully, the electric company restored the power. Suddenly he remembered the old man's warning and the vial of liquid he had given him. He began to wonder if it could have anything to do with his strange dreams. But that just didn't make sense. None of it made sense to him, really. That old man was simply crazy. And why did he have all that garlic hanging on his windowsill, and what was with all the crucifixes?

As the morning went on, Zaine thought over and over about the old man. He just couldn't seem to shake the old man's warning. Maybe he should go see him, ask him to explain. The guys from the maintenance department said they'd be by later that afternoon to board up the window properly, but they had to get a glass company to replace the existing window, which could take a day or two. Zaine could see from his back door that the sun was shining behind the clouds. He grabbed his jacket, got into his car, and drove straight toward the old man's house.

A few minutes later, he pulled up in front of the small house. He sat there for a minute before he finally turned off his car and stepped out into the brisk morning air. He walked up the walkway and knocked lightly on the front door a few times. He hoped the old man was awake and would be willing to talk to him. He was just about to give up when it seemed he wasn't going to answer. However, a moment later, the door creaked open, and the old man stood in the doorway, peering out at Zaine.

"Mr. Brantley, What can I do for you?" The old man asked as he opened the door a little bit wider.

"Hi, sir. Sorry to stop by, announced. I know it's early, but I was hoping we could talk for a minute. Maybe you could tell me what you meant yesterday about people wanting to harm me." Zaine replied.

"Yes. I figured I'd be seeing you again. I just didn't think it would be so soon. Please come in." The old man stepped aside, and Zaine followed him through the small living room and into the even smaller kitchen. The house reeked of garlic, coffee, and medicated ointment. "Please have a seat. I'll pour you some coffee." The man said, gesturing to a chair at the round oak table set in the kitchen corner. He poured two cups of coffee from the coffee pot on the counter and then sat in the chair opposite Zaine at the table. He pushed one of the coffee mugs over to Zaine and mentioned for him to ask his questions.

"Well, you see, I've been having these nightmares lately, and I thought they had stopped, but then last night after that freak storm, I had another one. They just feel so real, unlike any other dream I've ever had, and it had me thinking about what you said to me yesterday. I know it sounds crazy, but I can't help but feel like they are somehow connected to your warning. Though I can't figure out how." Zaine started to tell the old man even though it was more of a statement than a question.

"Tell me about these dreams. What are they about?" The old man asked.

Zaine began telling the man all about his dreams. He started with the first one he had a few weeks ago when he had woken up with blood in his mouth. He told him how he'd been almost paralyzed in these dreams to where he couldn't move or form any words. He told him about Harper and how she'd gone missing and was never found. Of course, he left out the part about their argument in his apartment and how, in reality, he killed her. Instead, he told his version that he had not seen her for days before his so-called drunken accident, and he didn't know how he even escaped the car. He continued telling the old man the rest of his dreams, where Harper appeared to him again in his living room and the one where she was meeting others in a strange building. He described to the old man the dining room and the people she accompanied. These were people he had never seen before. He described the dark wine on the table and the man with the bloody fangs. He told him about the strange phenomenon when he thought he saw a figure when the lightning flashed during the storm the other night. Last he told him about last night's dream with the fog, the scraping and the cold air on his neck, and the voice whispering his name.

"This girl Harper, you killed her, did you not? The story you told the cops, the one you just told me, is false. Correct? No bother lying to me. I am here to help you, not judge you. We all make mistakes, son." The old man finally said in response as Zaine sat astonished at his perceptiveness.

"It was an accident," was all Zaine could manage to reply as he looked down into his coffee cup.

"This Harper, there is a reason no one ever recovered her body. She is dead, of course, but not the way you think."

"What are you saying? That makes no sense." Zaine replied.

"She walks in the shadows among the undead."

"You are a crazy old man!" Zaine shouted as he began to rise from his seat.

The old man grabbed hold of his wrist, but Zaine snatched his arm away and stormed for the front door. He couldn't believe he had even entertained the idea of coming here. This old man was undoubtedly certifiable with accusations like that.

"She is coming for you! There are others too. Vampires! They will kill you if you do not take precautions! Listen to my words!" The old man pleaded after Zaine, but he'd only turned his head for a moment and stormed out of the house, slamming the fragile door behind him. The old man slumped down in his reclining chair, defeated.

Zaine stormed back down the walkway, got in his car, instantly started it up, and drove off. What the fuck? Harper, undead, vampires. The words kept circling in his head. Then the news broke through on the radio. Authorities have discovered two more bodies with puncture wounds on both of their necks near the collar bone. It appears someone drained the blood from the victims.

# Thirteen

Zaine sat on the couch with the whiskey bottle in front of him. Images of his dreams and the old man's words were reeling through his mind. How could any of this be true? It made no sense, yet at the same time, it did. But vampires aren't real, and Harper was dead. He couldn't explain why her body was never recovered, but that wasn't his job, and if he had to be honest about it, he was glad it hadn't been. Had her body been found, that would have proved he had murdered her. However, he hadn't wanted to kill her. That part indeed was an accident. He never meant to push her so hard. It all just happened so fast in the heat of the moment. She had been snooping around his things. She was questioning stuff he wasn't ready to answer. He hadn't meant to hurt her. He was just angry and wanted her to back off, but then she fell and hit her head; he had no choice other than cover it up. He'd rather face a DUI charge than a murder charge, so he did what he had to do, and that was all in the past now.

He decided his dreams were just that dreams. They didn't mean anything except maybe his guilty conscience was getting the best of him. As for the old man, well, he was crazy, and

Zaine made up his mind to stay away from him. It was time he decided to make things up to Nita and apologize.

He grabbed a stash of money from the box hidden in his bedroom closet. He had been holding on to as much as possible since he knew the upcoming winter months wouldn't bring him much work, but he had another game coming, so he was reasonably sure he'd be making it back. Besides, he had enough stashed just from that first game and the money from the old man to cover him most of the winter. Taking a few hundred dollars wouldn't hurt too much.

Zaine walked up to Nita's door with the box containing the bracelet he'd just bought her in his jacket pocket. It had cost him just under two hundred dollars, a sterling silver diamond accented heart link bracelet. Nita wasn't the flashy type, so he was sure she'd like it. He just wanted to offer her something with his apology, and he didn't feel flowers were enough. He wanted something that would last, something that would make her think of him every time she looked at it.

Nita's young son Caleb answered the door. "Hey, little man," Zaine said in response to seeing Caleb. "How you doing, buddy? Where's your mom?" He patted Caleb on the head and knelt down to hug him. After a moment, Nita appeared in the doorway behind them.

"What did I tell you about answering the door," Nita yelled at her son. Then looking up at Zaine, she ushered her son back into the house and closed the door in Zaine's face without saying a word.

Zaine got up and knocked on the door again, trying to control his disappointment and frustration. When Nita didn't return, he sat on the ground in front of her door to wait. He pulled the box containing the bracelet out of his jacket pocket and flipped it over and over in his hand. He knew if he were just patient enough, she would eventually come out the door and he was right. Moments later he heard the latch on the door unlock. He looked up and Nita was standing above him, her hands on her hips and a smile she was trying to hide forming on her face. She held out a hand to him. In return, he reached for her hand while standing up from his seated position on the ground and pulled her into a tight hug. He held on to her tightly for a few moments burying his face in her hair, smelling the flowery scent of her shampoo. As they pulled apart from each other, Zaine handed Nita the box with the bracelet, and she led him into the house.

Nita lived in a small three-bedroom home with her mom. They had moved in just a few short years ago after Nita's father had passed away. Things had been particularly hard on Nita's mom, so they moved to this small shore town to put some distance between them and all the memories that surrounded them. The front living room contained a couch, loveseat, and a large wooden chest that made up the room's main focal point. A small flat screen tv rested atop the round table in the corner of the room. Family pictures and other artful collections hung along the wooden paneled walls. Tiny porcelain figurines adorned various shelves and bookcases placed around the living room and the hall leading to the three bedrooms in the back of the house. Surprisingly not many books were on the bookshelves, just a few romance novels, and some old magazines.

"Where is your mom?" Zaine asked as he looked around the dark living room. It had always seemed dark inside Nita's house, no matter what time of day it was. He had only been in this house a few times. Normally they would spend time together either at his apartment or at the bar.

"She's working today. You're safe from her for now." Nita said with a laugh. "I've missed you." She looked down at the box in her hand and opened it. Even in the darkness of the room, the sterling silver and diamond accented bracelet shined against the dark velvet cushion it rested on. "It's so beautiful. Thank you so much. Though you didn't need to do this." Her face lit up as she pulled the bracelet out from the box, and Zaine helped place it upon her wrist.

"You're welcome. I've been such a jerk lately. I wanted to get you something nice to make up for it." He kissed her lightly on the lips knowing Caleb was somewhere nearby, then they both sat on the couch.

"Well, you have been quite a jerk lately." She said playfully as she looked down at the bracelet that now adorned her wrist.

Zaine put his arm around her and pulled her in close. They sat together in comfortable silence, listening to Caleb play in his bedroom.

Zaine left Nita's house minutes before her mother returned home from work, relieved to have missed any confrontation with her. The evening chill was settling in, and Zaine turned up the heat in his car. Turning onto the main road, he pretended not to notice Nita's mother passing him by as she turned the corner towards the same house in which he had just left.

When he arrived back at his apartment, he noticed his front window had been repaired. *That was quick,* he thought to himself. He hadn't expected it to be fixed so soon though he was grateful it had. He tossed his keys down on the kitchen counter and thought about heating himself up some dinner when his phone buzzed in his pocket. He didn't recognize the number that appeared across the screen. When he opened the message, he was surprised to learn the text was from Jace asking to meet him. He agreed and headed over to the café where Harper used to work.

He hadn't been there since Harper was alive. It felt strange to open the doors and walk into one of the places that were so important to the woman he had killed. He never could quite understand why Harper loved this place so much or why she continued working there when she didn't need to. To him, it was just another place that took her attention away from him. He managed to push his feelings aside as he stepped inside and scanned the room for Jace. The cafe hadn't changed that much over the past few years other than the new staff maybe. He didn't seem to notice anyone familiar from when Harper had worked here. Otherwise, everything else still appeared the same. The counter still sat at the back, filled with pastries and other sweet desserts. As always, someone was working at the back counter. The small tables scattered around the café sat the usual customer stopping by for coffee and maybe a tiny bite to eat after work or just to catch up with friends. It had always been pretty busy here, and Zaine noticed that hadn't changed much either as he scanned the crowd looking for Jace. He found him sitting at a table tucked into the corner of the café. He walked over to the table and sat in the chair opposite Jace. Jace had already ordered himself a coffee and was sipping it when Zaine approached the table. The waitress came over right away to take Zaine's order. He ordered just a regular black coffee and waved her off. Neither man said a word until the waitress returned with Zaine's coffee and set it on the table in front of him. He took a sip, then looked up at

Jace.

"So, what is this all about?" Zaine demanded.

Jace looked at him with a weary face, and that's when Zaine noticed the marks on his neck. Marks eerily similar to ones he had noticed on himself after waking from one of his nightmares. He thought he had somehow given them to himself. Now he was starting to wonder if it were something else. Suddenly the old man's words came rushing back to him. He took another sip of his coffee, trying to push those thoughts away. No way, he thought, this is crazy. Then Jace began to speak

"Listen, we both know I don't care much for you, and quite frankly, I think you should get whatever you deserve. But..." He began, then paused for a moment to gather his thoughts before continuing. "I received a warning about those people hosting the poker games. I don't know why, but I have a feeling they are behind those people turning up dead. I can't make sense of it or even try to begin to explain, but..." he paused again. "Just watch your back."

"Right, you don't like me, so then why the warning? Why would you care what happens to me?"

"I don't. I know you had something more to do with Harper's death and disappearance than you say, but at the end of the day, you were important to her. She cared a great deal about you, and I cared a great deal about her. Me and Cloe both did. She was our friend." Jace threw a few dollars on the table to cover the cost of his coffee and then left the café.

Zaine sat back, staring into the distance, thinking of what Jace had just said and the images of those marks on his neck. Jace had said he couldn't make sense of things, and neither could Zaine, but he knew in his heart all these strange things were somehow connected.

The waitress came back over to the table, breaking Zaine away from his thoughts. He let her know he was fine and didn't require anything else, waving her off once again. Just then, he noticed a dark figure pass by the front window of the café. He quickly dug a five-dollar bill out from his pocket, tossed it on the table, and ran out the door. Outside he looked around the parking lot and around the side of the building. He didn't see anyone but a few customers entering and leaving the café. Whoever or whatever he had seen was gone.

Zaine leaned against the side of the building and pulled out the pack of cigarettes from his jacket pocket. He took one from the box, put it to his lips, and lit it. He inhaled the smoke and the nicotine from the cigarette, finally feeling a little sense of calm. He stood there, watching the people coming and going. Something strange was going on around him, and he had to figure out what it was. Even though he didn't want to believe it, maybe he needed to pay another visit to the old man. What if there was some strange truth to what he had said. It seemed so unbelievable, yet it was the only thing that fit.

# Fourteen

Quentin stood on the side of the Aura Springs café, watching Zaine as he looked around the building and parking lot. Harper's plan was working. He was reluctant at first to join her in this little plot. In fact, he flat-out denied her request when she first came to him, but he knew this was the only way to keep her safe. She would never have stopped without someone else taking over, and Quentin knew she would have eventually taken things too far and probably killed him. He could see the dark, cold look in her eyes when she talked about Zaine. He had to do something to stop her. This way, Harper would stay safe at the house while Quentin continued to look for the vampires responsible for the killings and carry out Harper's revenge against Zaine at the same time. As soon as he finished with his investigation, he would be finished with Zaine too. By then, he would have driven Zaine mad, and Harper would be satisfied. At least Quentin hoped she would be.

Zaine's hand was shaking each time he lifted the cigarette to his mouth. He was very clearly worried about something. Quentin watched and waited until Zaine put out his cigarette and walked to his car. He concealed himself and moved in

Zaine's direction. Just as Zaine was pulling his car out onto the road, Quentin moved in front of his vehicle, revealing only a shadow of himself, causing Zaine to slam down hard on his breaks and swerve his car into the bushes lining the café's parking lot. He watched as Zaine got out of his car, knowing he couldn't see him. He smiled to himself, looking at Zaine's confused and angered expression. Quentin decided that was enough dealing with Zaine for the night, and it was time to search for the vampires.

The nighttime air seemed eerily calm. The sky was clear. The stars were visible all around, and the moon was shining brightly in the far distance of space. It would have been a beautiful night if not for the uneasy feeling forming in Quentin's chest. He had decided to check into the warehouses around the marina. He had been here the other night on the opposite side of the docks when he dumped that body in the water. He hadn't noticed anything usual then, but with more dead bodied popping up in the area not far from the marina, he figured it was a decent place to start. The warehouses were mostly empty and windowless. The chances of anyone being around this time of year were pretty slim. It would be a good place for a vampire to safely hide out.

As he approached the marina, it appeared vacant as he had expected, but then he sensed a presence. He ducked into the surrounding wooded area, camouflaging himself within the darkness of the trees. Across in the distance, he could see two figures standing there. They appeared to be in some type of argument or heated conversation. He tried to get a better visual of them. One of the two was definitely a woman. She was of average height, wearing dark pants and heels. She had long dark hair peeking out from under the hood of her jacket. As Quentin strained to get a clearer look, he realized she looked remarkably like Harper. But who was that she was arguing with and why? It was a man. Quentin could be sure about that. He had his back to Quentin so that he couldn't see his face, but he could hear his deep accented voice. He couldn't make out the words this man was saying, as he seemed to be speaking in another language. A language he didn't understand, although it sounded familiar. Then he realized where he'd had heard it before and the accent too. He heard it from Dac and Nikolai. They had both pretty much lost their accents and rarely ever spoke their native language, but when they did, usually when they didn't want the others to know what they were saying, their accents really came out. That was what Quentin heard now. The woman, too, made Quentin realize that she couldn't possibly be Harper, but how could she look so much like her. Almost identical even. What was going on, and who were these creatures? It just didn't make sense. Could it be some type of trick, maybe? Did they know he was near, watching? Was this the same person he saw the other times he thought he'd seen Harper and couldn't explain it?

Quentin stood back and continued to watch this exchange for a while longer. The temperature around him was cooling, and the precipitation was beginning to build in the air. A dog was howling in the distance, probably someone's pet begging to get back indoors. The two figures across the way were finally done with their argument. Quentin wished he could know what they had said. The woman was now gone from sight, and the man stood alone in the otherwise empty parking lot. Quentin contemplated approaching him, but he thought better of it. Though he didn't know anything about these vampires, he knew they were older and stronger, and he could sense something dangerous about them, though he wasn't sure why. Maybe it was because of the sudden careless killings or the argument he had just witnessed moments ago. More likely though, it was because at that very moment when the man turned to face Quentin with the dark shadows of the surrounding building hiding the features of his face, his eyes glowed bright red. Quentin knew he had sensed him there. He was giving Quentin a silent warning.

As Quentin turned to walk away, a dense fog began to form around him. He felt himself suddenly paralyzed, unable to move. His knees began to buckle as he felt the energy being drained from him and he fell to the ground. The dirt beneath him was cold and moist. He tried to grab hold of something, anything to help pull himself up. He had to get out of the grip of the fog and back to the house somehow, but it was useless. His limbs grew heavier and heavier. His energy was fading and was growing weaker. He could feel himself in a losing battle between awake and unconsciousness and then his eyes closed and the world around him grew dark and silent.

\* \* \*

Harper stood at the other end of the marina watching in terror as this dark figure wrapped himself around Quentin's lifeless body and carried him away. She could tell he was still alive, just in a state of unconsciousness brought on by this other being. She knew she had to do something, but what could she do? If she went back to the house to get Dac, he would know she was still out here chasing Zaine and that she had recruited

Quentin's help. Even though she knew this had nothing to do with Zaine, Dac would still know because what other reason would Harper be doing here. Quentin was here searching for other vampires, that she was sure of, but she was here searching for Zaine. Now she began to think somehow all of this was somehow connected, but how and why? That was what she had to find out. How was Zaine connected to the vampires and why did one of them just take Quentin? Then she remembered she had seen Jace that night at the warehouse. She had gone to him that very same night and warned him to stay away. She had sensed the evil in there and wanted to protect her old friend but now she needed his help. Maybe he could tell her about these guys. Find out what he really knew about them and what he had really been doing there. She set out in the direction of Jace's house. That was going to be the first step in finding Quentin.

Harper was standing outside of Jace's house. Cloe was there, inside. Cloe and Jace were sitting at a small table in the kitchen, appearing to be having dinner. They were eating, drinking, and laughing, having a good time. Harper didn't want to interrupt that, and most importantly, she couldn't let Cloe see her even though she missed her old friend. The pang in her heart was deep, just as it always was whenever she thought of her old life. Heat raced through her cold body from head to toe. She took a few deep breaths, pushing the anger and resentment aside. She had to gain control of her emotions. After what had happened the other night at Zaine's apartment and after Dac's warning, she knew she had to be careful now. Her powers were growing more potent, and she needed to be in control of them. She also needed to get Jace outside and alone so she could talk to him and ask him what he knew if he knew anything. She decided it was best to try to send him a silent message and hope he received it.

# Fifteen

Inside the house, Jace and Cloe sat enjoying their dinner together. He looked across the table at his longtime girlfriend and now fiancé. She was the most perfect person in the world to him. He knew he had been acting differently since he had seen Harper that night, and he hated that he couldn't tell Cloe about it. Harper had warned him against it, and if he were honest with himself, he wasn't even sure if it was real or some kind of bizarre hallucination. All he knew for sure was he had felt different since that night, as if he were walking around in a dream. He had moments where he was feverish, and he had a wound on his neck he couldn't explain. All this was causing tension between him and Cloe. She wanted him to go see a doctor, but he kept refusing. When she would ask why he would just say he was fine. She knew he wasn't, but he couldn't exactly tell her why. What would he say to her anyway if he did tell her? Would he just say, your old best friend Harper came back from the dead as a vampire and then bit me on the neck? She would think him certifiable, and if he said that to a doctor, they would undoubtedly commit him. So he just kept it to himself and told her he got the wound from some freak accident with a pair of scissors at work. It would all be ok, he assured her, though he knew she didn't really believe it. But she accepted it, and for tonight they were actually laughing together, and things were feeling normal for the moment.

Then suddenly, Jace heard a voice whisper his name, a voice that sounded distinctly like Harper's. It couldn't be her again, could it? Would she really come back? She said she had just come to warn him away from those people at the poker game, and he hadn't been back there since. He hadn't even heard from them again, so why would she come back. He looked around the room but didn't see anything. He was probably just hearing things, but then he heard it again. He looked at Cloe.

"Did you hear something?"

"No. I didn't hear anything. Are you ok? You look a little pale all of a sudden."

He shrugged. "Yea, I'm fine."

Then he heard the voice a third time. He was convinced now it was definitely Harper. What could she want? Maybe if he ignored her, she would go away. What was it they said of vampires? They couldn't come in if you didn't invite them. Except he hadn't invited her the first time so that apparently wasn't true. He felt the sweat start to form in the palms of his hands, and his heart began to race in his chest. He rose from his chair.

"I'm just going to get some air." He said as he looked down at Cloe, taking notice of the concern in her eyes, but she just responded with "Ok," and he turned towards the door.

Jace walked down the front steps and began walking to the side of the house when he saw Harper standing there. She was so pale, her skin almost glowing in the darkness. Her expression was blank. He took a deep breath, trying to slow his heart rate. *Calm down; she wouldn't hurt you*, he thought to himself, though he wasn't sure if he genuinely believed it. She hadn't that first night, but then why had she come back tonight? Why was she looking at him the way she was with her eyes so intense? She just stood there, not moving like a lioness ready to pounce on her prey. He stopped a few feet away from her, frozen in his tracks. Finally, she smiled at him. Her fanged teeth glistened in the light from the moon above them. It was then he noticed there were no outside lights on. He swallowed hard and took another deep breath.

Harper let out a quiet laugh. "I'm not going to hurt you, Jace." She reassured him. "I just can't let Cloe see me."

She turned and signaled for Jace to follow her. She led him farther back behind the house where it was darker, and she could speak to him with less chance of Cloe overhearing.

"Listen. Another vampire took a friend of mine tonight—an older and more dangerous vampire. I need to ask you a few questions. I'm hoping you could help me find him."

"More vampires?" Jace asked with alarm. "How would I be able to help? I don't know anything about any vampires."

"Keep your voice down a little, please." She demanded. "The people you were with the other night, the ones at the warehouse, I think they are the ones who took my friend. I just need to know what you know about them."

"Are you saying they are vampires? Are they the ones doing the killings? Were they going to kill me?"

"Jace, please calm down. But yes, I think they are the vampires responsible for the killings. No, I don't think they were going to kill you, or Zaine either for that matter, or they would have that night. I'm not sure what they want with either of you, why they chose you and why they let you go, but I am sure they took my friend, and I'm pretty sure it's all connected somehow. So please just tell me anything you know."

"I don't know much. I'm not sure I'll be much help."

"Anything you know, tell me, no matter how small. It may be able to help. How did you meet them? How did you end up at the warehouse?"

"I was waiting for Cloe one night at the café. We've been going there on the anniversary of your disappearance. This was the third year we had done this. I guess it's our way of celebrating your life and mourning you at the same time. As you know, since there wasn't a body to find, there is no grave to visit, so we go to the café since it was a place we know was special to you. Anyway, Cloe was running late that night. Some guy came in. I hadn't noticed him at first and had never seen him around town. Figured he was new in town or something, and he was dressed kind of fancy for the café. But I didn't think much of it. He came up to the table and dropped a piece of paper in front of me. He said I looked like I could use a little help, and he could help me. I took a look at the paper, and it only contained a phone number. He told me to text that number, and I would receive a message back in a few weeks with a place and time to meet."

"So, what you just texted some stranger and met at the warehouse? Didn't your mother ever teach you not to go to strange places with people you don't know?" Harper asked with more than a hint of sarcasm.

Jace rolled his eyes and continued with his story. "I wasn't going to at first. I went to hand the paper back to the guy and tell him no thanks, but he shook me off. He said it would be in my best interest if I just did what he said. I got up from my chair, started to argue with him, told him what he could do with his little piece of paper and his help, but then he stuck his arm out, placed his hand on my shoulder, and pushed me without much effort back into my chair. This guy was stronger than anyone I'd ever met before, and then I'd notice Cloe walking into the café, so I just looked at the guy, said fine, and slipped the paper in my pocket. He left after that. I never text the number. I figured I'd never actually see him again, and I'd just ignore him, but I got a message a few weeks later anyway. I wasn't going to go at first, but I figured if they could find out my phone number, they could find out where I lived too, and I didn't want anything to happen to Cloe." Jace stopped for a moment to catch his breath before continuing.

"I went to the warehouse that night and found out it was some kind of underground poker game. Some woman came to the door and ushered me to a seat at the only table. She brought me a drink, and I sat there for a few minutes. I wanted to leave but also didn't want to offend any of these guys since, like I said, I was worried about Cloe. Then Zaine walked in and sat beside me. He had been spending time with my cousin Janice, and I told him to stay the hell away from her, but other than that, the night was uneventful, except Zaine did seem to make out pretty big from what I could tell. It also seemed to me that they fronted him the cash."

"I see. Is there anything else you can tell me about that night? Something maybe about who was hosting?"

"I'm sorry, Harper. I don't know much about them. I only saw the guy once before and the others only that night, but I didn't really interact with any of them. I spoke with Zaine, played the game, and pretty much got out of there as fast as possible. The whole thing seemed way too shady for me, and well, you know what happened after."

Harper gave a slight grin before asking her next question. "That's ok. Can you just tell me how many there were? Can you describe them, maybe?"

"There were four, maybe five. The guy from the café, he just sat in the back corner all night. I never really saw his face. Come to think of it. I didn't get a clear look at his face at the café either. He kept a hat on the entire time and was gone so fast I barely saw him leave. Then there was the bartender, and again I barely saw his face. The whole place was pretty dark, and I never actually went up to the bar. Then there were two women, maybe three. I'm not sure."

"Maybe three? How are you not sure? Was it two or three? I need you to remember?"

"Well, there was the dealer and another woman who mostly stood near the man in the back. Then there was possibly someone else. I'm fairly sure it was another woman, but I only caught a quick glance of her a few times."

"What was she doing?"

"I'm sorry. Like I said, I only got a quick glance at her. I don't know I even really saw her for sure, you know."

Harper did know. Some vampires were good at concealing themselves and only being seen when they wanted to be seen. Quentin had done this often.

"Give me your phone for a sec."

"My phone? What for?" He asked as he handed the phone over to Harper.

She took the phone from his hand and began typing something into the notes section. Jace looked at her for a moment, then said. "One more thing." Harper glanced up. "Zaine, it seemed like he had been there before. Like he had been familiar with them. I got the feeling he had definitely been there more than once."

Harper handed the phone back to him. "Thank you Jace. You have been more helpful than you probably realize. By the way, the fever you've been feeling lately, it will pass in a few days as your own blood restores itself."

"So, this is normal? You didn't infect me or anything, did you?"

"Infect you?" Harper laughed. "No, there's no infection, and you're not going to become a vampire. There's a little more to it than that, but I do want you to go see Sarah Higgins."

"The gypsy girl?"

"She's not a gypsy. She's a spiritual advisor, but she sells things in her shop that can protect you."

"What do you mean? Like crucifixes and holy water? Wouldn't I go to a church for that?" Jace asked with a laugh.

"This is serious, Jace. Go to her first thing in the morning. Ask her for the essential oils, frankincense, and peppermint mixed with salt, and keep this mixture on you at all times. Promise me you'll do this."

"I'll do it. First thing. I promise."

"Good. Now just one more thing. I put a few names and an address into your phone. If anything happens to me, I want you to go to this address and ask for one of them. You'll be able to help them find me."

"How will I know if something happens to you, and how will I know where you are?"

"Don't worry. You'll just know."

Before Jace could say another word, Harper lunged at him like she had the other night. She kept a firm grip on his neck as she sank her fangs into his flesh before she disappeared again.

# Sixteen

Zaine looked at the front of his car, sitting in the bushes. Smoke was escaping out from under the hood, and the front tire was flat. Obviously, he wasn't going to be able to drive it home. He'd have to have it towed. He called his friend Chris since he worked at a mechanic shop, and Chris arranged for the tow truck and agreed to pick Zaine up at the café and drive him home. A crowd of people from the café began to form around him.

"Are you ok?" Someone asked.

"Yea, I'm fine. Thought I saw a cat." Zaine lied. Physically he was ok, but he was angry about his car, and that was definitely not a cat that he saw.

"Do you need a tow truck?" asked another.

"No. No. I called already, and I have someone picking me up. They should be here soon."

The crowd began to disperse as people went back into the warmth of the café. Zaine followed since there was nothing more he could do but wait. He sat down at a table near the front window to look out for Chris and the tow truck. The café manager came by and offered him a cup of coffee. He graciously accepted it, and he sat there sipping the coffee, letting the warm liquid calm his nerves a bit. He took a few breathes and leaned backed in the chair as he impatiently waited.

About twenty minutes later, Chris finally arrived. The tow truck was still nowhere in sight. Zaine let out an impatient sigh.

"Sorry, man, I got here soon as I could. Had to finish up some paperwork before I could
leave work."

"Yea, don't worry about it."

"Tow truck not here yet, I see. I saw your car out front. Man, what happened?"

"Swerved to avoid a cat."

"Right. Well, don't worry. We'll have it towed to the shop, and it'll be fixed up in no time."

Zaine could tell his friend knew he was lying about the cat, but he was glad Chris wasn't the type to press him about it. Chris was usually perceptive of his friend's moods and not one to initiate an argument. He'd just want to help his friend, so he'd keep quiet about his suspicions and accept Zaine's explanation about the cat.

Finally, the tow truck turned into the café parking lot. The two men got up and walked outside to meet the driver. Zaine gave the guy his payment, signed the paperwork, and watched as his car was attached to the back of the truck. The truck drove off. Chris slapped his friend on the back, and they walked over to Chris's car and headed off towards Zaine's apartment.

Inside the apartment, Zaine grabbed two beers from the refrigerator. He placed the bottles on the countertop. Chris took one walked over to the couch in the living room, sat down, and turned on the tv. He could hear Zaine sniffling in the kitchen and yelled over to him.

"You know that's probably why you've been paranoid lately. You really need to leave that shit alone."

"Mind your business," Zaine grunted back at him.

"I'm just saying you've been unnecessarily suspicious of some guy you've never met. You were so distracted the other day you nearly jumped out of your skin when I came up to you at the bar. Maybe that stuff is getting to you. That's all I'm saying, and you know what happened last time you got like this." Chris said, referring to three years ago when Zaine lost all his money, was disowned by his family, and went to jail for a DUI.

"Everything's fine. Drop it, ok." Zaine walked out of the kitchen and sat on the opposite end of the couch. Chris took a sip of beer and dropped the subject.

\* \* \*

Harper left Jace standing in his backyard. She got whatever information that she could get from him. He didn't know very much, but he did mention that Zaine seemed to know the vampires even if he himself didn't know they were vampires. Maybe she could get some information from him somehow. Harper couldn't exactly go to Zaine and just start asking questions as she had with Jace; however, she would have to get answers from him some other way. First, she would have to go back to the house and get some type of protection. If she couldn't find out from Zaine where she might be able to find these other vampires and where they may have taken Quentin, she would go back to the warehouse, but either way, she'd need some way to protect herself.

She planned to sneak into the house, undetected by the others. She didn't need them asking her any questions or delaying her mission. She needed to be in and out. She knew Nikolai and Dac kept weapons in the house. She just needed to sneak in, grab one, and sneak back out. After that, she would go to Zaine's apartment, and somehow, she'd get the information she needed. Finally, she would go and save Quentin.

Maybe this wasn't a super well thought out plan considering she didn't know for sure if Zaine would know where the vampires were or how she would get the information from him exactly. Maybe she could make him think he was dreaming like the other times she appeared to him. Even if that worked and she could find Quentin, how exactly was she going to save him? She didn't know. All she knew for sure was all this was somehow her fault, and it was up to her to save him.

Quentin and Emmaline were right the other night, she thought. Her getting revenge against Zaine must have somehow brought them out here. They must have sensed it somehow, and if it weren't for her, they wouldn't be around here, and Dac wouldn't have had to send Quentin looking for them. Besides that, Dac had already warned her to stay away from Zaine, and he seemed more serious than ever the other night. He had never threatened her like that before, and she knew he meant it. It was because of this that she couldn't go to him now. Otherwise, he would know she hadn't let go of her plan to get revenge on Zaine. She couldn't go to Nikolai either. He'd go straight to Dac. He and Dac were too close.

He felt like he owed too much to Dac. While he cared a lot for Harper, she knew he would never defy him to help her. As for Emmaline, she didn't trust her enough right now. She'd probably tell the others, so Harper was on her own.

The more she began to think about Zaine, the more she felt the anger grow inside her. As guilty as she was feeling for her part in Quentin's disappearance, Zaine was more at fault. Zaine was the one who had killed her; therefore, Zaine was responsible for setting all of this in motion.

The winds were beginning the howl around her. Dark clouds started rolling in. Thunder roared in the distance. It seemed this happened every time she thought of Zaine. She needed to gain control of her anger. The last thing she needed was to alert Dac. He had already warned her once. She was risking enough already. She just needed to quietly get into the house, gather the things she needed, then get to Zaine's. She breathed in deeply, clearing the toxic thoughts from her mind switching her focus to the task at hand. The winds began to calm, the sky started to clear, and Harper started out towards Aura city and the house she shared with the other vampires.

Once outside the house, Harper crept around and in through the back door and up the back staircase to the second floor. She walked silently down the long corridor towards the east end of the house. She could hear Nikolai in his office. She reached the end of the hallway and ascended up the next flight of stairs to the third-floor attic room. When she came to the landing, two large double doors leading to the only room on this floor stood before her. She stood on the landing for a moment longer, looked around, and saw no one. So far, so good. Still, at the top of the darkened stairwell, she listened for any sounds of movement nearby. She heard no sign of the others being near. She was alone in total darkness and silence.

She knew she shouldn't be there. Dac and Nikolai had forbidden anyone from going to the attic floor. It was the only place in the house where no one was allowed. Harper stared at the doors for a moment before entering the room, knowing that once she walked through them, there would be no turning back. Behind those doors laid the keys to her own undoing and everyone else's, but they also held the weapons that would protect her. She had no choice. She reached for the doorknob with a shaking hand, turned the handle, and opened the heavy wooden doors.

The room was dark and damp and smelled of mildew. Harper searched around for a light. While she could see well in the dark, for this task, she needed to see better than her vampire sight allowed her. After a few moments, she located a small lamp situated on the desk in the middle of the room. She walked over and turned on the lamp, which gave off little light, but it was enough. Next to the lamp on the desk lay an open book. The pages were old and worn, and when she looked closer at it, she noticed it was more than just a book. It was a diary written in Dac's handwriting.

The words on the page were written in his native language. She would need a translator if she wanted to read it. She pulled the phone she kept with her out of her pocket and clicked open the internet. There she could type in each word and translate it into English. It took a while, but as she translated each word, she realized what she was reading was the story of how Dac and Nikolai destroyed Dac's brother Luca.

Satisfied that she had learned enough of what she needed to know to destroy the vampires that took Quentin, Harper searched around the room for the weapons described in the pages of Dac's diary. On the walls hung various swords of different sizes. There were both metal and wooden stakes laid out on a large wooden table. She took a few and stuffed them in a knapsack she found sitting on the floor. On another table sat two clear jars filled with a clear liquid. Harper opened the first container. The smell of frankincense and peppermint immediately accosted her. She instinctively backed away from the container, but then she noticed a row of small vials on the shelf that hung above the table. She took a couple of vials down from the shelf and filled them with the liquid being careful not to get any of the mixture on her skin. She placed them each in separate velvet pouches and put them in the knapsack.

Just as she turned to leave the room, something on a separate shelf caught her eye. She moved over to the shelf, inspecting the glass casing that sat on top of it. Inside was a steel dagger. It was heavier than she had expected when she removed it from its case. Smooth black leather was wrapped around its cool steel handle. The blade was sharp and curved. Upon further inspection, she realized remnants of dried blood remained on the blade. It must be Luca's blood, she thought to herself. She found a leather case for the dagger, slipped it inside her jacket, grabbed the knapsack, and hurried from the room, carefully closing the doors behind her.

Sure that no one had seen her, and she had gotten out of the house without being noticed, Harper swiftly moved through the darkened night. Her next stop, Zaine's apartment. She decided she needed to get there quickly since she had already used up too much time tonight, and it was vastly approaching midnight. Sure, she could move fast, but tonight she would need more than her own speed. She decided the train could get her there quicker, and she had become accustomed to blending in with living people. She got to the Aura City train station and purchased her ticket just as the train was arriving. She pulled the hood of her jacket up over her head and boarded the train.

The fluorescent lights of the train car were bright in contrast to the dark night sky. She took a seat near the door so she could exit as quickly as possible without drawing attention to herself as soon as she arrived at her stop. She placed her bag on the seat next to her in hopes of discouraging anyone from trying to sit there. She sat inconspicuously as she watched the other passengers board the train and take their seats. Various smells of body odor, perfumes, and worst of all, human blood assaulted her senses. She had realized at this moment that other than the small amount of blood she had taken from Jace, she had not fed tonight. She missed the nightly feeding with the others. Would Dac be looking for her? She felt the anxiety rise within her, along with the hunger she was now feeling. Then another thought occurred to her. Had Quentin been at the table with others tonight, or had he missed it too? Did they notice he was missing yet? He'd be ok, though; even if he sometimes drank it, he didn't need blood like the others. He was an energy vampire. He fed off the energy of humans to stay alive instead of their blood. Harper wished she fed off energy right now. The pangs of hunger were becoming too much to resist. She had to hold it together.

Just then, an older woman approached her, almost breaking her from her thoughts. She was asking if she could have a seat next to her. Harper's heart was now beating harder in her chest. She managed to keep her head facing to the front of her directing her gaze off the woman standing beside her seat. She lowered her head and closed her eyes, pretending to be asleep. The woman walked off, muttering something under her breath about being rude. Harper laughed silently to herself. If that woman only knew how she had just saved her life. She easily could have let her sit there, drained her of her blood, satisfying her ever-growing thirst. The thought made her mouth water and her stomach ache. Her hands were shaking as she wrapped her arms around her stomach. She rested her head back against her seat and breathed deep.

Finally, the train arrived at the Aura Springs station. It had only been ten minutes, but it had felt like a lifetime. Harper grabbed her bag and hurried off the train onto the platform. Grateful to be back in the cover of night, she headed away from the station and in the direction of Zaine's apartment. A taxi had stopped her inquiring if she needed a ride someplace. She waved him off, deciding not to take any chances. She had surrounded herself with enough temptation for one night.

# Seventeen

Emmaline sat back in the dark, watching Harper as she descended down the back staircase and out the back door. It was apparent she thought no one had noticed her, but Emmaline had seen her come in, and she sensed she was up to something. Most certainly, that something was not good either. In the few years that Harper had been with them, she never came in through that door, and more than that, she never went upstairs. When she was home, she spent all her time in her room or the downstairs common room, claiming she liked the solitude. Ever the depressive one, she'd say it fit her new life. Now though, she was sneaking around, and more importantly, she left carrying a bag that she hadn't had with her when she first entered the house. Now Emmaline was even more curious. What exactly was Harper up to?

Emmaline had followed Harper out of the house and to the train station. She watched Harper board the train. She stood back and then boarded with the last of the passengers being careful that Harper wouldn't see her. She went into the opposite train car and watched through the tiny glass window for when Harper got off so she could follow closely behind her. Standing there as the train began to move, Emmaline started to think of when Nikolai had first brought Harper to the house to live with them. She thought it would be great to have another female around, like a sister. Emmaline had a real sister once, a twin, and she missed her. They were thick as thieves, their mother used to say. They went everywhere together. They would dress alike in the same clothes, never worrying about separate identities. As kids, they would have fun while people mixed them up and making them guess which was which. Then at the festival that day, they somehow got separated from each other. Emmaline remembered searching everywhere for her sister, asking anyone and everyone had they seen her. That's when the vampire snatched her. It had gotten dark, and she still hadn't found her sister. She was walking through a crowd of people trying to find a payphone or someplace she could call her mom when she felt someone grab her. A hand covered her mouth when she tried to scream. He dragged her off into a nearby cemetery, and that's where he bit her that first night, but he hadn't killed her, nor had he turned her yet. He locked her in a crypt and kept her there for three days. Each night he would come back and drink more from her. She had cried and pleaded with him to let her go. Finally, on the third night, after he had drunk one last time from her, he spit inside the wound on her neck, and when he left, he also left the door of the crypt open. As he left, Emmaline heard him saying something about how one day, she would have wished that he had killed her. At first, she didn't understand what he had meant by that, but then she tried to get up and run away. By this time, it was almost morning, and the sun was beginning to rise, and Emmaline realized she was too weak to move. She laid her head down on the cold stone of the crypt and slept. Later that night was when Dac found her and brought her to the house. At that moment, she realized what had been done to her and what she had become.

She had spent many years with only Dac, Nikolai, and Quentin. They had taken great care of her, and for that, she was eternally grateful, but she longed for a female companion, a sister. So, when Nikolai brought Harper to stay with them, Emmaline thought finally she had someone she could bond with as she had with her own sister. She tried so hard with Harper to be her friend, but Harper never truly opened up to her. She had tried in the beginning; Emmeline would admit, but that bond Emmaline was hoping for was just never there. Harper remained detached. Emmaline couldn't understand why the others seemed to protect her so much. She knew Quentin did because Dac and Nikolai cared for her. Nikolai, she understood a little bit. Harper supposedly resembles his late wife, so she guessed it made some sense he would harbor some type of affection for her, but it was a more familiar affection. Dac, on the other hand, for reasons Emmaline couldn't comprehend, was in love with Harper.

The train came to a stop breaking Emmaline of her thoughts. She saw Harper exit the train and followed her off onto the platform. Being careful to always keep a few people between them, Emmaline followed Harper out of the station and on the darkened street. Emmaline had rarely ever been on this end of town, but she was reasonably sure she knew where Harper was going. She was going to Zaine's.

\* \* \*

Harper continued walking, being careful to stick to the most darkened streets where the streetlamps were broken and porch lights were left off. The cold air filled her lungs with every breath she took. Dogs howled in the distance. A feral cat ran past her feet. She almost reached for it but held back and then instantly regretted it. The hunger and craving for blood were starting to consume her. The dizziness and weakness were beginning to take over her body. Her movements were beginning to slow. She tried to push the feelings of hunger aside as she soldiered on in her mission. Finding Quentin was the most important thing. She would have to be strong now. Suddenly, she thought she heard footsteps behind her, but she saw no one when she turned around. Everything was dark, still, and quiet. It reminded her of those moments she had had when she was still human, those moments of feeling as if someone was watching her, but no one was ever there. Then she remembered how Nikolai had told her how he had watched her for months before he rescued her from the water. Was someone watching her now? Had someone followed her from the house? Was it Nikolai or Dac, and she just couldn't see them? There was no time to worry about such things now. She held a tighter grip on the knapsack that hung from her shoulder and picked up her speed.

Finally, after what felt like an eternity, she found herself inside Zaine's apartment. The apartment was dark and quiet, but she could hear Zaine breathing in the back room. She dropped her knapsack on the floor, stood at the end of the short hallway, and whispered for him to come to her. She heard him rise from the sleep in which she had awoken him. He stood quietly at the other end of the hall just outside his bedroom door. Harper motioned for him to come closer. Obeying her command, he stepped slowly towards her, stopping only inches away from where she stood. He looked into her captivating eyes that glowed in the pure darkness of the room. He whispered her name, "Harper," and reached his hand out and touched her face. She placed her hand on his cheek in response. The smell of blood that coursed through his veins was compelling now that he stood so close to her. The warmth of his flesh was inviting against the coldness of her own skin. The hunger grew inside her, and her hatred for Zaine began to take over all her senses. A cloudiness had formed over her mind, and she'd almost forgotten why she had come here. Then in a brief moment of clarity, she realized she need not ask him any questions at all. She could get all the answers she needed from him without saying a word.

She ran her hand down the side of his face under his chin and around the back of his neck. She held him in a tight grip. Her fingernails broke through the surface of his skin. She could feel the warmth of his blood trickle down her fingers. She let go of her grip on his neck. She held her hand out in front of her staring at the bright red liquid covering her fingers. Zaine watched, horror stuck on his face. Harper put her fingers to her mouth, licking them clean of the sweet taste of Zaine's blood. Zaine wiped the back of his neck with his own hand. Blood was still dripping from the wound Harper had made. He moved to back up away from her. But it was too late. Harper lunged forward. She wrapped her body around Zaine, holding him in a tight embrace. He struggled to break free of her clutches. But her vampiric strength held firm. He continued to struggle in her grasp. Harper opened her mouth, baring her sharp fangs. Then sunk her vampire teeth into the salty sweat covered flesh of Zaine's neck.

The sweet and salty mixture of Zaine's blood and sweat filled Harper's mouth, rewarding her senses. Zaine's body began to relax beneath her as he succumbed to her and was no longer able to keep up the struggle. Harper continued to drink, draining the blood from Zaine's artery, quenching her vampire thirst. As she lost herself in this euphoric moment, the front door burst open, and a bitter cold rush of air entered the room.

"Harper! Stop!"

Emmaline's voice pierced through her eardrums as she felt Zaine's body ripped from her grasp. Zaine now lay weakened on the floor, blood spilling from the wound in his neck. Pieces of his lacerated flesh still attached to Harper's teeth. She licked them off and spat the bits of skin and what little blood remained onto the floor.

Emmaline grabbed Harper by the arm, trying to drag her towards the door. "What have you done? We have to get out of here!"

"No! You don't understand." Harper pleaded as she snatched her arm away and leaped toward where Zaine lay on the floor.

Emmaline dove after Harper and knocked them both to the floor. Harper kicked her away, forcing Emmaline to crash into the coffee table in the middle of the room. The force of the impact caused the wooden table to break and splinter into pieces.

Harper started to crawl near Zaine. A loud crash suddenly filled the room. Glass shattered around her. Emmaline was rushing towards her. She reached out, grabbed a piece of the broken wood, and thrust it at Emmaline.

The sharp end of the wood pierced the center of Emmaline's chest. She grabbed onto the wooden stake as she fell back against the wall and slid to the floor. She stared at Harper in what could only be described as disbelief. Blood began to spill out of the wound around the wooden stake still lodged in her chest, staining the cream-colored lace dress she had worn. A shadowy figure came through the shattering glass. He grabbed Harper and Zaine, wrapping them both in what appeared to be large black leathery wings. He faced Emmaline for a quick moment. Though she had never fully seen his face back then and could not now, she knew those red glowing eyes. Hardly able to move, she watched the creature carry Harper and Zaine away out of the broken glass door. Mustering all the strength she had left, she wrapped her hands around the wooden stake and pulled the wood from where it had lodged her in her chest. The blood poured out faster. Her body fell weak. The sounds around her seemed to be far off in the distance now. Her head began to spin with dizziness. There's was nothing more she could do. It was up to her body now to do the rest. Accepting her fate, she rested her head against the wall and closed her eyes.

# Eighteen

When Jace woke up the next morning, Cloe had already gone, but she had left a note on the pillow next to him. He picked up the small sheet of paper, reading it with a smile. She had said she hoped he would be feeling better today and that she would see him later. He placed the note on the nightstand next to him and looked at the time on his phone. It was almost ten a.m. He was glad he didn't have work that morning. He was still feeling a little bit feverish, but Harper said that would pass. He still couldn't believe any of this was happening. He decided to get out of bed, take a shower, and then see Sarah Higgins. Her shop was probably open by now, or at least should be by the time he got there.

Even though it was cold outside, he opted for a cool shower. He splashed the water over his face and hair. The cool water felt good against his warm, feverish skin. He turned off the shower water and stepped out of the tub when he had finished washing up. After drying off, he threw on a grey t-shirt and a pair of jeans. He rubbed the towel across his wet hair, drying it as best he could. He went into the kitchen to find a half pot of coffee still on the counter. He heated some of the coffee in the microwave, put it in a thermos, threw on his jacket, and headed out the door.

On his drive over to Sarah's store, Jace kept getting this feeling that he had dreamed of something terrible during the night. The more he tried the recall the dream, the more Harper's words from last night had echoed in his mind. "You'll know if something happens to me. Go to this address. They will help." She had told him. Was Harper in trouble? Was that what the dream had been about? He couldn't shake the feeling that it was somehow important to recall the events of that dream.

He pulled up to Sarah's store and entered through the front door. The bells above the door rang out, alerting her to his presence. Sarah Higgins had come out from another room in the back of the store. She had long wavy coppery hair. She wore a long-printed skirt and a white top with a long cardigan over it. She had combat boots on her feet, large hoop hearings dangled from her ears, and an array of long necklaces were layered around her neck. She reached her hand out to greet him. Her fingers were clad in large rings made of multiple precious stones. Jace shook her hand and introduced himself.

"What can I help you with, Jace?" She asked as she studied his face.

When he explained what he was looking for, she listened intently, never giving any indication of judgment. She asked him to wait a moment while she went to the back and prepared the mixture of oils he asked for and offered him a seat in the corner of the shop. He graciously accepted the opportunity to sit while waiting since he was still not feeling a hundred percent well.

A few minutes later, Sarah emerged from the back room

with a small container holding the essential oils. She also had a bottle containing orange-colored capsules and a tube of ointment.

"Take these pills for the fever. They have iron to help repair the blood, and this you can rub on the wounds to heal them quicker." She said as she handed him the three items.

Jace instinctively put his hand to his neck as she mentioned his wounds.

"Don't worry." She told him. "I have a great wealth of knowledge on such sensitive subjects. I will never judge you. Everyone who comes to me comes for a reason. While most are just looking for spiritual guidance and holistic medicines, others such as yourself require something much greater."

Jace looked at Sarah for a moment. "What can you tell me about...um...." He paused, and before he could finish his thought, she answered, "Vampires? Come with me. I'll tell you all I can."

Jace followed her through the store into the sparsely lit back room, where two tall lamps stood on opposite sides. There was an old-fashioned red velvet sofa against one wall. A red tablecloth covered the small table in the center. Jace mused that this was the room where Sarah would meet with her clients for spiritual readings and such things. Sarah offered Jace a seat on the couch. She grabbed a book from a shelf and sat down next to him.

She held the book in her lap and clasped her hands together. Then she began to speak.

"As you can tell, they do exist. Many different species exist amongst us, natural and supernatural. To think otherwise is naive. Mostly they are no more dangerous than any other predator, including humans. They must survive just like anyone else, and they have plenty of means for survival. They are also not all blood drinkers. Some survive purely on the energy of others. There are, however, a few you must be wary of. I sense you are in search of such individuals in particular. Is this true?"

"Sort of." He answered.

"Please tell me your story. How did this vampire come to see you, and why do you seek them out now?"

Jace hesitated at first, but then he began to tell Sarah the recent events that had occurred.

"See Harper, that is her name. I knew her before she was a vampire when she was human. We were friends, her and I, and she was best friends with my fiancé. That was three years ago. Then she disappeared. We assumed someone had murdered her, but her body was never recovered, and there was never any proof. Her case just went cold, I guess. It was devastating for her family and my fiancé; Cloe has never really been the same since. Any way Harper came to me a few nights back. She wanted to warn me of something. She had seen me someplace, a card game I had been invited to. She wanted to tell me the people hosting this game were dangerous and never to go back there. I've wanted to tell my fiancé, but Harper, she begged me not to, and I have kept my word." Jace paused to take a breath.

"Please continue. I feel there is more to this. You have seen Harper again since that first night?"

"Yes. She came again last night. I was having dinner with my fiancé when suddenly I heard her calling me. It was as if she was in my mind."

"She bit you that first night?"

"Yes. I've been feverish since then. I was beginning to feel a little better, but then like I said, she came back last night. At first, I wasn't even sure I was hearing her, but then the sound of her voice got louder and more urgent, so I went outside. She was standing on the side of my house. We went into the backyard to talk. That is when she told me her friend was missing. I think she was going to look for him. She put an address into my phone. She wanted me to go there if something was to happen to her. I don't know how I am supposed to know if it does, but she told me I would just know, and that's when she bit me again. Then she was gone. Oh, she also told me I should come here."

"Yes, for the oils. That is for your protection. I do not believe the ones she sent you to seek out will harm you, at least not so long as they believe you can help them. But remember, I said there are some you need to beware of. One, in particular, he is believed to be dead, but it may be possible that it is not the truth. He is extremely dangerous and incredibly old. He comes from a family of vampires though they are not born vampires. Within this family, it is said that the seventh son of the seventh son would become a vampire. The one who goes by the name of Luca, he is a part of this family. He is not the seventh son, but somehow, he became a vampire and killed the one before him. The lineage would have then died with him, but it is believed that he captured his youngest brother, the true seventh son, and turned him. This action started a conflict between the two brothers. Legend says the younger brother killed Luca. However, there has been evidence throughout the years that this may not be true. Have you heard of the recent killings? The police believe it is a wild animal, but I think you can see now that it is not the case. It may not be Luca, but the brutal attacks against these victims suggest that it very well could be. You see, Luca was an immensely powerful vampire and an even more brutal killer."

Jace listened nervously as Sarah told her story. He wondered how she knew all these things. He needed to learn so much more, and no one has yet to explain how he would know if Harper was in trouble. Yet, somehow, he was beginning to sense that she was, and he hoped it had nothing to do with whoever Luca was. Finally, he decided just to ask.

"So how would I know if Harper is in trouble? That is the thing I don't understand."

"She has bitten you. That bite connects you to her. You will be able to see what she sees and hear what she hears so long as she allows you."

Jace thought about that for a minute, then said. "I fear something may have happened. I had a dream last night, or rather a nightmare. When I woke up this morning, I could hardly remember it though it seemed so real at the time, and all morning it's been in the back of my mind. I think someone may have taken her, and I think someone else may be dead."

"What did you see in this dream? Can you remember it now?"

"Vaguely. But I will try to recall as best I can. I saw Harper; she was biting someone." Then suddenly, as the dream became more lucid, Jace realized who that someone was. "It was Zaine!" he explained.

"Zaine is someone you know? A friend?"

"Hardly a friend. Harper dated him before she disappeared. He killed her."

"Oh, I see," Sarah said.

"She had her body wrapped around Zaine. She had her teeth in his neck. It was dark, but I could see everything as if it were happening in the daylight. Then someone came in through the door—a girl. I have never seen her before. She snatched Zaine from Harper. Harper and the girl fought. Harper killed her." Shocked by this realization, he continued. "No, that can't be right. But I see it. She threw something at her. It pierced her chest. The girl fell back. There was so much blood. I don't understand. That doesn't seem like Harper."

"You must remember, Jace, she is not the same Harper you knew three years ago. Is there anything else you remember?'"

"I don't know. It goes dark. But I think I hear a crash, sounds like broken glass. Then I feel like I am suffocating, and I can't breathe. That is when I wake up."

"I feel you must be extremely careful with whatever you do next, but I think you must go to that address she left you. It sounds like she is in grave danger." Sarah got up from her seat on the sofa. She moved over to the table in the center of the room. She lifted the tablecloth and opened a drawer connected to the table. It was a crucifix hanging from a black cord. She handed it to Jace.

"Please take this. Wear it around your neck. The crucifix itself will not protect you, but the contents inside will."

Jace took the necklace from her and put it around his neck. As he examined it, it was then that he realized the thickness of the crucifix and the tiny screw at the bottom, which would open it.

"Keep the oils with you. They will burn the vampire if it is to touch his skin. If they sense the oils on you, that should keep them at a safe distance for now. But please be careful."

"I will, and thank you." Jace shook her hand and then left out of the store.

# Nineteen

J ace parked his car next to the curb and stepped out onto the sidewalk. The sun was beginning to set, painting the sky in hues of red and orange. Sarah had told him to come at sundown, but before the sky had turned completely dark. He hoped this was a good time.

He had never before been to this part of Aura city. He had also never gone looking for vampires before. Here the buildings were taller, and the streets were more crowded than in his small shore town. He looked down at the address on his phone. Could this be right? He would think vampires would want to live someplace more secluded where they could hide. Then he thought of that saying about hiding in plain sight. Maybe it made sense they would live here. No one would probably notice if they seemed a little bit strange. Everyone here seemed like they stuck to themselves, he thought to himself as he noted the people were walking with heads down and earphones stuck in their ears. Aura City was nothing like his little town, only a short twenty minutes away. No one here smiled or greeted one another. It was a world full of literal strangers.

The house he was looking for was a large three-story home

that sat atop a steep hill. A high brick wall and massive iron gates surrounded the property. He walked up to the gate and was surprised to find it wasn't locked when he tried to open it. Nervously he walked through the gate and up the long driveway to the front door. He used the heavy brass door knocker to knock on the thick wooden door when he couldn't find a bell. He wondered if anyone could even hear him. Then the door opened. In front of him stood a young girl. She couldn't have been more than eighteen or nineteen years of age. Her long red hair fell around her pale face as he looked at her in shock.

"I thought you were dead." He said to the girl.

She looked at him, puzzled. Then without warning, she grabbed him by the throat and pinned him to the side of the house. "Who are you? What do you want?" she demanded.

"Harper sent me." He managed to choke out the words despite the girl's tight grip.

"Get in here." She said, her voice harsh. She loosened her grip on Jace and dropped him in the open doorway.

"Now, Emmaline, is that any way to treat a guest?" Came a voice from down the hall.

Jace was picking himself off the floor when he noticed the owner of the voice he had just heard.

"It is you!" He shouted. "You took her!"

"I'm afraid I don't know what you are speaking of." Said the man.

"I saw you. Last night. You came in through the broken glass door, and you took her."

"I'm afraid you are mistaken, but please come inside. Tell us why you are here."

Maybe his memory was betraying him. Jace followed the

two into a side room. The room was furnished with two chairs and a sofa. A bookshelf had been built into the inside wall and was filled from top to bottom with various books. The heavy drapes that covered the windows were drawn closed. Wall sconces adorned the walls giving off minimal light in the room. Jace had noticed that the same sconces hung in the front foyer and lined the walls leading up the grand staircase. The man motioned for Jace to have a seat in one of the chairs. Emmaline and the man sat on the sofa across from him.

"Now tell me who has sent you here?" The man questioned.

"Harper. She came to me last night and gave me this address. She said to come here and ask for someone named Dac or Nikolai. She is in trouble." He said, then turned his head towards Emmaline. "I saw it. She stabbed you. I thought you had died. There was so much blood."

"Well, as you can see, I am fine. She missed my heart." Emmaline responded

"I'm so glad you are ok. You were there to help her. I don't understand; that's not like Harper. I have never known her to be so...so evil." He said.

"When did you know her?" The man asked him.

"We were good friends years ago," Jace answered.

"I see, and you know what she is now? I can assume that means you know what we are, too, then?"

"Yes." He said nervously, then added, "But I only want to help Harper. That is all. Is either Dac or Nikolai here? She said they would know how to help her."

"I am Dac." The man responded. "Tell me, why is it you thought you had seen me take her, and why is it she believes any of us will help her? I haven't seen her since the night before last. Long before she snuck in and out of here stealing from my attic and almost killing Emmaline here."

"She was looking for a friend. She said someone took him. She came to my house last night and told me that if anything happened to her, I would know and that I should come here, and you would help her. So, will you help her?"

"We have all warned her not to let her contempt for Zaine get the best of her. If her quest for vengeance has gotten her in trouble, then she is on her own. She has done enough to put the rest of us in danger. Need I remind you she's already tried to kill one of us." Dac said, pointing towards Emmaline. "We will not help her. Now leave here and forget this place, or you will regret it. Your trinkets and potions will not save you." Dac bluffed as he turned toward the door and began to walk out of the room.

"What about Quentin?" Jace asked in desperation.

Dac turned in surprise. "What do you mean? What is this about, Quentin?"

"I'm not sure, but I think he is the friend Harper is looking for; his name just came to me just like the visions or dreams about Harper. It's like she communicates with me somehow."

Dac moved closer to Jace, being careful of the necklace he wore. Could he smell the oils inside the pendant, Jace wondered? His hands trembled in his lap despite the knowledge and weapons he had been recently armed with. Jace was not a threat to the vampires, but the vampires could be a threat to him. Dac walked around the chair where Jace was seated, surveying Jace's neck as if searching for something. He pulled down the collar of Jace's jacket. His sharp nails grazed the skin of Jace's neck. Jace thought about the bite marks Harper left. His muscles stiffened.

Dac moved in front of Jace. He grabbed Jace by the throat,

lifting him from his chair. Jace trembled in his grasp; his eyes grew wide. His body froze, too terrified to react. Dac held Jace up. His feet lifted slightly off the ground. Dac's eyes pierced through Jace's. A crushing sensation took hold of Jace's head as if the vampire could reach into his brain and extract the very thoughts from his mind with his venomous stare. Seemingly satisfied, Dac let go of Jace's throat and let him fall to the ground.

"If you want to be a vampire hunter, you will need to control your fear and learn to react more quickly," Dac said to him.

"I don't want to be a vampire hunter," Jace replied as he peeled himself off the ground and tried to regain his composure.

"You will, my friend," Dac said with a wink as he turned and walked out of the room.

Jace brushed his hands across the sides of his pants. He moved towards the door, ready to leave this house, when a hand reached out and grabbed his arm. His heart sped up for a minute, and he looked back to see Emmaline standing almost beside him, still holding a firm grasp around his wrist.

"You can't leave." She demanded though her voice appeared softer this time, and her face betrayed the expression of her youth and innocence. Jace wondered what her story was.

"I will tell you if you stay and help us." She said to Jace reading his mind. "If you do not stay, Dac will find you. He will not let you alone until he is sure you are no threat to us. He does not want to harm you, but I cannot promise your safety if he believes you are a threat."

"I am no threat. I want nothing to do with any of this. I only came here because Harper needs help. I've done my part.

Now I just want to go home and forget all of this and all of you."

"I do not believe that is true. You want to help Harper. She was your friend. I want to help her too. As you know, that is why I followed her last night. I know she did not intend to kill me."

"But Dac just said that none of you had any intention of helping her."

"Yes, but he saw something when he looked into your eyes that has changed his mind."

"How do you know that?" Jace asked her.

"I have known him for a long time. Just wait here. He will return with Nikolai. Then they will tell us what to do."

Emmaline motioned for Jace to sit back down. He nodded in acceptance. They both moved back into the room and sat quietly while they waited for Dac to return with Nikolai.

A moment later, the door opened. Jace looked up and saw the man entering the room was alone and not Dac. He was tall with very dark hair that fell to his chin. He showed a somber look on his face. This must be Nikolai, he thought to himself.

"This must be our guest. I was not sure he would still be here." Nikolai said to no one in particular.

"Yes," Emmaline replied. "Where is Dac? I was sure he would have come back with you. What are we going to do about this uh situation? I know he saw something. Do you know what it was?"

"Yes, Emmaline. He did see something, and what he saw has disturbed him very much, but you mustn't concern yourself with it. He and I will take care of the situation, as you put it. You will remain in this house where it is safe until Dac says otherwise."

"Is it Quentin? Is he hurt?"

"We don't know."

"And what about Harper?" Jace interrupted, his voice catching in his throat.

"Our primary concern is getting to Quentin. We are sure that he has been taken by the same one who has taken Harper. We do not know if Harper was taken against her will or if she knew he was coming and went voluntarily."

"You know Harper didn't go voluntarily!" Jace yelled back in outrage.

"We do not know any such thing. All we know is Harper has repeatedly defied our warnings against her recent behavior. She has stolen from us and almost killed one of us. If she has turned against us, she will get what she deserves." Nikolai then turned to Emmaline, tossed her a key, and said, "Take our guest downstairs and lock him in Harper's room. We will need him nearby if Harper chooses to communicate."

"But…" Jace stood up and started to protest, but Nikolai was already out of the room, and Emmaline was grabbing him by the arm again.

"It's best not to fight it," Emmaline said to him.

Jace couldn't believe her strength as she dragged him across the room. He watched helplessly as she pressed a switch on the wall, and the wall began to open up, revealing a hidden entrance. Still holding a tight grip on his arm Emmaline dragged him into the wall and down through a dark stairway. He tried again to protest as he struggled to free himself of her grip, but she just pulled him along.

"I don't know what's with Nikolai tonight. He's usually the calm one. Maybe he feels guilty." Emmaline said in an attempt to distract Jace.

"Why would he feel guilty?" Jace asked her.

"Because he brought her here. He was the one who made Harper a vampire. She apparently looks a lot like his dead wife, you know."

"So, that's why he turned her, then?"

"Yes and no. I mean, she would have died if he hadn't. Sure, she is a vampire now, but at least she's not dead."

"But isn't that the same thing?"

Emmaline laughed. "Not really. We live and breathe just as you do, just differently."

"Very differently," Jace replied.

They continued to walk the rest of the way in silence and darkness. The air around them felt damp and cold. When they reached the end of the hall, Emmaline opened the door to Harper's room and pulled Jace inside. She turned on the small lamp that stood on the bedside table. Jace wasn't sure exactly what he had expected the room to look like but probably not the way it had actually looked. It was a bit fancy for what he remembered of Harper's taste, and well, it looked like it belonged to a human, not a vampire. Not that Jace knew exactly what a vampire's room would look like. Emmaline must have noticed his reaction because she said to him. "Were you expecting a coffin?"

"I guess. I don't know. I just thought," he trailed off before finishing his sentence.

"I suppose some vampires may sleep in coffins, but we don't. Except for a few differences, we pretty much live the same way we did as humans."

Jace didn't know how to respond, so he just shrugged his shoulders as he let his eyes adjust to the dim light and continued to look around the room. It felt strange for him to be in Harper's room while she was out there somewhere, probably in danger.

"You should probably text your family. Give them some excuse why you had to leave town, a business trip, or something. I don't know how long you'll be here and I'm sure you don't want them to worry. Once they find out where Quentin and Harper are, Dac and Nikolai will let you go home. In the meantime, make yourself comfortable. I'll be back to bring you some food and water."

Emmaline walked out of the room, closing the door behind her. Jace heard her put the key in the lock and the severity of his situation finally began to sink in. He was a prisoner here.

# Twenty

D ac knew he and Nikolai needed to come up with some kind of plan. The visions Dac had seen when he looked into Jace's mind had profoundly disturbed him. He had heard the story of what had happened from Emmaline. She had come home injured and weary from the ordeal the night before, but seeing it tonight made him sick to his stomach. That wasn't the only thing that was disturbing to him, though. What bothered him most was the red eyes that glowed in the dark and the face that looked like his.

Sitting at the desk in the middle of the attic room, Dac scanned the pages of his old journal. At one time, he had chronicled every detail of his life. He kept notes on all he had studied and learned about vampires when he had first become one. He noted everything he learned on how to survive as a vampire but also how to destroy another. He pulled down the books from the shelves, books that he had collected in his early years. He frantically searched through the pages for something he could have missed. Where had he messed up?

"You really think he survived?"

Dac looked up to see Nikolai standing in the doorway. "I don't know, but I know what I saw."

"But why show up now after all this time?"

"I don't know that either. How about you be useful and help me go through these books."

Nikolai stepped into the room. He snatched a book up from the desk and sat on the floor while he started flipping through its pages.

"I'm just saying, are you sure what you saw was real? Could it have just been Harper showing you what she wanted you to see?"

"You think this is some type of trick? I thought you would be the first to jump to her defense. You've always been her greatest protector."

"And you've been her lover, and yet you're just as ready to condemn her as I. Have you had a change of heart?"

"Her powers have grown stronger over the last few weeks. But I just don't believe she knows enough to produce that type of trickery."

"Well, let's say the vision was real, and he is alive. Do you think he's behind recent bodies found? Do you think he has Quentin? According to Harper's messenger, Quentin was taken by someone. Maybe Quentin found him but was taken before he had a chance to report back to us."

"That would be a logical conclusion."

"What I can't figure out, though, is what is his connection with Harper and Zaine?"

"That is what we need to find out. Let's go." Dac swiftly rose from his seat and darted out the room and down the stairs with Nikolai not far behind.

"Where are we going? What's the plan?" Nikolai asked.

"First, we go see our little visitor, find out what else he knows. Then we go search Zaine's place."

They reached Harper's room, where they were keeping Jace locked away. Dac reached for the key above the door frame, where he knew Emmaline would have left it, and unlocked the door. He and Nikolai entered the room to see Emmaline had already brought Jace a pitcher of water and a plate of food. Jace jumped to his feet from where he'd been lying on the bed.

"Sit. We need to ask you a few questions." Dac said as he pulled over the vanity chair. He turned it around and straddled it folding his arms across the back of the chair. Jace sat back down on the bed. Nikolai stood with his back against the closed door as if guarding it so Jace wouldn't try to escape.

"She hasn't sent me any other images yet."

"That's ok. We want to know everything Harper has said to you. How many times has she come to you? Has she ever said anything about a man named Luca?"

"Luca? No. She's never mentioned that name to me. She came by twice, but she never mentioned anyone named Luca in either visit. Who is he?" Jace asked, even though he already knew who Luca was from Sarah Higgins. But what he didn't know was why these two were asking about him.

"Never mind who he is. He is extremely dangerous; that is all you need to know. Just tell us about these visits with Harper. What did she want the first time she came to see you?"

Jace told the two men everything he remembered about that first time Harper appeared at his house. He told them about the invite to the poker game, how Zaine had been there, and Harper had followed Zaine, and that's how she saw Jace. She had gone to his house to warn him not to return. When asked, he described the people at the poke game, though there was one person he couldn't recount since she stood back mostly out of sight. Although he was fairly sure it was a woman by her silhouette. He remembered she appeared to be wearing a long gown.

Dac asked him one last question. "Did it seem like Harper had known any of the hosts of that game?"

"No. She didn't know them. That's why she came to see me last night. She was sure one of them had taken her friend, and she wanted to know what I knew about them. I told her I had never met any of them before that night but that Zaine seemed to be well acquainted with them."

"Interesting." Dac got up from the chair and returned it in front of the vanity.

As Dac walked out the door, Nikolai turned back to Jace, observing the untouched plate of food on the dresser. "You really should eat that. You'll want to keep up your strength." He said to him. Before Jace could respond, Nikolai was out the door.

"What do you think about that?" Nikolai asked Dac once they were back out in the hallway.

"It sounds like it's time to make a trip to Zaine's house and see what we can uncover there."

\* \* \*

Outside of the apartment building where Zaine had lived, Dac and Nikolai stood quietly and discreetly, taking in their surroundings, knowing that a perilous enemy could be nearby. It was an unusually still night. The air was cold and bitter. The area around the building complex was empty and quiet. Only a few street lamps lit the outside. With both hands in their jacket pockets, Dac and Nikolai walked carefully to Zaine's apartment.

The evidence of the previous night's events was still displayed inside the apartment. Clearly, no one reported the disturbance or bothered to clean up the mess or even fix the shattered sliding glass door, which the two had just entered. The shards of broken glass scattered over the floor crunched under their feet. Traces of dried-up blood, both Zaine's and Emmaline's, covered the floor and walls. Leaves and dirt had blown in from outside.

Nikolai went straight to the small kitchen area and began rummaging through drawers and cabinets. Dac started to make his way to the back bedroom when a voice stopped him in his tracks.

"What have you done with my son?" The old man shouted as he flung a liquid from a small tube in Dac's direction.

The liquid smelled of frankincense and peppermint and burnt when it hit the exposed skin on Dac's neck. Luckily only a tiny amount of the liquid had managed to reach his skin. The rest had landed on his jacket and onto the floor around him. Dac swung his arm out, knocking the old man into the old worn couch next to where he stood.

"Relax, old man. I don't have your son. Now get out of here." Dac said with a stern warning to the old man.

But the old man jumped up from where he had fallen onto the couch and shouted back. "I know you have him! I've seen how you've been watching and toying with him. Then last night, you took him, you and your little helper!"

Dac snatched the old man up by the throat, and that's when he noticed the two scars on the man's neck just above his collarbone. They were two identical scars perfectly parallel to each other, and the words the man was saying were now beginning to register in Dac's mind. This man thought he was

Luca, and this was just more evidence that Luca was, in fact, alive, and Harper was with him. His mind was now spinning out of control. He dropped the old man to the ground.

"I am not the one you think I am. Now, if you want your son back here alive, you will leave and let me find what I came here to find." Dac watched as the old man scraped himself off the floor and scurried out of the apartment.

"Dac, look," Nikolai said, pointing towards the door. There lying on the floor near the front door was the knapsack Harper had taken from the house, and it was still full of everything she had taken from the attic. Wherever Harper was, it appeared she was unarmed.

"Come on, let's keep searching."

"That man, he thought you were Luca, didn't he? Luca's alive?" Nikolai asked.

"Seems that way," Dac replied back as he headed off towards the bedroom again.

Nikolai followed behind but then trailed off into the bathroom. After having found nothing in the kitchen, he didn't expect to find anything in this room either, but the apartment was small. There weren't many places for storage, but it was best to be sure to search the entire home. People hid things in strange places sometimes. There had to be some evidence somewhere revealing more about the dealings Zaine had with Luca. Jace had said it seemed he and Zaine were pretty well acquainted.

He started by searching through the cabinets below the sink. Then he noticed a small linen closet. He opened the closet, pulled out the few towels and washcloths, and threw them onto the floor. A few boxes were stacked up on the shelves. Nikolai looked through the first box finding nothing other than a few photos and some old CDs and DVD videos. The next box held various travel-sized toiletries, shampoos, body washes, colognes, but still, nothing linking Zaine to Luca. The third appeared to be some old bills and bank statements. Nikolai was just about to close the box and give up his search when he noticed something on one of the papers. He removed it from the box and studied the substance that had stained one of the corners. He held the paper to his nose. What he smelled on the paper was blood, Harper's blood. This was the paper that Harper and Zaine had been fighting over the night he had killed her. Some of her blood must have gotten on the paper. Nikolai frantically started riffling through the rest of the box. At the very bottom, hidden under all the papers, was an old cell phone. Nikolai tried to turn it on, but its battery had died. This phone had probably not been used in years, but it could have crucial information on it. He had to find a charger for it. What if Zaine had been meeting with Luca way back then?

In the other room, Dac was sitting on the bed, searching through a different cell phone. This one was charged and powered on. Dac was reading through the text messages. Nothing from Luca, which didn't surprise him, but there were messages from another name he did recognize, Lizbeth. His heart dropped as he began to scroll through the messages. Unfortunately, all of the texts were short and vague, revealing nothing useful, only that they knew each other. They all said the same thing, *be here at a specific time; you know the place.* Dac wasn't surprised to see the times were always late at night, but he was frustrated that nothing contained an address. The only thing he had so far was the warehouse Jace had told them about and now a sure confirmation that they were dealing with his supposedly dead brother.

"Find anything?" Nikolai's voice came in from the doorway, breaking Dac's attention away from the phone in his hand.

"Just some messages with times to meet but no addresses. They just say he'd know the place and nothing from Luca directly.

"Well, maybe the addresses will be in here." Nikolai held up the old phone he had found for Dac to see.

"Where'd you find that?"

"In the bathroom closet. It was inside a box under some old papers from about three years ago."

"When he and Harper were together?"

"Right. Harper's blood was on one of the papers. That's what made me search the box deeper, and then I found this. We need to find a charger, but maybe it can tell us something if we can get into it. I have a feeling their acquaintance might go back that far."

"Let's go back to the house. I think we've found all we're going to find here." Dac stuffed the phone he was holding in his pocket and pushed past Nikolai out of the room. Nikolai followed on Dac's heels, snatching up the knapsack as they both left the apartment.

# Twenty-One

J ace awoke the next morning to find a new plate of food, and a fresh pitcher of water had replaced the one from the night before. He lifted the cover and took in all the fresh fruit scents, toasted muffin, and scrambled eggs and bacon that covered the plate. To his surprise, it was all still warm. Someone must have brought it in only a short time ago. He wondered who could have left it. He hadn't noticed any other humans around. He sincerely hoped they weren't keeping anyone else hostage here. He shuttered at that thought.

Suddenly he heard his stomach begin to rumble and realized how hungry he actually was. Due to his current situation, he hadn't had much of an appetite until now, so he hadn't eaten the food they left for him last night. He sat on the chair in front of the vanity, picked up the fork on the tray, and started to eat.

After he finished eating, he wiped his mouth and hands with a napkin. He walked back over to the bed, picked up his phone from the bedside table where he had left it, and checked the time. It was only 6 am. He breathed out a sigh. Then he noticed something on the nightstand that he hadn't seen before. There was a phone lying on the table, along with a note. He read the message under the dim light of the small lamp he kept on. It was instructing him to go out and find a charger for the phone. There were directions to a store not far from the house, and thankfully he realized directions to the bathroom upstairs.

Jace jumped up from the bed and practically raced to the door. He turned the doorknob and felt the excitement rise within him as he realized the door was unlocked. He found his way down the dark hall and up the stairs to the front room he had been in when he had first arrived here yesterday. The bathroom was down the hall behind the grand staircase. Not much was inside the room. He found a towel and washcloth hanging on the towel rack and a change of clothes folded on the closed lid of the toilet seat. He moved the clothes, placed them on the countertop of the sink, and lifted the toilet seat lid to relieve himself. Afterward, he moved over to the shower and turned it on. The steam from the hot water quickly filled up the bathroom. Jace removed his clothes and got into the shower. He stood with his eyes shut, letting the comforting warm water spill over him before washing up and getting out.

As he was getting dressed, a muffled noise came from the other side of the door. He pulled the sweatshirt provided for him over his head, grateful for the little bit of warmth it provided. The house was quite drafty. He slowly opened the door peeking around the other side out into the hall. It seemed quiet now. He didn't notice anyone else around. The thought had occurred to him; this would probably be a good time to escape, but he decided at that moment that he wanted to stay. He needed to help Harper even if no one else would. So, for now, he would do as the vampires asked. There must be something important in that phone they'd left in his room if they were looking to charge it. Figuring he had a few more hours before any stores would open, he decided to take a look around the house.

Across from him was a large room, much like the other room in the front part of the house. The difference was this room, like Harper's, had no windows and was slightly larger. Two large sofas and a large plush chair furnished the room. A coffee table was centered in the room. Two small end tables were placed, one between both sofas and the other next to the large chair. The same wall sconces that were elsewhere in the house adorned the walls, along with a few pieces of barely noticeable wall art and a large flat screen tv.

Jace moved on to the next room, which was a rather large kitchen. It was surprisingly modern compared to the rest of the house that he had seen so far. In the large window hung bamboo shades to keep out the light, but there were no drapes, unlike the window at the front end of the house. There was a large island with a quartz countertop in the center of the kitchen. Stainless steel appliances and white cabinets were situated along the inner walls. Curiously Jace opened the refrigerator. He wasn't surprised to see it hadn't contained much food. There was a carton of eggs, a loaf of bread, and some lunch meat. A container of orange juice sat towards the back of the top shelf. He guessed vampires didn't need much food.

In the other corner of the room, Jace noticed a pantry door. He wandered over and opened the door, realizing this was not exactly what he was expecting. Not that he knew what to expect, but this was not a pantry at all. Behind this door was another door to what appeared to be an industrial-sized freezer, but when he put his hand against the door, it was warm to the touch. It wasn't a freezer at all but a heated vault of some kind. Upon further inspection, he noticed a keypad on the door that locked and unlocked it, preventing anyone from opening it who didn't have the access code from discovering whatever was kept inside.

"What are you doing?" A voice yelled from behind him. Startled, Jace turned around to see a middle-aged woman standing at the entryway of the kitchen. She was of average height. Her greying dark brown hair pulled back into a tight ponytail. She was standing with her hands on her hips, waiting for an answer. She at least looked human, Jace thought as he let out a small sigh of relief.

"Sorry, Hi. I'm Jace. I was just, uh, having a look around." He said, finally settling on telling the truth. He reached out to shake her hand as he introduced himself.

"I'm Charlotte. So, you must be the guest Dac mentioned in his note for me this morning. Well, you can't go in there. Not that you'd be able to if you tried, and trust me, I don't think you'd want to anyway." She'd said sternly.

"Oh. Do you live here? I didn't see anyone else last night."

"Oh, no. I'm the housekeeper. I come in the mornings to let the delivery guy in, do whatever cleaning needs to be done, and then I'm gone before sundown."

"Delivery guy? Do they get a lot of deliveries?" Jace asked.

"Every morning. They got to eat, you know." She answered with a wink.

Unsure of what to say to that, Jace didn't reply. Images of dead bodies being delivered and stuffed in the vault, then later devoured by vampires, were racing through his mind. Thankfully, a knock on the back door broke him from his thoughts. On second thought, realizing this must be the delivery man, a sickness began to build up in his stomach. Charlotte moved to answer the door. Jace sat down on one of the bar stools surrounding the kitchen island.

A burly man walked through the door, pushing a hand truck with two large boxes. He went over the vault and punched a code into the keypad on the door. Jace wanted to look away, but his curiosity had taken over any feelings of anxiety. Charlotte and the man exchanged pleasantries while he unloaded the contents of the boxes into the vault. Jace noticed multiple clear containers containing vials and bags of dark red liquid being placed on the shelves. The red liquid was blood, he realized, but now he wondered where it had come from, and his stomach began to feel sick all over again. The man shut the door and locked up the vault. Charlotte handed him an envelope containing what appeared to be a large sum of cash. She ushered him out of the house and locked the door behind him.

"I'm sure by now you know what they are."

"Yea."

"It's not as bad as you think. Dac and Nikolai run a blood donation center nearby. People come by and donate their blood. They think it's just another typical blood bank, as do most people who work there. Garrett then brings the donations here. Dac and Nikolai pay us very generously to keep their secret." Charlotte explained.

"Oh. I see. That's clever, I guess." Jace responded. "How did you end up working for them?" He asked

"My mother, she worked for them for years. My whole life growing up, she would take me to this house. I would come here after school and do my homework right here in this very kitchen. It didn't always look like this, but the girl, Emmaline, she had wanted to remodel a few years back, so they let her update the kitchen. Anyway, when my mother got too old and tired to continue working here, I took over. It's simple work, and the pay, as I mentioned, is incredibly good."

"You were never scared?"

"Oh, no. At first, I didn't even know what they were. I just thought they were some strange rich family. It wasn't until I got a bit older when I began to realize that they never seemed to age, even as I'd seen my mother aging and even myself. So, one day I asked my mother about it, and she told me. If I'm honest, I was more intrigued by them than scared of them. You see, by this time, I had known them all my life even though I had only actually seen them on a few occasions. It certainly explained why they were so reclusive, and we always had to be gone by sundown."

"And you or your mother even have never wanted to become one of them? I mean, it seems like it'd be tempting to never age and not have to worry about sickness."

"Aging and death are all a part of life. What they are, it is not natural. Besides, they face other dangers that we, as humans, do not. So, no. I would never want to live as they live, having to go through the centuries always in hiding and taming their natural instincts. It's a heavy burden to carry."

"What do you mean by taming their natural instincts?" Jace asked

"They are vampires. Naturally, they are hunters and killers. The thing with this group is they have never lost their human conscience."

"The reason for the blood donations?"

"Exactly. They drink the blood from the donations, so they have no true need to hunt."

"What about those vampires I've heard of that don't drink blood."

"Ah, like Quentin. He carries his own burdens, you see. Imagine having to go out every day and feed off the energies of others. Imagine you walk past someone taking all of their energy away. Then that person gets behind the wheel of a car driving off somewhere, most likely home. This person is so tired now they fall asleep behind the wheel, causing an accident, an accident that kills that person or the others in another car. It may not be your intention to kill, but by draining another's energy, you just inadvertently caused someone's death."

"Well, I guess when you put it like that."

"Listen, I have to get some work done and go to the grocery store. I'm sure you're going to want some actual food to eat. As you can see, there isn't much in here." She pointed to the almost empty refrigerator. "There is an envelope of money left for you by the front door. I understand Dac has asked for you to find something for him. Until the stores open, there is a tv in the other room and a library on the second floor if you like to read. Other than that, I would advise you to stay out of any other rooms and especially the third-floor attic. It's always locked anyway, but still, I feel I should warn you that room is and has always been forbidden." Charlotte walked out of the kitchen up the back stairway, leaving Jace alone to ponder the things he had just learned.

# Twenty-Two

Harper awoke to find herself in a darkened room. Looking around, she saw only a small window with bars across it. The light of the moon outside shone in through the tiny window. Harper felt closed in, and then she realized she was laying a tight-fitting box. No, not a box, a coffin. Frantically she sat up and climbed out of the casket. The lid sat against the wall next to her. Her bare feet hit the cold concrete ground beneath her. Where were her shoes, and what was she wearing? Someone had changed her clothes. She examined the dress that she now wore. Its fabric was soft like silk, and it was the color of a light blue sky. It had a squared neckline and puffed sleeves trimmed in lace. The gown flowed all the way to the floor, grazing the tops of her feet. She looked around for her own clothes, but the room appeared empty except for the coffin and a pair of silver-colored ballet flats that sat next to the door. She rushed to the door pulling on the handle. The door didn't budge; she was locked in. She sunk to the floor, sighing in defeat.

She sat on the floor for a while, staring into the darkness, her arms locked around her knees, rocking herself back and forth. Her head felt dizzy, and her body was weak. She was cold and shivering. Her skin felt like ice, even to her vampire touch. She imagined that's how Jace perceived her.

How long had she been in here? She tried to rack her brain for the last thing she could remember. There was Zaine's apartment, Emmaline, a loud crash, and then total darkness. Dac had said if she would not stay away from Zaine, that he would destroy her. Oh god. Is that what is happening? Did he lock her in here? He was going to leave her here until he decided the best way to end her life, she thought as tears started to stream down her face.

No. It couldn't be Dac. He would have just killed her on the spot. This wasn't like him at all, and why dress her in this old-fashioned dress. It just didn't make sense. Then she remembered Quentin and the one with the red eyes. Yes, it was him, with the red eyes. OK. So now she needed to figure out how to get out of here. She got up from her position on the floor. The window was too high for her to reach. She placed the lid onto the coffin and pushed it under the window. She climbed up onto the coffin, hoisting herself up toward the window. The steels bars were clearly going to prevent her from climbing out. What now? Jace! She had bitten him. She could show him where she is. He could get a message to Dac and Nikolai. Now she remembered. She went to see him. She put the address in his phone. It was all starting to come back to her.

She looked around, studying the room while concentrating on thoughts of Jace in order to communicate with him. Then she climbed back up to the window. Grabbing hold of the bars, she pulled herself up and peered out the window. The window was at ground level, indicating she was in some type of basement. She could see a thin stone-covered walkway and then what appeared to be miles of grass. Beyond the endless yard appeared a stone wall. She wasn't sure any of this would be helpful, but it was all she could see through this tiny window. She let go of the window bars and sank down onto the coffin. She'd have to wait. Maybe someone would come for her. Hopefully, not to kill her before she could get more clues of her whereabouts to Jace. She sought comfort with the idea that if they wanted her dead, she would be by now. The question was, who were they, and what did they want?

She sat there on top of her coffin, trying to hear any sounds around her. There was the wind outside, a few howling dogs far off in the distance; otherwise, all was quiet. Then she heard voices. She had to concentrate hard. There were two voices, both male, very heavily accented. She couldn't understand the words, but it sounded like one was giving the other some type of instructions. She heard footsteps along with the voices as the sounds had gotten closer. Suddenly the voices were right outside her door. She stiffened up in anticipation as she listened to the click of a lock and realized the door was opening.

Two figures stood outside the doorway, but then one of them turned back and walked away. The other stepped into the room. He was young in the face appearing to be only about 17 or eighteen. Harper figured he had to be around the same age as Emmaline. Only by the hardened look in his eyes and the clearness of his skin could Harper tell that he was much older in his vampire years. He looked at her with a hatred she had never seen, but one that she herself had felt. It made her wonder what his story was. How did he come to be a vampire, and how did he end up here, holding her prisoner?

"It is true. You do look a lot like her, I wasn't sure if you would be able to pull it off, but it looks like you'll do perfect."

"What is going on? Who are you? What do you want with me? Harper demanded.

"Never mind. Here. Just drink this. It will help you sleep during the trip." The boy said as he handed her a cup filled with an amber-colored liquid.

Harper threw the cup down, spilling its contents on the floor. "I'm not drinking anything!" she yelled at him.

"Suit yourself then. Don't say I didn't warn you. It's a long trip in a box." He turned and walked out the door locking it behind him.

Harper hurried towards the door after him, but she was too late. She banged against the hard steel door with her fists, yelling for the boy to come back. After a moment, she realized it was no use, he wasn't coming back, and neither was anyone else. At least not for now. She turned around to face the coffin, the one she had just awoken in after some unknown amount of days. The boy's words were now echoing in her mind. *It's a long trip in a box.* Tears began to fall from her eyes. Her mind was racing with overwhelming thoughts. How had she gotten herself into this mess, and how was she going to get out of it? Where were they going to take her? Who are they anyway? Then she thought of Quentin. Where were Quentin and Zanie? She hoped they were both ok somewhere. Zaine was taken along with her, that much she knew. She hated Zaine, but somehow the thought that he might have been killed and used for food for these vampires made her feel something else. Maybe it was sadness or guilt, but whatever it was, it was definitely something other than hate.

180

* * *

Earlier that afternoon, Jace had found his way to the store and picked up a charger for the phone as he had been asked to do. With the newly purchased phone charger in his pocket, he headed back towards the house but then decided he should take advantage of this unseasonably warm day and his current freedom.

As he continued walking down the street, he noticed a small bakery and decided to go inside. The bakery smelled like coffee and sweets. Jace ordered a coffee and a cupcake then took a seat at one of the small round tables against the wall. As he sipped his coffee and ate the cupcake, he thought about his fiancé Cloe and her close friendship with Harper. He felt guilty he couldn't tell Cloe about Harper, but he'd promise to keep her secret, and besides that, how could he ever explain any of this anyway. It was all so surreal.

He pulled his cell phone out of his pocket and stared at the screen for a moment with his finger hovering over Cloe's name. He had wanted badly just to hear her voice but decided it was probably best not to call her. Instead, he sent her a text to let her know he was ok and thinking about her. She had already called and sent him numerous texts since last night wondering where he was. It was unlike him to not respond and definitely unlike him to not come home at night. He had been sick and distracted lately, and Cloe was understandably concerned. He hated that he couldn't tell her the truth, and saying he was away on some business trip would be too easy to verify. He decided it was best just to tell her he needed some time away, that he'd be back in a few days, and not to worry. As expected, she responded immediately, demanding an explanation, but he just answered with *I Love you* and then turned off his phone.

His heart sank down into the pit of his stomach as he put his phone away. Instead of making wedding plans, he was out chasing vampires and possibly chasing his fiancé away. He rose up from his chair and walked out of the bakery. The air was still warm but beginning to chill with the evening approaching. Jace decided it was time to head back to the house. He just hoped Harper would contact him soon.

Back at the house, Jace placed the charger on the front table by the door. The sky had already grown dark, and Charlotte was already gone for the day. She had left a note that there would be dinner for him in the kitchen. On the stove was a casserole and a few dinner rolls. Jace scooped out some of the casserole onto a plate he found in the cabinet and buttered one of the rolls. He sat at the large kitchen island to eat the food, and once finished, he cleaned up his dish and put the remaining casserole in the refrigerator. He was almost surprised to see actual food in the fridge this time, even though Charlotte did say she would go to the grocery store. He grabbed a bottle of water he found in the fridge and decided to go back down to his room, Harper's room, that is.

His mind was still quiet, aside from his own thoughts. He laid on Harper's bed, hoping it would give him a closer connection to her. Where was she? Why hadn't she sent him any clue as to where she was yet or that she was ok? He lay there trying to clear his mind from any thoughts, hoping it would help her get through to him. Then finally, he saw it, the tiny window, the bars, the large yard, and the stone wall in the distance. Then he heard the words, something about a trip. Nothing else was said, but it was a start, at least. Hopefully, Dac and Nikolai had found something useful in that phone they had found. Then maybe they'd be that much closer to finding Harper, and he could go back home.

Jace raced out of the room and down the hall to look for one of the others. He knocked on a few doors downstairs, but when no one answered, he moved on to search the rest of the house. Indeed, the vampires would have risen from their daytime sleep by now. He checked the main floor first but found no one around. He ran up the front stairs to the second floor and looked around, unsure which direction to go in, until he heard voices coming from one of the rooms. He followed the voices to a large set of double doors. Behind the doors, he could hear the voices getting louder. His heart was pounding now, he didn't want to interrupt whatever they were talking about, but this was important. He put his hand on the brass doorknob and opened the double doors to what appeared to be a formal dining room. Inside, the others were seated around a large dining table, talking and sipping from fancy glasses.

"I'm so sorry to interrupt." Jace began, "But Harper, she's come through."

Dac looked up in Jace's direction and motioned for him to enter the room. "Please come in. Join us. Tell us what she's said."

Jace took a seat at the end of the large dining table. He told the others what he had just seen from Harper. They all sat for a while, trying to determine where this place was that she was describing. Finally, Nikolai sprang up from his chair. "I know where it is!" He shouted as he bolted out the door.

# Twenty-Three

J ace and Emmaline sat staring at the dining-room door. Dac had run after Nikolai but not before telling the two of them to stay behind.

"What was that?" Jace asked.

Emmaline shrugged her shoulders. She stood up and moved towards the door. As she exited through the doorway, she turned back to Jace, who was still seated at the table.

"Are you coming?" She asked him. This time, Jace shrugged, but he got up and followed her out into the hall.

As they walked down the hall, Jace took the time to notice the elegant wallpaper and dark hardwood flooring. Except for the kitchen, the whole house appeared so old-fashioned. Emmaline stopped in front of a door at the end of the hall and entered the room. Jace stood in the doorway, watching as Emmaline searched the desk in the middle of the room.

"What room is this? What are you looking for?" Jace asked her.

"Isn't it obvious? I'm looking for something that will tell us where they went."

"And you think that will be somewhere in that desk?"

"Yes. This is Nikolai's office. If he believes he knows what this place is that you described, he must have seen it before. I'm guessing he's got a record of it somewhere in here. He and Dac record everything."

"What will you do if you find it?"

"Go after them, of course."

"But Dac told us to stay here and isn't snooping around and following people what almost got you killed the last time?"

"I know this is all new and probably very weird to you, but you really need to toughen up, Jace. Besides, I survived, didn't I?" She tossed a handful of photos she found in the desk drawer at his feet. "Look through those and see if anything looks familiar."

Jace picked up the photographs and flipped through them. Nothing seemed familiar to him in any of them. He tossed the pictures on the side table next to the door and entered the room. Besides the desk and the side table, the room had two floor-to-ceiling bookshelves. Each shelf was full of books. This house had more books than Jace had ever seen in his life outside a library. The window on the outside wall was covered in heavy drapes, just like every other window in the house had been. There were two large chairs on either side of the room and a chair behind the desk. Emmaline was still rifling through the desk drawers. Jace walked along the perimeter of the room, staring at all the books on the shelves.

"This place sure has a lot of books in it." He said more to himself than to Emmaline.

"Yes, well, Dac and Nikolai have been around for a long time. Long before there was any tv, or radio, or probably even electricity for that matter."

"So, they've read all of these?"

"Most likely, yes. Some for entertainment and some for

education and research, I assume."

"Research?"

"There's a lot of things you still don't know, Jace. Dac and Nikolai, they are vampires who hunt vampires. Well, I guess just three in particular. One of whom they believed was dead up until last night when you arrived here, that is."

"That's who they think has Harper and your friend Quentin?"

"Yes, and if that's true, they will need our help even if they won't admit it. Now help me look for something that'll tell us where they ran off to."

Jace moved to look at some books that appeared to be journals. He pulled one of them from the shelf. The book was bound in soft leather and tied with a black ribbon. Jace opened it and flipped through the pages. The words on the pages were written in elegant cursive, but unfortunately, he couldn't understand what they said. He picked up another book and then a third. It was the same with each book, each page filled with possible information that he couldn't read.

"I can't understand any of these; they're written in some other language, I guess." He said to Emmaline as he tossed the books onto the chair next to him.

"Romanian." She replied

"Romanian?"

"Yes. That is where they are from, Romania."

"Romania? Like Transylvania?"

"Possibly. I don't know exactly where in Romania. They don't talk much about it." She replied, but then she noticed the amused expression on his face as she looked up at Jace. "What?" She asked.

"Nothing," He said, trying to contain his laughter. He could feel the stress finally getting to him, and the absurdness of the situation was settling in his mind. "It's just you know this whole thing; it just seems so unreal. I mean, this is like some shit you would see in a movie or read in a book or something."

"Yeah, well, maybe there's some truth in all those stories and folklore."

"I suppose there is."

They continued in silence, their search of Nikolai's office for the next serval minutes. Jace took out his cell phone and turned it on. He had forgotten for a while that he had turned it off earlier that day. As soon as the phone came to life, it started pinging with text messages and missed voicemails. Most of them were from Cloe, but a few were from his mom. Great, Cloe must have called his mother, he thought. He decided to leave the texts unread and ignore the voicemails. This, he figured, was the best way to keep them safe.

He clicked open his internet browser and searched for a Romanian to English translator. Then he began to look up the translation of each word. After realizing this would take too long to translate each of these journals, he decided he needed to take a different approach. He remembered the voice saying something about a long trip. This made him think that Harper was being held nearby, at least for now. That would mean the place they were looking for was probably someplace Nikolai had seen recently or at least since he'd been living at this house.

"Em, when did Nikolai and Dac move into this house?"

"Oh, it's Em, is it now?" She asked with a hint of sarcasm though she had to admit she liked him calling her Em. If she were honest with herself, she was starting to like Jace. Had she been human, Jace would've indeed been someone she'd be interested in. Except she wasn't human and hadn't been for years, and once Jace wasn't needed anymore, Dac would send him on his way, and she would never see him again. "Anyway, I'm not sure exactly. They were living here before I came, and that was 1969."

"1969, huh? So, were you like a hippie or something?"

"Something like that."

"I'd like to hear your story one day." He said to her, his tone sincere.

"Someday." She brushed him off, knowing he'd probably never get the chance to hear it.

They both were quiet again for a while. Jace began flipping back through the pages of the journals. This time he was checking the dates at the top of each page. The first two books were all dated in the mid to late 1800s and early 1900s, so he placed them back on the shelf. He decided he needed to start with the most recent date he could find, so he went back to the bookshelf, searching for something more recent.

Suddenly Jace noticed a change in Emmaline. Her head shot up from the files she was looking through. She sat still for a moment as if she were concentrating hard, like when a dog hears a voice in the distance before its owners do. Is that what was happening? Did she hear something that Jace could not yet hear?

"What is it?" He asked

"Shh." She put her forefinger to her lips. "They're home. We need to get out of here."

Jace snapped some pictures of as many pages as he could, then put the journals back in their place on the bookshelf. "Hurry up." He heard her say. He put his phone in his pocket and followed Emmaline out the door and down the back stairwell.

* * *

Dac and Nikolai walked up to the door of the brick colonial house. There were no lights on inside the house as far as either of them could tell, but that wasn't very surprising. Luca always preferred the darkness. Nikolai tested the door; it was unlocked. As quietly as he could manage, he opened the door and stepped into the front entryway. Dac followed closely behind him. The house was too quiet, but they crept along in search of a door that would lead to the basement until they finally found it just off the kitchen.

They descended the steps one at a time. Each of them being especially careful not to make any noise. The smell of freshly burnt-out candles lingered in the air. There were two other rooms within the basement. Both of their doors were left slightly ajar, making it clear no one was in either space. Both Nikolai and Dac knew Luca wouldn't be so careless, but they decided to check inside the rooms anyway. The first room was small and windowless, meaning it was not the room Jace had described. The second, however, had a tiny barred window close to the ceiling. The space was empty except for a small wooden chair in the corner. Dac pulled the chair over so he could see out the window. Peering through the bars, he could see the ground outside. The tall grass went on for what seemed like a mile. A stone wall stood at the end of the yard. This was definitely the room Harper was in, but where was she now? They continued to search the rest of the house, but no one was there, just as they had feared. They had been too late.

Jace and Emmaline were in the kitchen when Dac and Nikolai returned home. Their laughter radiated through the house and made Nikolai smile a little bit. It was nice to hear some normalcy amongst all the uneasiness that had been surrounding them in the last couple of days. Dac made a face as if in disapproval and walked straight up the front stairs to his office while Nikolai went into the kitchen to meet the others.

"What's so funny?" Nikolai asked as Jace and Emmaline straightened up like two kids caught getting into trouble.

"Nothing," They both said in unison, and they smiled slyly at each other.

"It's ok. I know things really suck right now, but you're still allowed to laugh once in a while."

"Just trying to make the best of a bad situation. I'm guessing you didn't find Quentin and Harper." Emmaline replied.

"No, we didn't. I was right about the house, but they were gone before we got there. I just wish I knew where they were going and whether or not Quentin is still alive."

"I'm sure he is. I mean, Harper was sure he was when she saw him taken at least." Jace said.

"I hope you're right. Have you gotten anything else from her?"

"No. Not yet."

"There has to be more to this that we're just not seeing yet. I mean, if it is Dac's brother, do you think he's after some sort of revenge or something? I just don't see why he went after Quentin and Harper. Why not just come after you and Dac?" Emmaline concluded.

"He's definitely after revenge. I think that's why he left those bodies to be found like that. He wants us to know that he's back. The question is, how long has he been here, and where has he been hiding out all this time?"

"I think he's been close by for quite some time. I think he's the one who made me." Emmaline said, surprising Nikolai.

"What? Why haven't you said something before now?"

"I only just realized it. I never actually saw his face back then, only his eyes. Then the other night, it was the same thing. He looked right at me. I was so weak and dizzy from the blood loss. I could hardly see a thing, but those bright red eyes were unmistakable. I'd never forget the evil I'd seen in them, not back then and not the other night."

"Come on. We got go tell Dac." Nikolai grabbed Emmaline by the wrist and led her up the stairs while Jace followed right behind them.

# Twenty-Four

The four of them sat in Dac's office while Emmaline told her story. Jace chimed in when she was finished, telling them everything he knew about Zaine and Harper three years ago before Harper was killed. They were hoping maybe they could figure out a clue from back then. Somehow, they agreed, it all had to be connected.

"Has anyone else found it more than a strange coincidence that Harper looks exactly like Nikolai's dead wife?" A familiar voice came from the doorway. Everyone looked up at the same time to see who was standing there.

"Quentin!" Emmaline shouted as she ran over to Quentin putting her arms around his neck. Quentin wrapped his arms around Emmaline's waist, embracing her in a tight hug. Nikolai got up and patted his friend on the back, but Dac sat silently in the chair behind his desk, showing no emotion at all.

"Listen. I need to tell you both something. Dac's brother isn't dead. Luca is alive. He's here with his little crew, and he told me to give this to Nikolai." He handed Nikolai a plain white sealed envelope. "I don't know what's in it. I also don't know what, if anything, Harper has to do with all this, but I saw her lurking around the area the night Luca grabbed me, and it looked like she knew him, and they had been arguing right before that. I've also seen her a few places lately that just didn't make sense." He said as he explained the night he tripped over the dead body and how he'd thrown it in the Marina. "I should have said something then, but I wanted to be sure about whatever was going on before I accused her of anything. Then when I got home that night, she was waiting for me in my room. I have no idea how she could have gotten back here so fast, but there she was."

"What did she want?" Nikolai asked.

"She wanted help with Zaine. I refused at first, of course, but then I figured if I humored her a little bit, she would leave him alone and keep herself out of trouble, but I see now that was a mistake. I think maybe she was just trying to distract me. Where is she now? We need to question her find out what she knows because she's either a pawn in whatever game they are playing or she is working with them. Either way, we need to find out." Quentin said, thinking it was more likely the latter.

"You didn't see her then?" Nikolai asked

"No, I haven't seen her." He answered.

"Quentin, Harper was taken by Luca also. The same night as you, and we haven't seen her since." Nikolai informed him.

Quentin didn't react to the news but instead asked, "What's in the envelope?"

Nikolai peeled open the envelope he held in his hands. He pulled out a small yellow piece of paper and unfolded it to read the words written on it. His face looked puzzled as he read the words on the page. He held it out so others could see what it said.

*You're next.*

"What is that supposed to mean?" Emmaline asked, but before anyone could think of an answer, there was loud thump downstairs.

"What was that?" Jace asked in alarm. The others turned to him, forgetting for a moment that he had even been in the room.

Just realizing this for the first time, Quentin asked, "Who is he, and what is he even doing here?"

While Jace, Nikolai, and Dac filed out of the room to see what the noise was downstairs, Emmaline stayed behind to explain how Jace came to be visiting the house. She told him about the night Harper stabbed her and how Jace showed up the next day, claiming Harper had sent him there. Quentin could hear the admiration in Emmaline's voice as she described how he had been trying to help them find Harper. He didn't like it one bit. He didn't trust this human, and he no longer trusted Harper.

Just then, they heard one of the others call them from the bottom of the steps. They put their conversation on hold and walked out into the hall. As they descended the stairs, they could see the others crowded at the front doorway. On the floor of the entryway lay Zaine's dead body, his eyes wide open, staring blankly into nothingness. Emmaline let out a small gasp. Quentin noticed the paling complexion of Jace's face, and it looked like he might vomit at any moment. He put a hand on Emmaline's back and quietly said to her, "Take your human out of here."

Obeying Quentin's request, Emmaline moved to where Jace was standing. She grabbed him by the arm and dragged him off towards the kitchen. Quentin moved closer to his friends.

He placed his arm around Nikolai's shoulder. Everyone was thinking the same thing, but no one wanted to say it out loud. The timing of it was too perfect. This is what the message meant, and Nikolai's life was in danger.

Dac kneeled down to examine the body more closely. There were multiple puncture wounds on his neck, but when Dac turned him over, he realized the right side of his neck had been torn from his collarbone to his ear, and a piece of his right ear was missing as if he had been mauled. Then he noticed the large tear and bloodstain on the front of Zaine's shirt. He leaned in for a closer look, and that's when he saw it—the gaping hole in Zaine's chest where his heart had been ripped out.

Dac fell back in disgust. Quentin and Nikolai came over and helped him back to his feet. They would have to do something with this body. Obviously, they couldn't just leave it here in the entryway.

"Do all we agree now that Harper is a part of this?" Quentin asked.

"It certainly looks that way," Nikolai said solemnly. They both looked over at Dac, who didn't say a word, but they both knew he was thinking it too.

"I guess first we have to figure out how to dispose of this body, then decide what our next move is going to be," Quentin said

"I think we should return him to his father," Dac said.

"His father?" Quentin and Nikolai asked at the same time.

"The old man at his apartment." Dac turned to Nikolai, "That night, we went to search through Zaine's things. That old man was there. I believe that's his father."

"That's right. I remember now, but do you really think that's a good idea?"

"It's not like he's going to report it. He knows who and what we are. I don't know how, but he has the mark. I saw it, and do you remember he threw the oil at me? Look, it's the honorable thing to do."

"If he's the same man I told you about that first night into the investigation, I know where he lives. I followed him home that night. I thought he may have been hiding who we now know is Luca, but I realized he wasn't once I got there. I wasn't sure how he fit into this at the time, but if he is Zaine's father, it makes sense. He wasn't working for any vampires; he was looking after Zaine." Quentin said.

"OK, so it's settled then. We return Zaine's body to the old man, but how do we get him there?" Nikolai asked.

"Garrett's delivery Van. We'll call him, ask to bring it over here, and have Jace drive us to the old man's house." Dac explained.

"Why bring the human along, though? We can just drive over there ourselves. I don't see any reason he needs to come, and I don't trust him." Quentin protested.

"You don't have to worry about him. He isn't any threat to us. He doesn't have the stomach for it. Besides, he really has been trying to help." Nikolai said, patting his friend on the back as they all started off for the kitchen where Emmaline and Jace were waiting for them.

Dac remained in the entryway of the kitchen as he made his phone call to Garrett. Quentin reluctantly explained the plan to Emmaline and Jace, who were sitting at the kitchen island. Jace had a half-empty glass of water in front of him.

"You're going to need something a little stronger than that tonight, my man," Nikolai said as he reached up into the cabinet above the refrigerator and pulled down a bottle of whiskey. He poured some into a glass and handed it to Jace. Gratefully, Jace accepted the glass of whiskey and drank it down in one gulp.

"Thanks." He said. "But what do vampires need whiskey for?" He asked.

"It's Charlotte's." Nikolai laughed. "She thinks we don't know about it, and we let her think that, but it's ok." He added.

"Garrett is on his way with the van. I told him to call Charlotte and have her meet him here to drive him back home. I told him not to come up to the house. He'll park the van in the back of the house and leave the keys in the ignition. When he and Charlotte are gone from the driveway, he'll text me. Then we can load Zaine's body into the van. We'll take him to the old man and then drop the van off at the donation center. Garrett can pick it up there in the morning." Dac explained to the group.

"Why don't we have Garrett and Charlotte take Jace home?" Quentin asked

"I don't need a ride. My car is just outside." Jace replied.

"Jace is not going home yet. We don't know if Harper will send any more messages through him, and even if she doesn't, we still don't know her or Luca's plan and how Jace fits into it. Jace could be in just as much danger now as the rest of us, and since he's human, he could be in more." Dac said

"I don't need to go with you tonight, though. I can just stay here." Jace said, sensing Quentin's hostility.

"No, you're coming. It's best we all stay together. We can't protect you if we're not here." Dac said.

A few minutes later, they saw the lights of the van outside the kitchen window. They all looked at Dac as they waited for Garrett's text to come through. Quentin and Nikolai went out into the front hall to gather Zaine's body, ready to load it into the van soon as Dac gave the word. Then it came. Dac's phone pinged with the message from Garrett. "Time to go," Dac said.

# Twenty-Five

They all sat in silence on the drive over to Zaine's father's house. There were only two seats in the delivery van, so they had Emmaline sit up front with Jace while Quentin, Nikolai, and Dac sat in the back with Zaine's dead body covered in a sheet. After what had felt like hours, though, it had only been about thirty minutes, they pulled up in front of the old man's house. They had decided Jace and Emmaline would stay in the Van. Dac would go to the door first and speak with the old man. When he gave the signal, Nikolai and Quentin would bring over Zaine's body.

The house was mostly dark, except for one window that showed a light on inside. Dac knocked on the door. He only had to wait maybe a minute before the old man answered.

"What are you doing here?" The old man said with both hostility and fear in his voice.

"Are you Mr. Brantley?" Dac asked the old man.

"You know who I am, and I know who you are, vampire. Now, what do you want with me? You have been taunting me for years. Please just kill me or leave me alone," Mr. Brantley said.

"I'm not who you think I am, Mr. Brantley. Though I'm

afraid, I know the one of who you speak. Unfortunately, I cannot help you with that matter, and that is not why I am here."

"Then why are you here?" The man shouted at him. Dac placed a hand on his shoulder.

"I have some rather unfortunate news," Dac said, and he proceeded to tell him what had happened to Zaine, trying his best to leave out the goriest details. Although he knew he would see for himself soon enough. The old man dropped to his knees. He covered his face with his hands as he began to sob. Dac turned his face back towards the van and silently signaled for Quentin and Nikolai to bring Zaine's body over.

Quentin and Nikolai got out of the van carrying the body over to where Dac stood over Mr. Brantley. They placed Zaine down as respectfully as they could at Mr. Brantley's feet. Mr. Brantley removed a portion of the sheet covering Zaine's face. He sobbed louder, now cradling Zaine's lifeless body in his arms.

"I don't know why we had to do all this. I can't feel sorry for Zaine. As far as I'm concerned, he got what he deserved and should have just been thrown out in the woods and left to rot somewhere for what he did to Harper." Jace said as he and Emmaline watched from the van as the events outside unfolded.

"I hear where you're coming from, but Dac is not like that. He has respect for all human life. That is why he and his brother did not get along." Emmaline said

"That sounds like you're putting it mildly. Looks to me like it was more than just not getting along."

"Yea, I guess you're right. Even still, we don't know anymore what really happened between Zaine and Harper."

"We know he killed her."

"We only know what she let us know. How do we know she hasn't been working with Luca all along? For all we know, she could have manipulated this whole situation, including her death." Emmaline reasoned.

"Are you turning on her now too? I thought you were her friend. How do you know Luca hasn't manipulated her? For all we know, she is still in danger or, even worse, dead for real this time."

"All I know is a dead body showed up on our doorstep today along with a message for Nikolai that said you're next. The only way Luca would know where we live is from Harper. So, I can't help be at least a little bit suspicious."

"How do we know you're not the one who told him. Maybe you're the one manipulating everyone. Luca did make you a vampire, didn't he? Isn't that what you said earlier?"

"Luca tortured me for days before he turned me. I would never work for that monster. I owe everything to Dac. If not for him, I don't know what would have become of me." Emmaline yelled at him.

"I'm sorry. I shouldn't have said that." Jace apologized.

They sat quietly in the van, now waiting for the others to return. Jace nervously rubbed his hands across his thighs. Emmaline reached over, placing one of her hands on his in an effort to comfort him. Her skin felt cold and soft over his. He looked over in her direction, though they both remained silent. It was only a moment later that they heard the others get back into the van. Jace looked over out of the driver's side window and saw the old man at his doorway, carefully dragging Zaine's body into the house. Jace started the van back up and drove off.

The donation center was only a mile from the house, so they walked back home after dropping off the van. Emmaline, Quentin, Nikolai, and Dac all walked at a human's pace so that Jace could keep up. When they arrived back at the house, Jace immediately left the group. It had been a long day for him, and he retired to Harper's room, where he had been staying. Emmaline watched as he descended through the hidden passage down the stairs. Quentin, of course, took notice of this.

"He's still a human, you know." He said to her.

"Shut up." She said back and went into the side room. She plopped down on one of the large sofas and turned on the tv.

Upstairs, Dac sat in his office, his head in his hands as he thought about Zaine's father. Zaine was indeed not innocent, and maybe he deserved some form of justice for what he'd done to Harper, but Dac couldn't help feeling bad for the old man, especially knowing what had happened to Zaine was not for justice but was just some part of whatever game Luca was playing. Dac knew he had to figure out what Luca was up to and how to find him, and he had to do this sooner rather than later.

A knock on the door interrupted his thoughts. He looked up to see Nikolai and Quentin standing in the doorway. He hadn't even realized he didn't shut the door behind him.

"Come in." He said as he gestured for them to sit.

"We were just thinking we need to figure out how everything and everyone is connected to Luca and what it all means," Nikolai spoke first.

"You're right, and I was just thinking the same thing," Dac

said. He pulled out a notepad and pen from his desk. "Let's write out everything we know first and see if we can then put some of the clues together."

"Ok, well, let's start with Emmaline. We just found out today that Luca was the one who left in her that graveyard. That would be the first we would know of his reappearance." Nikolai said as Dac wrote it down on the paper in front of him.

"And the old man, I think he would have been his next victim," Quentin added. "I think we need to go talk to him and get his story."

"I think you're right. We'll send Jace over to his house in the morning." Dac said.

"The human? You really want to send him? I don't see why we can't just go ourselves." Quentin questioned.

"Yes, the human. If we send him out in the daylight, he'll be safe, and Mr. Brantley is more likely to talk to him than any of us. As far as he's concerned, we're all responsible for what happened to his son. Anyway, let's get back to the list. What else do we know?" Dac answered.

"The next apparent targets were Zaine and Harper. It seems they met around the same time that Nikolai noticed her. I don't think that was a coincidence. I also don't think it was a coincidence that Zaine was the old man's son." Quentin said next.

"I'd have to agree with that," Nikolai said.

"Is that everything?" Dac asked the other two.

"I think it is, but how does it all fit together?" Quentin answered.

"Well, we know how Harper, Zaine, and the old man fit. They were all connected. The old man was Zaine's father, and

Harper was Zaine's girlfriend. I'm guessing, as you said, this is no coincidence. We know Luca marked Mr. Brantley, and he must have noticed Harper too at some point and somehow manipulated it that I would notice her. He'd know her likeness to Una would grab my attention and likely make me want to protect her, which I did. Now the question is, how much was Harper aware of, and what is her part in this?"

"You mean, is she helping him, or is she just another one of Luca's victims?" Quentin asked.

"Precisely."

"I know you want to think the best of her, but I thought after tonight, we all agreed she's working with Luca," Quentin argued.

"It certainly looks that way, but I think we need to keep an open mind either way about her." Dac interrupted, quieting the tension beginning to build between Quentin and Nikolai.

"Ok, You're right," Quentin said. "But what about Emmaline. How does she fit?"

"I think she was probably one of his first victims here. I don't think it was his intention to turn her. From her story, I think he intended to kill her and leave her for me to find. The deliberate way he tortured her should have been and probably was meant to be the first clue that he had survived. She was so traumatized by the ordeal she never talked about it. She was always just grateful to us all for taking her in. I also don't think she was the only one. I'm betting there have been other victims left behind, and we've just never noticed." Dac said.

"And when Luca realized he wasn't getting our attention, he had to come up with a new plan. That's probably when he marked the old man. Then it seems Mr. Brantley left his family but probably continued to keep an eye on them. Luca would be able to see everything that the old man was seeing. That could be how he saw Harper and why he approached Zaine." Nikolai added.

"That's a good theory. Now, all we need to do is confirm if it's true and, more importantly, find Luca before he makes good on his threat to Nikolai." Quentin stated, and they all agreed.

# Twenty-Six

J ace awoke the next morning to see a piece of paper on the floor near the door. He picked up the note and read it. It said for him to visit Zaine's father and gather as much information as possible from the old man. He was to report back here at the house later that evening as the note warned him to be back before sundown.

Jace decided he'd better get an early start, no point in wasting time. The sooner this was all over, and they no longer needed him, the sooner he could get back to his everyday life. He went upstairs to the main floor bathroom to wash up. He could hear Charlotte was already at the house and in the kitchen. In order to avoid making pleasantries, he snuck quietly out the front door, deciding he'd grab a quick breakfast on the way.

He had located his car exactly where he had parked it on the first night he got here. He unlocked the doors and got into the driver's seat. He had only been to the old man's house once before, and that was last night, and it had been dark, but he thought he could still remember the way. Not bothering to turn on his phone, which he had been keeping turned off to avoid Cloe, he drove off with no navigation to tell him the way, just his memory.

He pulled up in front of the old man's house just as he had the night before. Last night's events replayed in his mind as he peered out the window of his car. He pictured Zaine's father on his knees, cradling Zaine's dead body, then dragging him into the house as Jace and the others drove off into the night.

He took a deep breath as he got out of the car and walked up the pathway leading to the front door. He knocked lightly on the door at first. When he received no answer, he knocked again, a little harder this time. A shuffling came from inside the house, so he just stood at the doorstep and waited. A moment later, Mr. Brantley was standing in front of him, staring at him from the open door.

The old man's eyes were still red and puffy from the night before. His face looked like it had aged another ten years overnight. He clearly hadn't gotten much sleep, not that Jace expected he would have.

"Who are you? What do you want?" The old man asked.

"Hi, Mr. Brantley. I'd like to express my condolences about your son." Jace said as sincerely as he could muster.

"Thank you, but I know that's not why you're here. Now tell me what you want or get off my doorstep." Mr. Brantley said. Jace swallowed hard before he replied.

"I'm sorry. You're right; that is not the reason I came by this morning. Please excuse me. I don't mean to be inconsiderate, but the man from last night asked me to come here. He and his friends are looking for information."

"The vampires. I see. And they sent you, their human pet, to get this information."

"I am nobody's pet." Jace protested

"So, you think. I warned my son to watch out for them. He didn't listen, and well, you see what that got him. I suggest you get far away from them while you still can."

"That is all I want: trust me. I just want to get back to my normal life when vampires were only fiction, but they won't let me do that until I help them. So, please will you help me by telling me what they want to know, then I promise I will leave you alone." Jace pleaded.

"Fine, but I don't know what they think I know that could help them out." He paused before saying, "Come in." Mr. Brantley moved out of the way so that Jace could enter the house.

Jace stepped into the tiny living room. He took in a deep breath looking around the room, praying he wouldn't see Zaine's dead body lying there somewhere. He hoped it wasn't still in the house at all, but thankfully he didn't see any signs of it anywhere. He followed Mr. Brantley through the living room into the kitchen. The old man gestured for Jace to sit down at the table while he poured two cups of coffee for the two of them.

"So, what kind of information do these vampires think I have for them?" Mr. Brantley asked as he placed one of the coffee cups on the table in front of Jace and took the seat opposite him at the table.

"I don't know exactly what it means, but they tell me you've been marked by a vampire. They believe that vampire is Dac's brother Luca. Basically, they want to know your story. How did it happen to you?" Jace answered him after taking a sip of the warm coffee.

"And why do they want to know? How can my story be of any help to them? Why should I help any of them? I just want to be left alone."

"It seems Dac and Luca have been in some type of long-term battle with each other. I don't know the whole story, only that Dac and one of the others, Nikolai, thought they had destroyed Luca years ago, but it seems they were wrong, and Luca has resurfaced."

"And I suppose Dac and his friends are supposed to be the good guys?"

"Yes, they are."

"How can you know that? Can any vampire be good? You say they won't let you go until you help them, as if they are holding you prisoner. How can that make them the good guys? How are you even involved in this in the first place?"

"I used to know one of them before she became a vampire. Her name is Harper. She and my fiancé and I were all really good friends once."

"Ah, Harper."

"You know her?"

"No, not personally."

"Oh well anyway, are you going to help us or not? Please can you tell me what happened to you? How do you know about the vampires, and what does it mean that one marked you?"

"I will tell you my story, but first, I will tell you that you have the mark too." Jace looked at the old man in surprise as he pointed to the mark above Jace's collarbone. "This mark right here. It means you have been bitten by a vampire. For whatever reason, this creature has left you alive. It did not turn you, nor did it kill you, but now you are forever linked to this one vampire. It can communicate through your voice and see through your eyes as if they were its very own. You say you want to go back to live your normal life. I'm sorry, my dear boy, but that is no longer possible. Your life now belongs to the vampire." Jace swallowed hard as he listened, holding onto the coffee mug in front of him with both his hands. The old man then began to tell his own story.

"It was years ago. I had a wife and a young son," Mr. Brantley began. "I remember the very day like it was yesterday. We were having an enjoyable day walking along the boardwalk. The weather was warm and breezy. I remember the flower my wife had worn her hair. The three of us walked together hand in hand, never knowing that that would be the last time.

"Later that night, after we had returned home, my wife noticed she had lost the shawl she'd been wearing earlier that day. I offered to go out and look for it. I went back to the boardwalk, to this spot we had stopped to take some photographs. I remembered she'd had with her then, and we had left shortly after that, so it was most likely in that spot. When I got there, I realized it was unusually empty for that time of year, but I got out of my car and began looking around for my wife's shawl.

"A thick fog began to roll in. I remember thinking I heard footsteps behind me. When I turned back to look, there was no one there. I hadn't found the shawl yet, so I continued looking for it. Finally, I saw a glimpse of something white down on the sand. I climbed down over the railing onto the beach, and there it was hanging from a nail on one of the wooden planks of the boardwalk now above me. She'd be so happy I found it; I remember thinking. It was her favorite accessory, she said. Our son had given it to her on her birthday earlier that year. I took him to the mall one day, and he had picked it out for her. Anyway, the fog was getting thicker, and the winds were beginning to pick up at this point. I figured I'd better hurry up and start heading back home. I grabbed the shawl and began to climb back over the railing. That's when it grabbed me.

"I struggled my best to break free, but it was no use. Whoever had me was much too strong. Then I felt the sharp pain in my neck, and the pressure against my ribs as this thing had me in its grasp. I think I screamed, and for a moment, everything around me became a blur. When the fog cleared up around me, I stayed lying there on the sand, trying to get my vision back into focus and understand what had just happened. I had gone back home that night and cleaned up. Over the next few weeks, I began having these terrible fevers accompanied by all sorts of delusions. I didn't know what was happening to me. I went to a couple of different doctors and had all types of bloodwork and tests done, but no one could tell me anything. It felt like someone or something else was controlling my thoughts and movements. My moods were becoming increasingly irritable. The littlest things would set me off. Finally, I decided to check myself into a psychiatric hospital.

"It was there that I met Max, the orderly. He noticed the wounds on my neck and began asking questions. At first, I was reluctant to tell what had happened, but Max was so patient and unjudgmental that I eventually opened up and told him everything about the attack. He started to tell me stories about these vampires. I knew it all sounded far-fetched and crazy, but at the same time, it all made so much sense, so I listened intently. Max started to bring me these books that told all about the superstitions and how to protect yourself, but also what to do if you'd been bitten and survived. I read each and every one of them until I finally learned how to quiet the voices in my head. I was beginning to feel almost like myself again. I checked myself out of the hospital a few weeks later. I knew I couldn't go home, that one day the vampire would be back for me. I had to protect my family, so I stayed with Max for a little while until I found and moved into this place. It was far enough away that my wife and son would be protected but close enough that I could keep an eye on them without them ever knowing."

"So, that's what you have been doing all this time?"

"Yes, but what good did it do? My son is still dead, and for what?"

"That is what we are trying to figure out. Had you ever had any other contact with the vampire who attacked you?"

"No, not until recently when I ran into your friend at Zaine's apartment, then he showed up here last night. But he said he's not the same one who attacked me. You say it was his brother?"

"That's right. Well, thank you for your time. I am sincerely sorry for your loss." Jace rose from his chair to take his leave. The old man followed to show him out. As they reached the front door, Mr. Brantley grabbed Jace by the shoulder.

"One thing before you go, the girl I just remembered, I have seen her recently."

"Harper? You've seen her? Where?"

"By the warehouse a few times. Then here last night."

"Last night? She was here?"

"Yes, last night. She appeared as you were leaving. She was standing right there beside that tree." He said, pointing to a tree on the side lawn. "She didn't do or say anything. It was almost like she was an apparition. She just stood there smiling, and then she was gone."

"That's strange. How did any of us not see her?"

"She must not have wanted you to. Be careful, please. I don't know what's going on, but none of this is right."

"Thank you. I will." Jace said as he turned down the walkway back to his car.

Inside his car, Jace thought about everything the man had told him. Nothing really made sense to him. What had Luca wanted with him? He still didn't see the connection. Was he just some random victim, and was Harper meeting Zaine a coincidence or not? More importantly, what was Harper doing there last night? Hadn't she been kidnapped? Were the others right in suspecting she was working with Luca? This visit left Jace with more questions than answers. He needed to get back and tell the others, but it was still early when he looked at the time. He decided to take a little detour and visit Cloe.

# Twenty-Seven

W hy was it so dark? Where was she? She couldn't move. There was no room. This space was too tight. She tried to feel around her. There was a cool silk underneath her. Her head lay on a soft pillow, but when she tried to sit up, she hit her head. Feeling round again with her hands, she felt the warm wood above her head and on both sides of her. A coffin. She was in the coffin again, but this time the lid was closed. That's what the boy meant about a box. She pushed up against the lid with her hands, but it wouldn't open. She was locked in the coffin. Her heart began to pound fast. She tried pulling in some deep breaths to slow her breathing. Was she going somewhere? Yes. She was moving. She could feel movement beneath her and hear the sound of wheels on tracks. She was on a train of some sort. But how did she get here, and where was she going? The last thing she remembered was being locked in that room.

\* \* \*

The container train pulled into the freight station at Noxwood.

The two men who made up this train's crew were given strict instructions to have the train unloaded and out of the yard by sundown, but they were running behind schedule. Evening was already approaching, and the sky was showing brilliant colors of red and orange as the sun was reaching the horizon. The freight yard was empty and quiet, and the two crew members quickly got to work unloading each container as instructed. Luckily, they didn't have many boxes to unload off their train. By the time they got to the last container, the sun had already set. They placed the container on the ground separately from the rest as they had been instructed to do. Then as they were getting ready to clear the yard, a sound came from one of the containers.

"What was that?" One of the men said.

"Probably just a raccoon or something. Come one, let's get out of here."

The ground crunched under their feet as they walked. The brisk winter night air had settled in, and the winds were beginning to pick up. A loud crash came from behind them as the lone container lid came flying open. Two dark creatures escaped from the opening of the container. The few lights that lit the yard flickered off. Total darkness surrounded the men. They started to run, but they weren't fast enough. The creatures had descended upon each of them, wrapping them in what felt like huge leathery wings. For a second, one of the men gazed into the red eyes of the creature holding him captive. Before he could scream or put up any kind of struggle, the creature opened his jaw wide and sunk his sharp fanged teeth into his neck. The man could feel the creature's grip getting tighter around him as it sucked the blood from his veins. He opened his mouth, but no sound came out. His chest began to feel like it was closing in on him as he gasped for his last breathes of air before he lost consciousness.

Luca dropped the now dead man on the cold dirt-covered ground. He licked the remnants of the man's blood from his lips. His counterpart, Alex, did the same.

"What do we do with the bodies?" Alex asked him

"Leave them. Go get the truck so we can load the ladies before they wake up and get out of here."

"Yes, sir," Alex said as he went in search of the truck that was supposed to be left there for them.

Luca looked down at the two dead men on the ground. "See what happens when you don't follow directions." He said to the corpses. He gave a slight laugh and walked back to the container while he waited for the boy to return with the truck.

When the truck arrived, they loaded the three coffins into the back. They got into the cab. Luca took the driver seat, Alex in the passenger, and they drove off to their next destination.

Not long after leaving the freight yard, they arrived at a large house that stood at the top of a steep hill in the mountains. The nearest neighbors were a few miles away. The house's location reminded Luca of his castle in Romania, which is why he chose it. The house itself was a bit different, but he'd fashioned the inside to resemble it as much as was possible. It had taken a few years to complete, but once it was done, it was better than he'd imagined.

A large stone wall and iron gate surrounded the grounds of the house. Luca stopped the truck outside the gate and ordered Alex out of the passenger seat to open it. He then drove up the long driveway to the front of the house. Outside the house, a young man no more than probably twenty years old awaited their arrival.

"Mr. Vladescu. It's nice to finally meet you. I'm Brian. I have brought two friends, Matt and Keith, just as you requested. They are inside." The young man greeted him.

"That's perfect. You guys can wait in the dining room. My associate and I will unload our truck and meet you there in a few moments." Luca replied.

Brian, the young man, wandered off into the house, and Luca and Alex removed the three coffins from the back of the truck into the garage. Once inside and the garage door was closed, Luca opened the coffins and awakened Lizbeth and the other two.

The five of them walked into the house and towards the dining room, where their guests awaited. Lizbeth walked gracefully over to where Matt sat at the table. She held out her hand and introduced herself. Matt smiled up at her, captivated by her beauty. She ran her hand up to his shoulder and around the back of his neck. Another woman came into the room. She was just as beautiful and elegant as Lizbeth. The young men watched as she circled the table, stopping next to Keith. He stood and greeted her. She greeted him in return, then motioned for him to sit back down. He did as she commanded. Slowly she reached a hand around his neck. At the same time, she and Lizbeth leaned into their victims. Brian sat wide-eyed and frozen in fear as he watched his friends struggling against the grip of the two women as they drank from their necks.

Harper stood against the doorway, watching as the two women took their victims. This is not how things were done in her world. Luca walked over to her. He leaned in close to her ear and whispered, "Your dinner awaits, my dear."

"I will not be a part of this." She snapped.

"You will starve then." He snapped back, losing his patience

217

with her.

Luca stepped into the dining room. Brian scrambled up from his seat and tried to run out past Luca. Luca grabbed him by the throat and pinned him to the wall. Brian's feet dangled in the air as Luca held him up. Luca looked up at the young man's fearful face with a sinister smile, then tossed him across the room. Brian hit the opposite wall hard and slid down the floor. His head was leaning far to one side as his neck broke—the look of fear frozen in his now dead eyes. Luca stepped over Brian's lifeless body and back to where Harper stood in the doorway.

"Don't wait too long, or the blood will get cold." He said to Harper, and then he walked away.

Harper stood there in shock, staring down at the dead body on the floor. Lizbeth and the other woman walked past her, not saying a word. Their victims lay lifeless at the table. Harper looked around at the death surrounding her for the first time, realizing what she really was. She had been a vampire for three years, but she hadn't experienced anything like this. The blood she drank had been provided for her. She never gave a thought about where it may have come from. The hunger inside her was growing, and she was beginning to feel weak, but the gruesome scene she was witnessing made her sick inside. How had she gotten herself into this, and what was she going to do now? If she was going to survive, she was going to have to play their game. She knelt beside the body on the floor. She took her nail and pierced the skin surrounding the artery in his neck, digging her nail deeper and deeper until the blood began to spill out violently from the wound. She put her lips to the boy's open throat and began to drink. As the blood flowed into her, the boy's heart began to beat in tune with hers. The essence of his life, of his spirit, filled her and satisfied her more than the blood alone ever had. That's when she realized he hadn't been dead yet. That is not until she had just killed him.

She let go of the body she had just cradled in her arms and held against her lips. She leaned her head back against the wall. Her breaths were shallow. She could feel the warm blood of this man now racing through her own veins. She thought about who this man could have been. Did he have a family somewhere that was going to be looking for him? Was he in school? Did he have a job? He looked so young. He should have had a full life ahead of him, and now instead, because of her, he was dead. The worst part was in that very moment that she was taking his life, she enjoyed it.

A shadow formed above Harper. When she looked up, one of the other vampires was standing over her. He reached out a hand to her, and she grabbed it as he gently helped her up from her spot on the floor.

"Welcome to our side." He said as he led her away from the dead bodies in the dining room and into the front parlor.

"I'm not on your side. I thought he was dead already." She snapped back at him.

"You shouldn't feel so guilty. That is how we survive. Your friends have raised you to be soft, but there is a predator inside of you. You feel it, and we see it in you. Now it's time to accept it. That is why we chose you; you know. Well, that and because of your looks." He said with a sick smile.

"Chose me?" She asked.

"Yes. I'm sure by now you have figured out who we are, at least."

219

"You are the ones at the warehouse. The ones Zaine owed money to all those years ago, I guessed, but I don't know who any of you are or why I am here."

"Well, in that case, let me formally introduce myself," came another voice as the other man entered the room. "though I'm sure you've heard of me. My name is Luca, and this here is Alex."

Harper gasped as her knees began to weaken and buckle beneath her. She sat down on the sofa next to where she stood. "Luca, Dac, Nikolai," she whispered under her breath as she began to put the pieces together. She started to recognize the man standing in front of her. How had she not seen the resemblance before? The man who stood before her had a face like Dac. He was the same man from the visions she'd had the night Nikolai had made her.

"But I thought you were dead." She finally managed to say.

"As I am sure, my brother and his sidekick did as well," Luca said. "Although I'm sure by now, they have realized that is not the case, and I am very much alive.

"What have you done?" Harper demanded to know.

"Just left them a little a present, that's all." He replied with a sinister smirk that made Harper's skin crawl.

"What kind of present?" She asked, rather quietly, afraid to hear the answer.

"Let's just say you no longer need to worry about your killer."

"Zaine? You killed him, didn't you? And where is Quentin?" She asked, trying to choke back the tears she could feel forming in her eyes.

"Oh, now, please don't cry for your killer. He doesn't deserve your tears. You wanted justice, and now you have it. As for your little bodyguard, don't worry about him. He is fine. We sent him home as soon as we had you."

"Yes, I wanted justice, but I never wanted Zaine dead."

Luca stepped closer to Harper. Standing directly in front of her, he placed his fingertips under her chin, lifting it slightly. He looked deep into her eyes and said. "You will feel much better once you stop lying to yourself. Stop denying who you truly are. You are a powerful vampire. You are a killer." He said to her.

Harper stood up and looked at him defiantly, staring back into his eyes, silently daring him to take back his words. Although deep down, they both knew that she feared he was right. She had wanted Zaine dead. She had just been denying it to everyone else for so long that she began to believe it herself. But she remembered the feeling of Zaine struggling in her arms, the scent and taste of the blood that spilled from his veins into her mouth. The truth was if Emmaline hadn't stopped her that night at Zaine's apartment, she probably would have killed him. But that made her no better than him, and now she was just as responsible for his death as if she had killed him herself. She sat back down on the sofa and watched as Luca turned and walked out of the room.

"I'm not a killer." She mumbled to herself.

Alex sat on the sofa next to her. He rested one of his hands on top of hers and then said, "He's right. Accept who you are, Harper, and join us."

# Twenty-Eight

"I knew we shouldn't have trusted him. He should have been back by now." Quentin was saying as he paced the room.

"Just relax, will you. He'll be here, if for no other reason than that he still believes in Harper and wants to help her." Nikolai said.

Nikolai wasn't so sure himself that Jace would be back. He just needed to calm Quentin down, although he was beginning to worry Quentin might have been right. Jace should have returned hours ago from his visit with Mr. Brantley. Where was he? Had he decided not to help them after all? Had Luca gotten to him somehow too? Nikolai was starting to worry, but he could not let his friend see it. Quentin had been against Jace being included in anything since he had gotten back last night and noticed him sitting in the room with everyone. If he noticed Nikolai was beginning to worry, it would only confirm his belief that Jace shouldn't be involved. But right now, Jace was their only link to Harper, so Nikolai wanted to keep him close by just in case Harper tried to reach out through him again. Although he had to admit it didn't seem likely. The only time she reached out so far had led them nowhere, just to an empty house. Nothing was making any sense at the moment. Hopefully, Jace would get back soon with some answers or at least some kind of clue from Zaine's father.

"What if Luca got to him too? Dac was right. The human is all mixed up in this now, so he's in just as much danger from Luca as any of us. Possibly more because he's human. He has no power against Luca. You think his little potions he carries around his neck and in his pocket are going to protect him from that monster?" Quentin said to Nikolai's surprise, echoing precisely the same worries.

"Look, I get it. If he doesn't show up soon, we'll go look for him. Let's just give him a few more minutes. I'm sure he'll be here." Nikolai said.

A noise from downstairs averted their attention. They both moved to see what was going on. Nikolai felt a sense of anxiousness in his gut after what had happened the night before. When they had heard a noise like this last night, it had been a dead body on their doorstep. He hoped that was not the case tonight. As he rushed down the stairs ahead of Quentin, he came to a stop when he saw Emmaline at the bottom of the steps. She was kneeling on the floor, picking up a pile of clothes from the ground and putting them into a basket.

"What on earth are you doing?" Nikolai asked her.

"I washed my laundry and dropped the basket when I was carrying it back to my room." She said with a sheepish smile.

"Um, we have Charlotte do that kind of stuff for us." He said as he bent down and helped her pick up the remainder of her clothes from the floor.

"I know. It's just I've been feeling so anxious since last night.

I needed to do something to distract myself."

"By doing housework?"

"Yea, my mother used to go crazy cleaning the entire house whenever she was nervous or upset about something. I guess I inherited that from her."

Nikolai nodded in understanding. He helped her gather her things and carried her basket down the stairs, where they all kept their rooms. As they walked in silence, Nikolai wondered if he should ask if she heard from Jace at all. She must be as worried about him as he and Quentin were, and he didn't want to make her anxiety any worse. He decided it was best not to mention it. When they reached the door to Emmaline's room, she opened it and took the basket of clothes from Nikolai. She thanked him and then asked him the question he didn't want to ask.

"Has Jace come back yet? I haven't seen him."

"No, he hasn't."

"Are you worried?" She asked though she could see from the look on his face that he was indeed worried.

"A little, but I'm sure he'll be back soon."

"Is that what you and Quentin were talking about upstairs? You two seemed kind of heated."

"Well, you know Quentin has always been a little uptight."

"What about Dac? What has he said?"

"I haven't talked to him yet tonight. He's been in his office all night with the door shut. I didn't want to bother him. He still has to process the fact that his brother, who we thought was dead all this time, is still alive and causing all this havoc."

"And how about you? How are you dealing with it?"

"I guess I haven't had much time to process it myself yet, but it's different for me. I'm not related to Luca. It isn't my family. My family is gone and has been for a long time. I've accepted that. Am I mad? Yes. But right now, my focus has to be on those of us that are here and protecting all of us."

"Well, whatever happens, please be careful."

"I will." He said as he turned away, closing the door behind him.

* * *

Jace looked over at Cloe, who was peacefully sleeping next to him. He slowly slipped his arm from underneath her, careful not to wake her. He glanced at the time display on his phone. He should have been back hours ago. He wasn't sure what was in store for him, but he had no regrets. He made his way to the kitchen to find a piece of paper and a pen, knowing Cloe kept a small notepad in the drawer to write her grocery list. He wrote a note to her and tiptoed back to her room, leaving it on the bedside table. He leaned over and softly kissed her forehead, then left the apartment.

In his car, Jace looked up at the window of Cloe's apartment. It was weird being there. Since he had bought his house, they had mostly spent their time at his place, but since he hadn't been there lately, he wouldn't have expected her to stay there. Of course, she would be at her own apartment. Someplace she could feel completely comfortable and not be reminded of him at every turn. He felt terrible for how he had been treating her and the uncertainty he was making her feel, but what choice did he have? He turned on his car's ignition and slowly pulled out of the parking lot. He didn't want to leave her, but he knew he didn't have any other options. He was too deep in this situation with the vampires, thanks to Harper, and he had to see it through.

Jace turned his car onto the street the vampire's house was on. As he had the first night he came here, he parked his car a few blocks down and walked the rest of the way to the house. He took his time walking down the darkened street. The winter air was getting colder, although the crisp freshness was welcoming. The scent of chimneys surrounded him, reminding him of times he had a child, like the drive home from his grandparents' house on Christmas eve.

It seemed the whole world around him was quiet save for the crunching of dead leaves under his feet. He bent down, picking up one of the dry brown leaves off the ground. He stared at the dead leaf he held between his fingers, thinking of all the dead that was suddenly surrounding him, both those still walking and those not. When he finally approached the front gates of the vampire's house, Emmaline came rushing out, grabbing him by the arm, nearly scaring him to death.

"Where have you been?" She asked as she dragged him into the house. "We've all been so worried."

"I know I should have been back earlier. I met with Zaine's father, but then I made another stop before I headed back here. I had to see someone. It was important."

"You shouldn't have done that." Quentin's voice came from the hallway as he walked over to greet them.

"I'm sorry. I just needed to see…." Jace started to say, but Quentin interrupted him.

"It doesn't matter who think you needed to see. Harper can see anything you see and do. Talking to anyone puts them in danger now. You shouldn't have even been talking to the old man, but that was Nik's and Dac's decision. I hope you found out something useful at least. Dac and Nikolai are waiting for you upstairs in Dac's office. Let's go." Quentin chastised Jace as he led him and Emmaline up the stairs to Dac's office.

Inside the office room, Dac sat at his desk with Nikolai standing to his right. Emmaline and Jace sat in the two chairs pulled up in front of the desk, and Quentin stood by the door with his arms folded as he usually did. Jace retold the story told to him by Zaine's father. The others were taking it all in, trying to make sense of it and find the connections. The one thing they all seemed to agree on was that Luca had been close by for much longer than they had first expected, and he had probably been using the old man as eyes looking for Dac and Nikolai. This meant that he probably had more human eyes lurking around and possibly even the eyes of animals. Luca had been known to use bats and wolves in the past to spy on Dac and Nikolai. The thing they still couldn't figure out was how had Harper and Zaine fit into all of this. Was it really just a coincidence? It was most likely that Luca had noticed her through Zaine's father watching out for Zaine. But then what had happened? The questions of Harper's involvement still lingered.

When Jace entered the room he'd been staying in for the past few nights, she was sitting there on the bed, still wearing the same clothes he had last seen her wearing. Her skin, however, was much more luminescent, and her hair seemed to have more shine. Her vampiric appearance was more like that of Dac or Nikolai than of herself. Before Jace could open his mouth to say something, she rushed over to him, putting her forefinger to his lips to quiet him.

# Twenty-Nine

J ace awoke to the morning sun lighting up the room. The particles of dust danced around in the rays of light peering in through the windows. He was in his own bed, in his own room, in his own house for the first time in days. It was a welcoming sight opening his eyes to daylight instead of a drafty, dark, windowless room. While he should have felt peaceful and relaxed, instead, he felt restless and uneasy. Something was weighing on his mind from the night before. Harper. There was something different about her, and why hadn't she let him speak or see the others before he had left. She had quickly and quietly ushered him out of the house and sent him on his way home. She had barely spoken any words to him other than go home, and even that had barely been a whisper.

He tried to push it out of his mind, telling himself to let it go. Harper was probably just trying to protect him, and whatever was going on was no longer his problem. He had only been there to help find Harper, and Harper had returned. Yet there was still this nagging voice in the back of his mind telling him that something wasn't right.

Jace pushed his blanket to the side, sat up, and planted

his feet firmly on the floor. He picked up his cell phone off the nightstand and glanced at its screen. No messages. He opened up his pictures and scrolled to the photos he snapped of Nikolai's journal pages. He had taken the shots when he and Emmaline had been searching through Nikolai's office, but he had never had a chance to interpret them.

He walked out of his room and into the kitchen to make himself some coffee. Once he had had his fill of caffeine, he searched unsuccessfully around his house for his laptop. Looking down at the phone in his hands and the pictures on its screen, he decided using the phone alone to translate would take too long. With that in mind, he got himself dressed and headed out towards the library.

As he drove through town on his way to the library, he passed Sarah Higgins' shop. A new thought came to him, and he turned his car around and pulled into the little shop's parking lot. He pulled open the door, and the sound of the bell above rang out as he passed through the doorway. He stepped into the shop. The various smells of wax candles and incense filled the room. He called out for Sarah figuring she was in one of the back rooms. Moments later, she appeared in the shop.

"Hi," she said, "I would've liked to say you look much better than the last time I'd seen you, but you look a bit disheveled. What happened?"

Jace hesitated for a moment before answering. He'd known that she somehow had knowledge of vampires and believed in their existence, but he didn't want to betray their trust by telling her too much. But he also needed answers, and she was the only one he knew that could possibly help. So, he told an edited version of the past week's events, leaving out details like Zaine's gruesome death. He recapped Harper's disappearance and then how she miraculously just showed back up last night. He explained the journal he had found while staying at the house with the vampires and then showed her the photos he had taken with his phone.

"Would you be able to help me translate this?" He asked Sarah.

"Let me see." She took the phone from his hands and examined the photos. "Would you allow me to print these? If I can make the images bigger, maybe I can help." She said.

"Sure," Jace replied, and Sarah plugged the phone into her computer and printed out the journal images.

She sat there quietly for a moment as she read through the pages that came out of the printer. Jace was curious if she could translate them. She turned to him and gestured for him to sit. He abided. She sat across from him, holding the papers up as she began to read the words off the page.

*I thought I saw a ghost today. Her hair the same jet black, but I couldn't get a good look at her face. Even though I know it's impossible, I wanted it to be her. I'm sure it was just my mind playing tricks on me. I miss her so much, even after all these years. But I saw him kill her. Right there in front of my very own eyes, and I could do nothing to save her. That was so long ago, yet it still hurts as bad as if it were just yesterday. I can only hope she is up there in heaven, if there even is a heaven, knowing that I tried to save her, knowing that I eventually avenged her death. Oh, how I wish I could go back to that night. I would never have left her alone. I would do anything to have just lived a normal life and grow old with her and then have died a normal death with her by my side. Instead, she is gone, and I am made to suffer in this eternal nightmare.*

"He seems so tormented," Sarah stated after she finished reading the first page.

"This must be when he first saw Harper. I've heard she looks like his late wife." Jace replied

"Interesting. Shall I go on?"

"Yes, please."

*I saw her again tonight, and tonight I saw her face. It was like a shock to the soul. The resemblance is unbelievable. I wanted to speak to her, but I knew that wouldn't be possible, so I just watched her for a while. She sat there on that bench for at least an hour. I could hear the music through her earphones. She seems so troubled. I just want to take all her problems away, whatever they may be. I know that's impossible too, but I can't help how drawn I am to her, and this feeling I have that makes me want to protect her. It's just overwhelming. I can't seem to rid her of my thoughts. I haven't told any of this to anyone else. I know what they would say, especially Dac. He would say to me I need to move on. He would say to me to leave the past in the past and leave this girl alone. It pains me to say that I know he's right. This girl is not Una, and pretending that she is will not bring Una back.*

*Nothing will. After Luca was gone, I thought that I'd be able to live my life in some kind of piece. I guess I thought that I would feel some type of justice or closure by killing him. But I felt none of those things. When we hunted him and fought against him, I had a purpose, something to focus on all those years. I can still remember what it felt like to hold that dagger in my hand, its cold steel against my cold skin. I remember the moment the knife went into his cold, undead heart. It was easier than I thought it would be. Then I watched as his evil red eyes turned black and empty. The blood that spilled from him went from red to black as it poured out from his chest, mouth, and eyes. I pulled the dagger out from his chest. His limp body fell to the ground, and that's when I noticed Dac standing there. He took the dagger from my hand. Together we dragged Luca's body out of the catacombs and outside to the grounds behind the castle. There we dug his grave.*

*I watched as Dac pulled on a pair of leather gloves. He pulled a small bottle of liquid and a clove of garlic from the velvet pouch that hung around his neck. He placed the garlic in Luca's mouth then rolled him into the ground making sure he was face down before pouring the liquid over his body. I could hear his flesh sizzle as it burned from the liquid. Then we covered the grave, and shortly after that, we said goodbye to Romania for the last time. All these details have been recorded in other journals that we keep locked up in the attic upstairs, along with the dagger and a few other things from those days of hunting Luca, but writing it all down again right here at this moment feels somehow therapeutic. So, I sit here writing down the same things I've written over and over again.*

Sarah paused for a moment. She continued reading aloud the printed pages of Nikolai's journal. Each page described in more and more detail his fascination with Harper. He wrote about his worry about her being in trouble. He wrote about the feelings he had developed for this girl he didn't even know and about wanting to protect her. He often mentioned Una, his late wife, imagining what their life could have been like had it not been for Luca. Seeing Harper had brought up so many feelings he had long ago pushed down, which were now coming out into the pages of his journal. Lastly, he wrote of the night he made Harper into a vampire.

As she read the last of the words on the page, both Sarah and Jace simultaneously looked up at each other. Jace not only wondered what Sarah thought of it all, but how had she gained so much knowledge of the vampires, and how had she come to believe in them in the first place? Had it not been for Harper and everything he had witnessed in the past few days since she first appeared at his house that night, he would have never believed anything like this could be true. And if he were honest, he would have rather gone the rest of his life, never knowing the truth. How did Sarah seem to handle it so well? Or was she putting up as good of a front as he was?

Finally, Sarah had broken the silence. "This is so fascinating." She said. "I would love to read more. It's like a true glimpse into their lives. I bet they are fascinating creatures."

"I suppose they are, but this isn't very helpful. I don't know what I expected to find or how I thought these pages could help with what's happening now."

"Well, if anything, it shows the legends are true and why Luca is after them now. They did try to kill him, you know, and by the look of things, they almost succeeded."

"Maybe so, but from what I've been told about him, he's evil and deserves to be dead."

"That may be so, but you must remember there is always more than one side to the story than what you know."

"But when I was here the last time, didn't you say...."

"Yes, but I only know of rumors and tales passed down through the generations. But you have been on the inside now. You have been closer than anyone has in a long time. I'm only saying we don't know for sure who really is the most dangerous one. It could be this Luca, or it could be Dac. Do not think they are your friends just because they didn't kill you. They are smart and calculating. They may think you are still of some type of use to them, but when they are truly done with you, they may look to kill you. You need to prepare yourself for that and prepare to defend yourself if it comes to that. You said yourself Harper snuck you out of the house before even telling the others she was back."

"Right. That's what I don't understand. Why would Harper do that when she's the one who sent me there in the first place?"

"That is what we need to find out. Do you think you could get back into the house? Possibly during the day when they are sleeping. If you could get more pages of more journals, and if you get into that attic, maybe we can find out more."

"We? Sarah, I will not betray them but tell me, why are you so eager to help and even believe in vampires for that matter?"

"I have grown up with the stories, knowing that one day the time may come when I would have to pick up where my ancestors left off."

"What does that mean, Sarah? Who are your ancestors?"

"Vampire hunters."

\* \* \*

Jace stood outside the vampire house, contemplating whether or not to go inside. It was still early in the day, and he knew the vampires would still be asleep, but he also knew their housekeeper Charlotte would most likely be there. She came to the house every day and cleaned and looked after the place during the day and would leave right before sunset.

He didn't want to betray the vampires. He still felt loyal to Harper. She had once been one of his best friends. And these were her friends, and in some sort of way, they felt like his friends too. The thing that bothered him, though, was Harper's actions the night before. Something about her just seemed different this time. Different not only from how she'd been in life but also how he'd seen her as a vampire. He needed to get to the bottom of whatever was happening, and maybe Sarah had a point. If he could get back into the house without any of them knowing and get a look at more of those journals, he could learn more about them. More importantly, he thought if he could learn more about their history with Luca, he could still help them because even with Harper back, he had a bad feeling they were still in a lot of danger.

He continued pacing along the sidewalk outside the house, trying to work up the nerve to go inside, when he heard footsteps coming towards him. He stopped, turning towards the house. A distraught-looking Charlotte was running towards him. She opened the gate meant to protect the home from outsiders, grabbed Jace by the wrist, and dragged him towards the front door. He followed her. That's when he noticed the blood on her clothes and the tears running down her face.

"Oh, I'm so glad you're here. I just don't know what to do." Charlotte said through breaths and sobs.

"What happened? What can I do?" Jace asked with concern.

Charlotte stopped in front of the open door as if she were hesitant to go back inside. She just stood there, shaking her head as her sobs grew louder. Jace put his arm around her shoulder and led her to the concrete steps to sit down.

"What happened in there, Charlotte?" He asked her again, but she just sat there, resting her head against her knees, unable to form any words. Jace tried his best to comfort her, but not knowing what was going on made it more difficult. "It's going to be ok." He said. "Can you tell me what's wrong?" He tried asking one more time. Finally, she looked up, wiped the tears from her eyes, and began to explain what had happened.

"I came in this morning and noticed a note left on the side table by the door in the foyer. When I picked it up and read it, the note said I didn't need to come back here anymore and that I should message Garrett and tell him not to come anymore either. I thought this strange because there was no explanation. Who is going to look after the house? I've been coming here for years, and before that, it was my mother. It's never been anyone outside my family, and the same with Garrett. Plus, if he doesn't bring by the donations, what would they do? It just didn't make any sense. I figured since I was here anyway, I would do my usual work around the house and talk to Garrett when he gets here. It was quiet as it always is. Nothing seemed out of place or out of the ordinary but then... Well then I went upstairs and when I saw the...." She trailed off, unable to finish her sentence as she began to sob again.

Jace took her hands in his. "It's ok. You don't have to finish. But do you mind staying here? I'll go check it out."

Charlotte shook her head. "It's just so terrible." She managed to say.

"It's ok. Just sit right here. I'm going inside to check things out. I'll be right back. Jace stood up and slowly stepped into the house. From inside the doorway, everything looked and seemed normal, just like Charlotte had said. He took a deep breath to gather his nerve up. He slowly approached the stairs and looked towards the top of the winding grand staircase. He took one more deep breath and crept up the stairs. Once at the top of the stairs, he looked to his left and then his right, unsure which direction he should go in, but then he noticed a light coming in through an open door down the hall. This was unusual since they usually kept all the doors closed, and this was sunlight coming in through a window. All the windows had heavy drapes covering them that were always tightly shut. The vampires weren't keen to let the sunshine in, so something definitely wasn't right. He walked down the hall to the open door. As he got closer, he realized this was Nikolai's office. He stepped into the room and gasped at the sight in front of him. The chairs were knocked over. Books had fallen from the shelves and onto the floor. But the worst was the blood splattered everywhere. It was on the walls, the chairs, the desk, and when he looked down, there was a pool of dark red blood on the floor beside his feet. Suddenly a voice came from behind him. It was Charlotte. "He's dead? Isn't he?"

# Thirty

Harper awoke that night in a dark room lit only by the candles that surrounded the place. The room seemed familiar though she knew she had never been there before. The ground beneath her was cold, and her arms hurt where they hung over her head. She rose from the spot where she was seated. A sharp pain shot across her wrist, and a solid, cold metal scraped against her skin. She struggled to get to a comfortable position, still not fully aware of her situation. After a moment, she finally started coming out of her sleep-filled daze and into wakeful consciousness. She tried to walk away, but something stopped after only a few steps. The clicking sound of metal against metal rang in her ears as the chains that bound her moved. The cold metal she felt around her wrists were the shackles that chained her to the wall. Suddenly she knew why she recognized this room. It was the room she'd seen three years earlier when Nikolai took her from the water when she and Nikolai exchanged blood, and he turned her into a vampire. But it couldn't be that same room. No, it was a replica. But why was it here? Why was she chained to this wall? Then she remembered Luca. She'd met him last night. He was alive. Then she knew he was recreating that night. He was going after Nikolai.

* * *

"Jace, wake up." The soft voice whispered in his ear. He felt someone shaking him with soft feminine hands, but they were abnormally strong. His eyes blinked open. His heart was beating rapidly. The cap to the tiny bottle he gripped in his hand flew off, and the liquid inside spilled out, splashing onto the girl's arm. He heard a loud screech come out from her mouth. His eyes now focused, he realized it was Emmaline. He quickly jumped to his feet, dropped the bottle to the floor, and rushed over to her.

"Oh my god. I'm so sorry. Are you ok?" He felt genuinely concerned. He hadn't meant to splash her. He hadn't even realized he had fallen asleep. Earlier that afternoon, he had sent Charlotte home after coming upon the scene in Nikolai's office. He had stayed behind, hoping the other vampires that lived in the house were safe and only resting. He was waiting for them in the front room when he must have dozed off.

"I'm ok. Just burns a little." She said as she wiped the oily liquid from her arm with the hem of her dress. Jace had removed the sweatshirt he was wearing and tried handing it to her to clean her arm, but she brushed him off. "I'm fine, really. I didn't mean to frighten you, but what are you doing here, and what happened to you last night?"

"After we were all done talking last night and I went down to Harper's room, she was there. She rushed me out of here, so I went home. Then when I woke up this morning, something just didn't feel right to me. Something about Harper, she just seemed different, and I couldn't understand why it seemed she was rushing me out in secret. It was like she didn't want anyone to see me leave or know she was here. The more I thought about it, the more I kept getting this feeling like you guys were in danger still, so I came back. Charlotte was here when I got here. She was hysterical. She said there was a note left for her this morning when she got here telling her she was no longer needed and to tell Garrett the same thing. Then she told me she went upstairs, but she couldn't tell me what she saw or why she was so upset. She kept crying, so I went upstairs to see for myself. That's when I saw Nikolai's office."

"That doesn't make any sense. Dac sent Charlotte a message the other night to only come to let Garrett in and then leave. He instructed her not to be in the house longer than needed until further notice. With everything going on, he doesn't want her in any unnecessary danger. Plus, why would we tell Garrett to stop coming?" Emmaline replied.

"Charlotte said the same thing. She seemed surprised by the note."

"Also, what is this about Nikolai's office? What did you see?" Emmaline asked.

"You don't know?"

"Know what?"

"Brace yourself. Something horrible happened up there?"

Jace took Emmaline by the hand and led her up the stairs towards Nikolai's office. They reached the top of the stairs and hurried down the hall. When they came to the room, they were looking for the door was closed, but Jace was sure he had left it opened earlier that day. It was still quiet throughout the house. Jace knocked on the door, then pushed it open when no one answered. What he saw inside shocked him. The room was clean, and everything was in perfect order. The chairs were upright, all the books were on the shelves in their place, and no trace of any blood splattered or pooled on the floor. It was as if nothing had ever happened.

"What is going on, Jace? Everything looks fine in here?" Emmaline asked in total confusion.

"I don't get it." He then proceeded to tell her about the mess and blood he'd seen all over the room earlier that day.

Emmaline stood there looking curiously at Jace. His words weren't making any sense to her. No one had seen Harper the night before. As far as she knew, Harper was still missing, and Nikolai had been fine when they all went to sleep in the morning.

"I don't understand. Could I have somehow dreamt of all this? It all seemed so real, though." Jace said.

"Come on. Come with me. Let me show you everyone is ok. Then I'll explain what I think happened."

Jace followed her out of the room. They walked around the house until they found everyone and confirmed all three were ok, including Nikolai. Then they went to Harper's room so Jace could see she hadn't been there either. Dac messaged Charlotte to see what time she came and went from the house earlier that afternoon and if she'd seen or spoken to Jace while she was there. Afterward, all five of them met in the kitchen. Jace stood leaning against the countertop holding the glass of whiskey Nikolai poured for him. Dac entered the room last with an answer from Charlotte.

"Charlotte was here around 2 pm. She said she left about thirty minutes later after Garrett arrived and finished putting the donations away. There was no note left for her on the front table or anywhere else, and she hadn't spoken to Jace.

However, she did say that she had noticed him sleeping in the chair in the front room, but she didn't bother waking him. She said he looked tired, and she didn't want to disturb him. I'm guessing that's where Emmaline found him."

"Yes, that's where I found him," Emmaline replied. "So, do you think I'm right?" she asked.

"Yes, Emmaline, I do. Jace, those images you saw and what you experienced today, as real as that all seemed, it was a trick. What bothers most, however, is the fresh bite on your neck." Dac said, pointing to the side of Jace's neck.

Jace instinctively put his hands to his neck and felt the fresh scab. He was even more confused now than before. He did not remember Harper biting him last night. Had she? Could it have been someone else? Could it have been someone in this house, someone in this room? Could it have been Luca or one of the other vampires he has with him? Suddenly the heat of panic rose inside him. His hands started to feel clammy and began to shake. He unsteadily held onto his glass of whiskey. His hand was shaking as he brought the glass to his lips and took a sip as he tried to calm his nerves a bit. Emmaline took notice and suggested he sit down. Taking her advice, he sat down on one of the stools that surrounded the kitchen island.

"It seems to me that someone doesn't want him here," Quentin said.

"And whoever it is didn't kill him, but I'm afraid if he continues to stay, they might do just that," Nikolai added. "I don't think it's safe for you to be here anymore. It may just be best for you to go home." He said directly to Jace.

"When I thought I saw Harper last night and she told me to go home, I'll be honest; I was glad to be getting back to my normal life. But when I woke up this morning, I could not shake the feeling that something wasn't right and that you guys are still very much in danger. That is why I came back earlier today. I may not fully understand what is happening, but I want to help."

"The most important thing right now is figuring out where Luca and his crew are, so unless you know the answer to that, there's nothing you can do, and it's best you just go home," Quentin replied.

Jace sat and thought for a minute, then suddenly he jumped up and said, "I don't know where they are, but I have an idea where to start looking."

Everyone turned to him in surprise. "What do you mean?" Quentin asked.

Jace pulled out his phone and opened it to the internet. He pulled up an article he saw on the news the other day. It hadn't meant much to him at the time since it was kind of far from where they were, so he hadn't paid much attention to it then. Now, however, he thought just maybe it held a clue to finding Luca and his friends. He placed the phone down on the countertop and pointed to the article about a gruesome murder discovered in a train yard a few hundred miles away in a town called Noxwood. One by one, they each studied the article displayed on the screen.

"Why is this the first time we're seeing this?" Quentin asked.

"I saw this the other day, but I didn't make any connection to it because, well, it's nowhere near here, but now I'm thinking, what if they traveled out there. You said they weren't at the house you searched. The place where they were initially holding Harper and Quentin. What if they went to Noxwood after they let Quentin go, and that's why we can't find them? Jace replied.

"I think that's a fairly good theory. It's worth checking out." Dac said.

"What about Harper or whoever is pretending to be her? Did she just stay behind then? How do you explain her just appearing and no one seeing her but that old man and now Jace?" Quentin scoffed.

"I don't think it's Harper at all. I think it's one of Luca's crew projecting themselves and appearing as Harper. It's all a part of whatever game they're playing. So, I agree with Dac. This is the best lead we have right now. It's worth us looking into it." Nikolai answered.

They all decided the first thing to do was search any place they would consider a good place Luca and his crew may have taken up. Dac and Nikolai retreated to Dac's office to research the area around the train yard. If they found anything promising, they would arrange travel plans to go out there and check it out in person. Quentin had decided to head out for the night. He could feel his energy depleting and needed to feed. He would go to his usual hot spots full of people and life, take what he needed, and return home to see what Dac and Nikolai found in their research. Emmaline and Jace remained in the kitchen.

"He doesn't like me much, does he?" Jace asked Emmaline about Quentin.

"He just isn't very trusting, and it's difficult for him to be around humans without taking their energy."

"Do you think they'll be able to find Luca soon?"

"I hope they do, but I think you really helped out tonight. It's a promising lead. The best we got right now."

"I just wish I would have thought about it earlier."

"Well, at least you thought of it now. That's what counts."

Emmaline said as she walked over to the pantry hiding the heated vault that held the blood donations.

Jace watched as Emmaline pulled out a jar containing the deep red liquid and poured it into a glass. Even as he was getting used to the idea that vampires existed, he still thought this was something he would never get used to seeing.

# Thirty-One

T he fluorescent lights flickered above in the car of the
train. Nikolai sat in silence in the seat across from
Dac, the hood of his sweatshirt pulled up over his
head. The night sky was a deep purple as the winter's first
snowfall was covering the ground outside. Nikolai watched
each delicate snowflake hit the small window beside him,
trying not to think about what may be waiting for them at the
other end of this trip. The world outside sped past him as he
stared out the window. Dac sat still with his face buried in a
book. Though neither said a word, they both knew what the
other was thinking.

The trip took up most of the nighttime hours. As soon as
the train came to a stop at the Noxwood train station, Nikolai
and Dac gathered up their bags and quickly exited the train.
They stepped out onto the platform. The air was cold, and the
fresh snow crunched under their feet. Garrett had a cousin
in the area and arranged for him to drop off a car for them at
the station. They spotted the black car with the dark tinted
windows in the exact spot Garrett said it would be, and they
quickly made their way there. A small magnetic box under
the driver's side door hid the key. Inside was a note with the

address of the place they were going to stay.

The town of Noxwood was situated high in the mountains. Luckily, the streets had been paved and salted. The snow had finally stopped, and they drove along the windy steep roads until they reached the address on the note. It was a small house sitting on a few acres of land surrounded by woods. There were no neighbors for at least two miles. The perfect secluded spot for them to hide away during the day. There was a small metal gate that blocked the entrance to the driveway. Dac got out from the passenger side of the car to open the gate. He shut and locked it again after Nikolai drove through, then got back in the car, and they drove the rest of the way up the driveway to the house. It was a ranch-style home with an attached carport where Nikolai parked the car. They got out of the car and retrieved their bags from the trunk. The sky became a lighter shade of blue and pink as the sun threatened to rise over the horizon.

Nikolai located the house key hidden in the lamp that hung above the door. They entered the house through the door next to the carport, which led them directly into the kitchen. They took a moment to look around the room. A small window above the sink looked out into the backyard. Nikolai pulled the shade down, covering the window. Next to the kitchen sat a small dining room with a small round wooden table and four matching chairs. To the right was the sparsely furnished living room consisting of just a plush couch, a chair, and a floor lamp that stood in the corner. Dark heavy curtains hung around the windows. Nikolai pulled out a box of clothespins he'd packed in his bag and pinned all the curtains so as not to let in any light. There was a small hallway that led to a bathroom and two small bedrooms. They each checked one of the rooms making sure they were empty, and pinned the curtains in there as well. Once they finished securing the house, they double-checked that all the doors were locked and set the alarm. Just off the kitchen was the stairwell leading to a windowless cellar. They locked the cellar door behind them and crept down the stairs. The room was dark and chilly. It was empty but for two small cots pushed against the wall. They placed their bags on the floor, and each of them choosing a cot they laid down to get some rest.

Nikolai lay restless on his cot. He looked over at Dac, who was lying there with his hands folded over his chest, and wondered if he was resting as peacefully as he had seemed. It had been a long time since Nikolai had been somewhere so unfamiliar. It reminded him of his early days as a vampire. He had found it hard to rest in those days too. His body was constantly fighting the daytime sleepiness. His mind would race with the anxiety of someone finding and killing them. He found himself having those same fears now as he lay in the silence of this unfamiliar room, listening to the creeks of this aging house in the mountains.

As the sun rose higher in the daytime sky outside, Nikolai finally gave in to the fatigue overtaking his body. His eyes finally closed, and his mind eased into a quiet sleep.

Hours later, when the new night began to creep in, the two men awoke from their vampiric sleep. Nikolai sat up upon his cot, put his feet on the floor, and listened carefully to the house. All was quiet. No noises came from the floors above them. Nikolai stood up, headed up the stairs, unbolted the cellar door, and stepped into the dark kitchen. His senses still on full alert, he carefully walked through the house, checking all the rooms as he had done earlier that morning. Once satisfied they were safe, he pulled out the laptop he had brought with him and sat at the wooden table in the dining room.

Nikolai sat staring deep into his computer screen as he once again looked through the properties he and Dac had researched as possible hiding places for Luca. The first house sat back on 3.5 acres. It had a stone façade and covered front and back porches. It was rather large for a temporary dwelling but perfect for a permanent living space. The second was a similar large estate with a large lower-level basement and a stone wall surrounding the property. The problem was they didn't know if Luca was in the area and, if so, had he been there long or had he just arrived. And if he had only just arrived, how long was he planning to stay? There was one smaller place they were also considering, set deep inside in the woods, much like the place they were currently staying. It wasn't much Luca's style, but for a short time, it would do, and it would hide him quite nicely.

Dac stood by the table and placed a glass in front of Nikolai. "You need to drink this."

Nikolai looked up from his screen at the glass in front of him. The scent of blood filled his nostrils. Immersed in his research, he wasn't even aware of how long it had been since his last drink. He picked up the glass and took a large sip. "Thanks," he replied as he set the now half-empty glass back down on the table. He wiped his mouth on his sleeve and went back to his research studying each floorplan of Luca's suspected hiding places. Dac sat down next to him, and they discussed their next steps.

The smallest of the three houses was only a few miles from

where they were staying, so they decided to start their search there. They got into the car and drove up the road. When they reached the place they were looking for, Nikolai turned off the headlights and pulled the car off the road, parking a few feet away from the property opening. A frigid breeze accosted them as they stepped out into the night air. Their feet sunk deep into the heavy snow that still covered the ground from the night before. They hopped over the gate that closed off the property. The snow fell from the trees. The crystallized flakes stuck to their exposed hair and eyelashes as they trudged towards the small house off in the distance.

When they finally reached the house, it appeared dilapidated and desolate. Loose tiles hung from the rooftop. Cobwebs still hung from the siding despite the wind and snow. Even in the dark, the peeling paint and graffiti were visible. Nikolai pushed on the fragile-looking front door, and it easily opened. They stepped carefully inside.

The wind blew in from the broken window across the room. A single rocking chair rocked back and forth. Something scurried across the room, a mouse probably. Piles of dust covered the decaying wood floors. From what they could tell searching the house's main floor, it didn't appear that anyone had been here in ages. They decided to check the cellar anyway despite the house's rather empty appearance.

The stairs to the cellar were flimsy, the wood rotting away from years of neglect. More cobwebs hung from the ceiling. Empty shelves lined the walls, and a single metal crate sat in the middle of the floor. It was clear that no one had been in this place in some time, not even vampires. Nikolai and Dac took their leave and moved on to the next house.

When they pulled up to house number two on their list

again, Nikolai cut the headlights before pulling the car to the side of the road. He parked a few feet away from the actual address, just as he had done before. A stone wall bordered the house; however, there was no gate blocking the entrance. They wandered up the freshly paved circular driveway. Lights were shining through the front windows. It was clear someone was currently here but was it Luca? Quietly they approached the house in front of them. Just as they arrived near the top of the driveway, a young girl about seven or eight years old came out of the front door. The girl descended the front steps. Clearly, this was not the house they were looking for, either, and both Nikolai and Dac stopped in their tracks as she approached.

The little girl wore a wool coat over her long nightgown, and she had a pair of bright pink rubber rain boots on her feet. The curls of her hair fell loose from the ponytail she wore. She glanced up at the two strange men in front of her, and her blue eyes sparkled with curiosity.

"Hi," she said innocently. "Are you here for the party?"

Nikolai and Dac stood silent. After a moment had passed and no one had answered her, the little girl continued talking.

"Your skin is pretty." She said to them. "It glows in the dark." She giggled.

Both men looked at each other, and then Dac started to turn around to walk away, but the young girl kept talking.

"You don't look at the other people at the party. You are so tall. My uncle is tall, but he never comes to the parties. My parents say he is too loud and causes trouble, so he isn't allowed to come here. What's your names?"

Nikolai knelt down to be more level with the young girl. "My name is Nick. What's your name?" He asked in return.

"Sophia." She answered, and she held her hand out for him to shake it.

"Nice to meet you." He said as he lightly shook the girl's hands, grateful for the leather gloves he was wearing.

"I like your hair. You should come to the party." Sophia said to him.

"Thank you, Sophia, but we really should be going. I think you should go back inside now."

Before she could say anything, the front door of the house opened again. A woman stepped outside and called out to the little girl Sophia. She was wearing a deep purple cocktail dress made of velvet fabric. The high neckline tied in a bow around her neck. On her feet were glossy pointy-toed pumps that probably added another 4 or 5 inches to her actual height. A faux fur pashmina was wrapped around her arms as she stepped down the same stairs the little girl had just come down moments ago.

"Sophia, go inside and back to bed." She scolded the little girl.

"Sorry, mom," Sophia said to the woman standing beside her. She looked up at Nikolai, who was standing up again. "Good night." She said, and she strolled back towards the house.

"Hurry up, Sophia." Her mother yelled after her. "And whom may I ask, are you?" She asked as she turned back to Nikolai.

"Sorry ma'am, my friend and I, we had some car trouble down the road. We were just looking for someplace we could use the phone to call for a tow. Phone is dead." He said as he showed her his conveniently turned-off cell phone.

"Here, you can use this." She said as she held out the cell phone she held in her hand.

Nikolai took the phone from her and pretended to look up

and call for a tow truck. "Thank you." He said when he handed the phone back. He and Dac began walking back down the driveway when the woman called out to them.

"Wait. Why don't you guys come wait inside?"

"Thank you, ma'am, but that's ok. We'll just wait by the car." Dac replied.

"No, please, I insist. It will be at least an hour before any tow trucks get way out here, and it's freezing. Please come on inside." The woman insisted.

The two men looked at each other and shrugged. They decided they would go inside for just a moment and sneak back out as soon as the woman was distracted with her guests, which they figured wouldn't be very long.

They followed the woman up the steps and into the large foyer of the house. The house inside was brightly lit. A large chandelier hung from the ceiling. The floors were a beige marble, and the walls were all painted in an off-white with cherry wood finishes. The stairs were made of the same cherry wood and covered with a thin running of white carpet. They could hear music playing in the other room. People were moving about laughing and talking with each other. The women were sipping from champagne flutes or wine glasses, and most of the men drank their whiskey or whatever from fine crystal rocks glasses. The heavy scent of the sweet red wine, champagne, fine liquor, and human blood filled their vampire scenes. Even with the blood they drunk earlier that night, this situation was undoubtedly going to test their restraint.

"Boys, let me take your coats and gloves." The woman said as soon as they entered the house.

"No, that's ok. We aren't going to be that long." Dac replied.

"Lucy, who is this?" A man came around from one of the other rooms placing his hand on the small of Lucy's back and questioning the new arrivals.

"They had some car trouble down the road. I told them to come inside while they waited for the tow truck. It's so cold out tonight, and you know how long these things can take." Lucy answered, then she turned to Nikolai and Dac and said, "I'm sorry. I didn't get your names."

"I'm Nick, and this is my friend Dac," Nikolai said as he offered his gloved hand and shook hands with both hosts.

The man introduced himself. "Mitch. My wife is right. It is much too cold to wait outside. You, young men, look so pale; why don't you come in and have a drink. That will warm you two right up."

Before either of them could refuse, Mitch had asked a nearby server to get each of them a glass of whiskey. He was leading them both into the other room with all the other guests. Nikolai and Dac both looked at each other, noticing the other's concern.

The room was full of so many people mingling and moving about that it took a moment for Nikolai to realize he and Dac had somehow been separated. He held tightly to the glass he held in his gloved hand, pretending to sip from it. Nikolai watched the people in their fancy clothes eating their little fancy foods off fancy silver trays and drinking their drinks. He looked down at his black jeans, black leather coat, and gloves, and aside from the fact that he was a vampire among all these humans, he felt completely out of place. He scanned the room, searching for Dac, ready to get out there. The smell of human blood was becoming more intense, and he could feel his thirst creeping up. It had been ages since he'd taken blood directly from any human, and he wasn't about to do it tonight. It was time to leave.

He moved about the room with his head down when someone bumped into him. He looked up quickly, but whoever it was passed by already. Then he saw the long, dark familiar hair across the room. It couldn't be her, could it? He tried to move to a place where he could get a better look at her, but the most he could see was the side of her face. She turned her face slightly towards him but quickly turned away again. She moved swiftly through the room, and he lost sight of her. He had to find Dac now. He made his way back to the front of the room and eventually back out into the foyer, where he found Dac waiting for him.

"There you are. Let's go." Dac said to him.

"Wait," Nikolai said, lightly grabbing Dac's arm. "I think I just saw Harper."

"What? Are you sure?"

"I can't be certain, but it definitely looked like her, except I could only see the side of her face, but it looked for a second that she winked at me. Then I lost her."

"You lost her?"

"Yea, she disappeared into the crowd. I couldn't find her again, so I came looking for you."

"Well, come on. We need to get out of here."

They rushed towards the door but stopped when they heard a small voice yell down from the top of the stairs. "Bye!" Little Sophia was standing at the railing, waving down to them. Nikolai waved back to her and gave her a slight smile, and then both men walked out of the house.

# Thirty-Two

Back outside in the fresh cold air of the night, Nikolai and Dac decided they should wait around and watch as each of the guests left the party. If Harper really were somewhere among them, they would be best to find her that way. They decided they could follow her as she left the party and find out where she was staying, and most likely, Luca was also staying since they believed more than ever now that she was working with him and not being held as a prisoner. There were just too many sightings of her for it to be anything else. The question remaining in the back of both their minds now was when and why had she betrayed them?

It was just passing midnight, and the sky was at its darkest. They found an inconspicuous spot on the wall surrounding the house to sit and watch for Harper. The nearby evergreens cast a dark shadow across the area. They concealed themselves in the darkness and waited.

One by one, people started to leave the party. Valets brought their fancy cars up the driveway nearest the front door, so not one guest had to walk too far in the cold. The front door opened and closed numerous times, flooding the driveway with light and then bringing it back into darkness. Cars with their bright headlights rolled down the pavement. Finally, the last guest had gone with no sight of Harper or anyone that even resembled her.

Dac and Nikolai hopped down from their spot on the wall, walked back to their car, and drove back to their tiny hideaway. Nikolai put the key in the lock unlocking the side door they used to enter and exit the house. Dac was directly behind, but as Nikolai entered the house, he put his arm out, preventing Dac from entering.

"Someone's here." He whispered.

They both stepped through the door as quietly as possible. Dac slowly closed the door behind him. They stood still for a moment listening for any movement when a noise came from one of the back rooms. They started to move carefully towards where the noise came from when a shadowy figure appeared in the hallway. Nikolai rushed over, swiftly grabbing the trespasser by the throat.

"Wait! It's me! It's me," Pleaded a familiar voice.

"Jace! God Damn! What the hell are you doing here? Fuck! I could have killed you." Nikolai yelled, and he loosened his grip, dropping Jace to the ground.

Jace retrieved himself from the floor, catching his breath and rubbing his neck. "Sorry, man. I followed you guys out here. I thought I could do something to help."

"You shouldn't be here. There's nothing for you to do. Go back home." Nikolai scolded.

Dac turned on the overhead light in the kitchen. "Maybe there is something he could do."

Both men looked over at him. Jace looked eager, and Nikolai puzzled.

"Jace could go over to the other house tomorrow and

check it out in the daytime," Dac said. "Just hear me out." He continued before Nikolai could object. "He'll have an advantage that we don't have. By going over during the day, they'll all be asleep, and he could see for sure whether they are there or not. We'll go over the floorplans with him tonight. We can come up with a plan for him to get in and out of the house undetected. Once he confirms if they're there, he leaves and comes back here."

"I'll do it," Jace said eagerly.

"Now listen. Don't be too eager. Even though it will be daylight, it will still be dangerous. If any one of them gets any sense of you being there and wakes up, they very well can and will kill you. Except for maybe Harper. So, you still need to be extremely cautious and don't do anything stupid." Dac stated.

As the three of them continued to discuss their plans, Nikolai sent a message to Quentin and Emmaline to come out and meet them. He then set up an arraignment with Garrett to drive them up in the van so he could make use of the daylight hours, and they could be there first thing the next evening. He had a very distinct feeling they were close to finding Luca, and they all needed to be ready when they did.

The next day Jace set out about his task right about noon. They had decided this would be the best time since the sun would be at its highest, and therefore the vampires would be at their weakest and less likely to hear him and awaken.

When he pulled up to the address given to him, he was surprised to find the property not gated. He would have thought they would have provided themselves with more security. The house sat back far from the road, but Jace still parked his car just off the shoulder and walked the distance over to the house. Luckily, most of the snow from the other night had started to melt, and the temperature was a bit warmer, so the walk wasn't that horrible.

There was a detached three-car garage behind the house, and Jace decided to start there. He was detouring off their plans a little bit, but he had noticed what looked like fresh tire tracks in the slush-covered driveway. This made him think whoever lived here probably weren't sleeping vampires.

Luckily, each door of the garage had a window. Wiping the snow dust and dirt away, Jace peeked inside and noticed two cars parked in the garage, but the third spot was empty. He wondered if this meant the owners of the other two vehicles were home.

He quietly moved up the path to the house and peered into the windows of the backdoor. It appeared to open into a mudroom where Jace could see three pairs of shoes resting on the floor. Two, which seemed to be children's shoes. He thought about Charlotte and Garrett and wondered if this could be the same type of arraignment. That thought just didn't sit right with Jace, however. From what he had heard about Luca, he didn't seem like the type to keep humans around. Well, there was only one way to find out.

Jace made his way to the front of the house. He walked up the front steps onto the covered porch and rang the doorbell. No answer. He rang it again. Still no answer. His heart started to pump harder in his chest. His hands and forehead began to sweat despite the cold. Had he misjudged? Did he make a mistake ringing the bell?

Going back to the original plan, he found the entrance they had decided he would use to enter the house. It was a small door on the backside of the house under the back porch that led to the basement. He entered through the tiny door, careful not to make any noise as he descended the concrete steps. The basement had a few small windows allowing for a bit of sunlight to shine through. While this provided Jace enough light to look around, it wasn't likely the vampires would be in this room.

Dac had told him that years ago, Luca and his friends had favored sleeping in coffins as added protection, and they likely still did. Jace looked around the basement, but no coffins. There was a door leading to a separate room, but when Jace checked it, it turned out it only held some weight benches and a treadmill. There was no sign of any floors lower than the basement, so Jace made his way carefully up the stairs into the main part of the house. He was surprised but happy there was no alarm system. He continued searching the rooms of the house with no sign of any vampires. He decided to check one more spot before he left, the attic. It seemed an unlikely spot for them to be hiding, but he wanted to be thorough in his search.

He crept up the stairs leading into the attic. It was seemingly darker up here than in the basement. A black sheet covered the only window blocking any sunlight from coming in. He pulled the sheet aside and tied it with a piece of rope he found lying on the floor. There were no coffins up here either, but there were four rather large trunks. Were they big enough to hold a full-grown person or, in this case, a vampire? Jace stepped towards one of the trunks and put his ear near the lid, trying to listen for any signs of breathing. He checked for a lock but didn't see any. The lid creaked as he lifted it open. The trunk only contained some old clothing and nothing else. Jace let out a breath he hadn't realized he was holding and checked the other remaining trunks. Each one contained much of the same thing except for one full of children's toys and stuffed animals. Convinced no vampire lived here, Jace decided it was time to leave before the owners of the house returned home.

Later that night, Jace reported to the others about his findings at the house, concluding that Luca was, in fact, not living there, nor any other vampire for that matter. Quentin and Emmaline had arrived just a short time ago. Garrett had made good time arriving just after sundown to drop them off, and then he headed over to his cousin's house, where he would stay the night before leaving the next day.

They were all seated at the dining room table when Jace delivered his news. Everyone could sense Nikolai's disappointment. He was so confident that it was going to be the place. He was sure they were close to ending this, but now they were back, starting from the beginning.

"Don't worry," Dac said to Nikolai. "Just because that wasn't the right house doesn't mean they aren't nearby."

"I know I was just so certain after last night. I know we didn't see her leave that party last night, but I know I saw Harper there last night."

"You saw Harper last night?" Quentin asked, having heard about this for the first time since arriving this evening.

"Yea," Nikolai replied, then continued to fill them in on the events from the night before.

They all agreed that Nikolai had likely seen Harper the night before, and if he did, Luca and his crew were likely nearby. And since Nikolai was in the most danger at the moment, based on the note a couple of days back, it was understandable that he'd be feeling a bit uneasy.

Nikolai got up from the table, walking away from the group.

Deciding he needed a little time alone, he left the house and just started walking. The temperature had dropped since earlier in the day. Grey clouds were threatening to cover the already darkened night sky. Nikolai walked for what felt like miles until he came upon what looked like a little cul de sac in the road. He leaned over the railing at the edge of the cliff and peered down the mountain at the city below. He imaged all the people out there living their lives carefree unaware of the dangers surrounding them. Then he looked out further into the distance at the mountains surrounding him. He thought about his life in Romania. Growing up and meeting Una and falling in love. He thought about their life together, the baby they were expecting. He thought about all the dreams they had before Luca came and stole their lives from them. He stared far off into the distance, and that's when he saw it, the house all alone high up in the mountains, the house that looked like a castle. He pulled out his phone and sent Dac a message. *I know where they are.*

# Thirty-Three

She was still in that same room and still shackled to that same wall. Her hair was matted, and her wrist and shoulders hurt. She wasn't sure how long she had been there. It could have been a day or two. It could have been a week. She didn't know. Time had seemed to cease since she had been locked up in this room. She watched a spider crawl across the floor and couldn't help thinking how free he was and how much she wished to be that free. In life, she, like so many others, had been afraid of spiders. Now she looked at this spider and thought, the two of them weren't that different. Both fearful and feared creatures, hiding in dark spaces, ready to devour their prey. She was now picturing that last night inside Zaine's apartment. The last time she knew freedom. It was also the first time she had felt free in three years. Free to give in to her vampire instincts. Her mouth on this neck, her teeth sinking into the vein. The blood flowed so freely into her mouth. Her thirst was strong, and her body weak. Why had none of her vampire family come looking for her?

"That's easy." A voice came from the other end of the room. Alex had entered and was now walking towards her. "They did go looking for you, but we were gone before they got there.

We knew what you had done and how you would try to warn them, so we remedied that, and now they think you are one of us."

"But why all this here? I see what you're doing. This room, this dress you put me in. The way I'm chained to this wall. If Luca wants revenge against Nikolai and Dac, why go about it this way? Why go through all this trouble? It's not like they would have seen him coming. They thought he was dead."

"Oh, my dear sweet Harper. There is so much more you still don't understand." Alex said.

"So, make me understand. Tell me what is going on here." Harper demanded.

"This was never about Luca. This was never about Dac, either. Everything Luca has ever done was for his brother. He was never the one with the vendetta. He has already forgiven him for his treachery. This here, all of this, is for Nikolai."

"But why? I still don't understand. He wasn't the only one to try to kill Luca. All he did was try to avenge his wife."

"Avenge, his wife! Maybe he wouldn't have had to avenge her if he would have saved her! Instead, he stood and watched like the coward that he is." Alex yelled.

Harper stared up at Alex, not responding to his sudden outburst. As she sat there trying to comprehend his words and fit the pieces together, Alex regained his composure and continued.

"Let me tell you a story, Harper. A long time ago, a woman was kidnapped from her home while her husband was off elsewhere. The woman was pregnant with a child and held as a prisoner in a room very much like this one while being feasted on by a vampire. When the husband eventually showed up, he did not try to save her. Instead, he stood helplessly in the doorway and watched as the vampire tortured her and drank her blood. He did nothing to try to rescue her. Instead, he walked away and let the vampire have her. Since then, he has become a vampire himself. He walks around all self-righteous and believing himself to be the victim." As the tension grew in his voice, Alex paused for a brief moment but then continued his story. "But what this man didn't know was that the vampire never killed his wife, and seven months later, she gave birth to a baby boy." Harper gasped, but Alex continued. "The two women that had tended to her were vampires too. They delivered the baby, and later they took the child away, abandoning him on some random doorstep to be raised by strangers.

"So, these strangers, they took in the boy and cared for him?" Harper asked.

"Yea, they took him in but care for him." Alex scoffed. "No, they did not care for him. They beat and abused him. While their real children were dressed in good clothes, he was dressed in rags. While they were in school, he was forced to work on the farm, and while they all ate good food, he was given scraps."

"And then what happened to him?"

"At the age of fifteen, he ran away from that horrible place in search of his real parents. Finally, after three whole years of searching, he found his mother learned what happened to her and how his very own father left them both there to die."

"But that's not what really happened. He went to the castle to save her and to save you."

Alex reached down and snatched Harper up by the throat. He pressed her against the wall. The rage he felt at her words defending Nikolai radiating out of him. The shackles around her wrist were cutting into her skin. Whatever blood that remained inside her was now seeping out the wounds turning black as it hit the ground. Her heart beat faster, and her head grew dizzier. Was she dying?

"He wanted to save you. I know he did. I saw it the day he turned me. When I drank his blood, I saw it, and I felt it. He tried to move forward, but he was frozen in that doorway by Luca, and that has haunted him ever since. If he knew you were alive, he would take you in and love you. It is Luca you should be blaming, not Nikolai." Harper pleaded as she struggled to get the words out of her throat.

Alex dropped her back to the floor. "You are foolish if you believe that. Just look at how easy it was for him to believe you crossed them. They stopped looking for you the minute we dropped Zaine's dead body at their doorstep."

"Then why are you still keeping me here? If you know, they stopped looking for me, why still set all this up? What makes you think Nikolai will still show up?"

"Because he knows that Luca is alive and just like you, he thinks Luca is looking for revenge. Do you really think he and Dac will just sit around and wait for Luca to show his face?"

"No."

"And with Luca's help, I've laid a nice little trail of breadcrumbs for them to follow."

"What does that mean? I thought you said Luca wasn't after revenge."

"He isn't, but he would use it as a chance to reconnect with his brother. As for Nikolai, he has no use for him either way."

"That is twisted. It will never work. Dac would destroy Luca all over again if he let something happen to Nikolai."

"And that is exactly what I am counting on."

# Thirty-Four

Dac and Quentin dropped Emmaline and Jace off at the Noxwood train station with strict instructions to get on the next train heading back home to Aura City. They had decided it was best to get Jace back home, and they were sending Emmaline to make sure he actually got there and stayed. They had become rather fond of him since the first time he showed up at their doorstep, and the last thing they needed was to have to protect him against whatever they were about to face.

Afterward, they met Nikolai at the spot where he had been waiting for them. The three men stared off into the mountains opposite them and marveled at the house that stood in the distance. Dac had to agree with Nikolai; this was the place. If his brother was living anywhere in this town, it was there. After determining how to get to that side of the mountain, the three of them got back into the car and drove off.

The drive over was tense with anticipation. No one spoke a word until they arrived in front of the house. They drove past discreetly and parked the car deep within the trees. They stood back as they watched two women leave out the large front gates.

"That's Lizbeth and Sonya," Dac whispered. "They must be going to hunt."

They watched the women disappear into the night, and they made their move. As planned, Quentin went to the back of the house, and Nikolai went around the side to each find his own way into the house. Dac was going in through the front.

Dac began his walk up the long stone driveway. Water streamed down from the large heated fountain that sat in the middle of the grounds. It seemed odd to Dac to have a water fountain in the middle of winter, but Luca had always been extravagant. The house ahead of him appeared dark, though some light peak out through the open front door. That's when Dac noticed the shadowy figure standing in the doorway. He continued walking, inching closer and closer to the figure he knew was Luca.

He saw Luca was moving closer to him as well. They both moved at a steady pace until they had finally come face to face. The sound of the waterfall from the fountain echoed behind them. The light of the moon shined down upon the vampires like a spotlight.

"It's been a long-time, brother," Luca said

"Where is Harper?" Dac demanded.

"If I were you, I'd be more worried about where Nikolai is."

"What is that supposed to mean?"

"Your friend did deliver the message, didn't he? Although I suppose I should mention that note didn't come from me."

"What are you talking about?"

"You see, my dear brother…." Luca began as he put his arm around Dac's shoulder, though Dac quickly shrugged him off. "This isn't about me or you for that matter, though I could see why you might think that it was after what you and your friend did to me. But I am a forgiving man. I can let that go. Unfortunately for Nikolai, others aren't so forgiving."

"Others? What others are you talking about, Luca? You're not making any sense."

"Why don't you follow me. Maybe we can still catch the show, and you can see for yourself."

Reluctantly Dac followed Luca inside the house. By then, Quentin had made his way inside and was standing in the entryway when Dac and Luca stepped into the house. Quentin prepared himself for a battle, but Dac set him at ease, at least for now. They both cautiously followed behind Luca down what felt to Dac like a familiar set of stairs. Although he knew they were not the same steps he once climbed down into the catacombs of his brother's castle, they looked and felt the same, cold and damp. Everything except the outside was built exactly like that castle Luca had taken him to so many years ago. So, if whatever were going on had to do with Nikolai, that could only mean one thing. It had something to do with the night his wife was killed. The pieces started falling into place, Harper, who looked exactly like Nikolai's dead wife, and this place looked exactly like the place she was killed, but something was still missing. Something still didn't add up because if Luca wasn't after revenge and Una was dead, then who was after Nikolai?

Instead of continuing all the way to the bottom of the steps, Luca led Dac and Quentin into a small room. It was not what Dac had expected, but then Luca flipped on the switch attached to the wall. An overhead light turned on, and Dac saw they were looking down into another room through a glass window. In the room below, Dac saw the scene he was expecting when they first descended down the stairs. Harper was chained to the wall. She was dressed in the same dress Una had worn that night all those years ago. Then there was Nikolai standing in the doorway. But who was that in the room with Harper?

"Looks like the show is about to begin," Luca said. "Hope you enjoy watching your best friend finally learn the truth." He said to Dac. Then Luca walked out of the room, locking the door behind him.

"We have to get down there and stop this," Dac said to Quentin.

"Your right, but first, what did Luca mean about Nikolai finally learning the truth? The truth about what?" Quentin asked.

"There's no time for this. We have to get down there." Dac protested.

"Not until you tell me what's going on here. What are you hiding, Dac?"

"Nothing. Now come on." Dac pushed past Quentin and went to work on opening the door. He pulled on the handle a few times with all this strength until it finally opened on the third try. But before he could get through the door, Quentin grabbed him by the arm and held him back. "What are you doing?"

"You have to tell me what's going on. I can tell you're hiding something. Now tell me, what the hell is going on down there?"

"Fine." Dac relented. "What you see down there is basically a reenactment of the night Nikolai's wife Una was killed. The room is set up exactly the same, and Harper is dressed exactly like Una was that night. Nikolai watched from the doorway as Luca drained and killed her. I don't know who that kid is down there now, but I'm not going to wait around to find out."

"Wait a minute. How do you know the details of that night? You were there, weren't you? That's what you don't want Nikolai to find out. You were there. Dac, what did you do?"

Dac started for the door again, ignoring Quentin's question. Quentin once again held him back. When Dac tried to fight him off, Quentin pushed him up against the wall holding his arm against Dac's throat. "Tell me what you're hiding, Dac," Quentin demanded one last time.

"Yes, I was there. Ok? Are you happy now? I admit I was there. I saw the whole thing happen. Now stop this, and let's go."

"No. Finish the story. What happened? What did you do?" He pressed his arm harder into Dac's throat.

"It was me. Ok? It was me that froze Nikolai in that doorway. It was my fault that Nikolai could only stand there and watch his wife get murdered." Dac finally admitted. "But you have to understand. I had to do it. Luca would have killed him too that night. He was still human then. He would never have been able to get past Luca, and I needed him. I needed him angry enough to come over to my side. I needed him angry enough to want to become a vampire himself and help me defeat Luca." Dac argued.

"You used him. All this time, he's thought you were his friend, but you used him. You helped Luca kill his wife, and you used him in your vendetta." Appalled by Dac's admission, Quentin drained enough of Dac's energy so he wouldn't be able to follow him. He then walked out of the open door in search of Nikolai, leaving Dac motionless on the floor.

\* \* \*

Nikolai stood still in the doorway, looking into a room built just like one he remembered from long ago. The whole thing was set up to remind him of the worst night of his life. Suddenly he felt a hand on his shoulder, and a voice whispered in his ear. "You're not frozen this time. Go in. Save her." He turned to face the voice. Luca was standing right behind him. He pushed Luca back, and he fell into the wall. Luca let out a small sinister laugh, and Nikolai entered the room, heading right over to Harper.

He grabbed Harper by her chained wrists. "Nikolai," she whispered.

"What's going on here? Are you a part of this?" Nikolai asked.

"No. You have to believe me. I had no idea about any of this. They took me that night at Zaine's apartment. Is Emmaline alright? I didn't want to hurt her, but she would have been taken too if they knew she was alive." Harper pleaded.

"She's fine. But I don't know what to believe right now. Here you are chained up like a prisoner, but you've been sighted around a few times since you're supposed kidnapping, and I was pretty sure I saw you the other night, so how do you explain that?"

"I don't know. I've been here the whole time." She answered.

"Ah, the man of the hour has finally arrived." A man's voice came from the corner of the room.

Nikolai looked at the young man emerging from the shadows. "Who the hell are you?"

"He's your...." Harper started to say, but Alex rushed over to silence her before she could get all the words out.

"Shut up." He yelled at her as he struck her in the face so hard that her head pushed back and hit the wall behind her.

Nikolai lunged at Alex. Both men fell to the ground, each struggling to gain control over the other. Alex pushed back at Nikolai. He flung back a few feet away, hitting the ground hard. His fanged teeth cut into his lower lip. The taste of salt filled his mouth. Nikolai spat out the blood onto the floor as both men gathered themselves up from the ground.

"Who the hell are you?" Nikolai asked again.

"Have a little patience. I've waited for centuries; you can wait for a few minutes. You'll find out soon enough, but first, I want to tell you a little story about why you're here. Then I will tell you who I am, right before I kill you."

"Ok then, let's hear your little story," Nikolai said, shrugging off Alex's threat.

"You see, it starts a long, long time ago in a room identical to this one. You stood right there in the doorway and watched as your wife was bitten and drained by a vampire—your pregnant wife, who was carrying your very own son. Maybe you didn't know at the time it was a son, but I can tell you it was. And you walked away that night. You turned your back on them. Then one day, they learned that you yourself had become a vampire. You had become the very creature that tortured her. You became the very creature that you allowed to destroy your family." Nikolai stood in silence, his jaw and fists clenched tight as Alex paced in circles around him, continuing to tell this story. "For centuries, we waited for the perfect moment, then one day we saw her—the one who would attract your attention and allow us to put our plan into place. We had eyes throughout the world, searching for her—the descendant who would look just like your precious Una, who you pretended to mourn. I have to admit we never expected you to make her a vampire too, but just as well, here we are. I heard you ask Harper if she was in on this. I can assure you she wasn't. All those times anyone thought they'd seen her, it wasn't her. It wasn't Harper, your friend saw arguing with Luca in front of the warehouse that night. She wasn't in front of the old man's house or at your place like your little human friend was led to believe. And it was not Harper you saw at the party the other night."

Nikolai's mind was running wild with confusion. Still, he stayed silent. It was as if no words could form in his throat as he pieced together what Alex was telling him. He was standing face to face with the child he thought had never been born. How was this possible? He saw Una die that night. How was the child born? And if it weren't Harper he'd seen the other night, then it had to be...

"Have you figured it out?" Alex asked him. "You know who I am, don't you, father?" Alex continued saying as he pulled a steel dagger from his jacket. It was the same dagger Harper had taken from their attic. The same dagger that had been used against Luca when Nikolai and Dac thought they had killed him.

Before Nikolai could even react, Quentin came flying in from across the room. Quentin knocked Alex to the ground. He tried to weaken Alex by consuming his energy, but Alex was stronger than he'd expected. The two of them struggled for the knife. Quentin was on top of Alex. He grabbed Alex's hand that he'd been holding the knife in, banging it harder and harder against the ground. The knife fell to the ground with a clank. Alex swung with his free arm connecting his fist with Quentin's face. Quentin fell backward from the force of the punch, dragging Alex with him. Alex struggled but broke free of Quentin's grasp. Though not for long as Quentin stayed right behind him. When Alex went to reach for the knife again, Quentin kicked it out of his reach. The steel blade clinked against the stone wall. The two vampires continued to struggle. Harper watched helplessly as she struggled with the chains that still constrained her to the wall. But none of that mattered because no one saw nor were they prepared for what happened next.

"Alexandru," Nikolai whispered the name he and Una had planned for if they'd had a son.

"That's right, Nikolai. That's our son, Alexandru." Said a soft familiar voice. In his ear, he felt the cold breath of the woman whom he loved his whole life. The woman whom he thought was dead all these years. He felt the vampiric strength of her hand on his shoulder. But before he could turn to face her, he felt the cold steel of her knife in his back. The pain shot through him as the knife pierced through his flesh. He looked down to see the long blade sticking out through his torso. The red blood turned black as it dripped to the floor. The world around him seemed to pause, and within moments everything went dark.

# Epilogue

J ace sat at the edge of his bed, looking through the box
of things he hadn't looked at in months. It contained
printed out papers of a journal, vials of essential oils, and
a cross pendant necklace. He had put all these things away
months ago after returning home from Noxwood. He and
Emmaline said goodbye for the last time that night at the Aura
City train station. They decided together it was best to part
ways there instead of him going back with her to the vampire
house. That was the last time he'd seen or heard from any of
the vampires except for one final message he received from
Emmaline. She had reached out with a text to say the others
had gotten home. Harper had returned with them, and while
things weren't great, she was sure they would work through
it. He sent a message back to her, wishing them all well.

Since then, he'd gotten back to his own life. He and Cloe
had begun planning their wedding finally. Together they were
picking out flowers, choosing a venue, and deciding where
to go on a honeymoon. Cloe had begun spending more time
at Jace's house than her own apartment. When things were
hectic and crazy, it was a normal hectic and crazy. He was
happy. So why was he sitting here now looking into this box

of peculiar memories?

Because a couple of weeks ago, Jace and Cloe were getting ready to go out, Cloe had a sudden dizzy spell and passed out on the living room floor. He drove her to the hospital to discover she was suffering a severe fever and mysterious blood loss. Up until a few moments before, Cloe had been in perfect health. That night they admitted her to the hospital, where she remained for two weeks.

Every moment he could be, Jace was at the hospital with Cloe. If he couldn't be there, one of her family members would be with her. Over the last two weeks, Cloe's fever had stayed steady, and it seemed no matter how many transfusions they gave her, they couldn't keep her blood count up. She had begun having hallucinations, which the doctors attributed to the fever and blood loss. Then suddenly, one morning, her fever broke. Her blood count began to rise back to normal. Once Cloe's condition remained stable for a couple of days, the doctors finally said she could come home.

Jace tried to convince her to stay with him while she recovered, but she wanted to go back to her own place. He had a key, and so did her mother, so they both agreed that it would be ok, and they would each go over and stay with her in shifts as they had at the hospital. They wanted to be sure she didn't relapse even though she insisted she felt much better.

Jace couldn't help remembering the fever he had experienced when Harper had bitten him. Even those first days of Cloe's sickness, he had thought about it. He had discreetly checked her neck for any signs of a bite every day for the first couple of days, but he never found any, so he told himself he was just paranoid. Still, something was worrying him. As much as Cloe claimed to be fine, he could sense something different in her. He'd seen a sadness in her eyes that he'd hadn't seen since the first few weeks after Harper disappeared three years ago. Only this time, it seemed to be much more profound, and even if she was doing a good job hiding it from her family, Jace sensed it, and it worried him.

It was time for him to head over to Cloe's apartment. Her mother would be leaving for work soon, and he didn't want to leave Cloe alone for too long. He scooped up the oils and put them in his pockets. He planned on rubbing the oils along Cloe's windowsills, just in case. He also intended on stopping at Sarah's shop on the way over to Cloe's to see what else he could get from her.

By the time Jace had gotten to Cloe's apartment, her mother had already gone. He used his key to unlock the door. Once inside, he could hear the water from the tub running. Figuring Cloe must be taking a bath, he decided he would get started on her apartment. He began wiping the oils along the windows and doorways. Sarah had given him some hawthorn branches to place in the windows. He put the branches into a couple of bowls and placed one on each of the windowsills in the living room. Now he was ready to move on to the bedroom, the only other room with windows that could be used for entrance into the apartment. He started off towards Cloe's bedroom, but as he started to pass the bathroom, the sound of water squished beneath his feet, and he stopped. The lukewarm water began to seep into his shoe as he glanced down at the puddle on the floor beneath him. Then he noticed the streams of red within the water that leaked from under the bathroom floor. The bowls that he carried in his hands dropped to the floor with a crash shattering into pieces. He banged on the bathroom door, calling out Cloe's name. When she didn't answer, he pushed against the door with his shoulder until he was finally able to force it open.

He froze at the sight in front of him. The water ran out from the overflowing tub. Cloe lay in the tub, her head resting against the side. The razor blade was floating above her in the water. Her arm hung over the edge; her wrist cut open. The blood poured out into the water. Jace rushed over to her, pulling her from the water. Not even noticing his own soaked clothing, he cradled her in his arms. His voice caught in his throat as he called her name a few more times with still no response. The tears that formed in his eyes ran down his face. He was too late. She was gone. He held onto her lifeless body, brushing the wet strands of hair from her face as her head turned to the side. That's when he saw it. Right at the nape of her neck, just below the hairline, were two round puncture marks. The perfectly hidden bite of the vampire.

www.ingramcontent.com/pod-product-compliance
Lightning Source LLC
Chambersburg PA
CBHW031701170626
46808CB00005B/1565